THE KREMLYOV INFECTION

ALLAN LEVERONE

Special thanks to:
Elderlemon design and Kealan Patrick Burke for the
outstanding cover art and to Jane Dixon-Smith for the
formatting and design of *The Kremlyov Infection* print edition.

PART ONE
SPRING 1984

Parties, plays, charity auctions, it seemed Dana had an event to attend nearly every night. With the events came expensive gowns and even more expensive jewelry. David was expected to attend as well, when all he wanted was to sink into his couch with a drink.

The problem was twofold. David had no interest in living a life among the Washington elite, but worse, even a man earning a salary that placed him near the very top of the government's pay scale could not hope to match the truly wealthy, dollar for dollar.

Both concerns seemed lost on Dana.

As debt began to pile up, so did the arguments, and before long David and Dana found themselves sleeping in separate bedrooms. They maintained the fiction of a happy marriage in public, at state dinners and other obligations, but away from the bright lights and society gatherings they rarely spoke, other than to bicker and fight.

Adding to the mounting financial pressures were college bills. Both their children attended Georgetown, one moving on to medical school and the other to dental school.

The education loans began coming due just about the time David moved out of the house, and he had absolutely no idea how the hell he was going to pay them.

Unfulfilled potential.

David Goodell was truly mystified at how his life had gone so completely off the rails, and how it had happened so quickly.

He sipped his drink and checked his watch again.

Nearly nine o'clock.

He smiled. As badly as things had gone over the past year, there was one bright spot.

Well, two if you counted the liquor.

Lisa Porter would soon be joining him for drinks and, with any luck, some bedroom gymnastics immediately afterward.

Lisa was younger than David by a lot. He'd never asked her age because he didn't really want to know. He doubted she was much older than his kids. A little voice occasionally whispered in his ear that she might even be younger, and that voice always made him feel guilty and ashamed of himself.

But not ashamed enough to break off their relationship. How could he consider ending it when she was the only thing keeping him sane?

Lisa was beautiful, with a tight body of which any Hollywood actress would be proud.

More importantly—or at least of equal importance to David— was the fact that she actually listened to him. When he unburdened himself about Dana, about her extravagances that were slowly bankrupting him, about the mountain of education loans hanging over his head, about how he feared his life and career had peaked before his fortieth birthday and then begun sliding inexorably backward, she *actually listened.*

Without rolling her eyes.

Without telling him he was being silly, or selfish, or dramatic.

If he was being truly honest with himself—and he could never *bring* himself to be honest with himself unless he was drunk, like now—he had to admit that were it not for Lisa Porter he might have considered ending it all by now.

"Suicide is painless," the theme song from *M*A*S*H* went. It was one of David's favorite shows, and while he didn't know whether the painless part was true, if nothing else suicide was permanent, and that was starting to look pretty appealing from his perspective.

A hand placed lightly on the back of his neck told him Lisa had arrived. Her touch was cool and brief, but it never failed to light in David a fire he hadn't felt since the very early days of his relationship with Dana.

He smiled and lowered his drink to the little round lounge table. He thought he was being careful, moving smoothly, but the glass thunked loudly and precious whiskey slopped over the top, running down the side and forming a small pool on the scarred wood.

Normally David would have been pissed at wasting even a drop, but not now. Not with Lisa here. Suddenly he didn't care much about his drink.

He rose to his feet, wobbling like one of his legs had grown longer than the other while he was sitting.

She laughed, the sound girlish and sweet. It never failed to turn him on.

"Sit down before you fall down, baby," she said. She wrapped an arm protectively around his waist and eased him back onto his chair, then crossed to the other side of the table and slipped into the seat.

"So," she said with a bright smile. "What are we drinking tonight?"

"Jameson's." Thanks to his three-hour head start, it came out more like "Shameson's," which struck him as appropriate. Also far more amusing than it probably should have.

"Really," she said, her megawatt smile clicking up another notch. "You only drink Jameson's when you want to be an extra bad boy."

Was that true? David had never thought about it before. But looking at the vision of loveliness and barely-contained sex appeal sitting across the table, he decided her observation was a good one. He really did want to be bad tonight.

And he wanted to be bad with her.

He raised his hand to get the attention of the overworked cocktail waitress. He needed to order Lisa a drink.

Hopefully only one drink.

And then they could stagger down the street—well, he could stagger while she walked—to his apartment and get bad.

2

Tonight would be the night.

Lisa Porter—whose real name was not Lisa Porter, although she had not used her real name since she was a very little girl—had worked hard to get to this point. She'd been given David Goodell's name by her handler more than six months ago and instructed to proceed slowly, with extreme caution. To avoid spooking the man at all costs.

Goodell was near the top of the CIA's management roster. If successful in turning him, Lisa would ensure KGB access to one of the highest-ranking American officials they had managed in years. Decades, perhaps.

And she liked her chances. Goodell had recently been exhibiting many of the classic signs the KGB looked for when identifying potential CIA moles: extreme financial difficulties, marital problems, and alcohol or drug abuse.

To prepare for her assignment, Lisa studied up on David Goodell, learning all she could about the CIA bigshot before ever approaching him: where he had grown up, where he had gone to school, when he'd gotten married, the names and ages of his children as well as where *they* went to school. She learned how many credit cards Goodell had (a lot). She learned how many cards his wife had maxed out (also a lot).

She practiced patience, maintaining as close to constant surveillance on the target as it was possible for one woman—one stunningly beautiful woman—to manage without being noticed, either by the subject himself or by his coworkers or family members.

It wasn't easy. It was lonely work, and dangerous, operating with minimal backup in the very society she had sworn an oath to overthrow. She'd moved to the United States as a very young child and the American version of society was all she knew. She never doubted the superiority of the Soviet system to the American one, but having grown up among the American people made her realize most of them were every bit as good and decent as the ones in the country of her heritage.

But that realization changed nothing. She had been well trained and was dedicated to her cause. She would follow her instructions to the letter, or die trying.

So she watched and waited, allowing Goodell to slip ever farther down the rabbit hole and into a hell of his own making. When she had finally determined the time was right—six weeks ago—she struck up a conversation with him at a bar very much like this one.

He'd been nearly as drunk that night as he was tonight, the desperation and hopelessness as plain to see as if he'd shouted it to the world. Even drunk he'd been clearly surprised that a girl as beautiful and young as Lisa would give him a second look, much less chat him up and drink with him and smile at him and talk quietly at a corner table until last call.

They made plans to meet again the next night, and the night after that, and by the fourth night, she'd allowed the man to bring her home and take her to bed. He thought it was all his idea of course, all his doing, and she was perfectly happy with allowing him to think that.

It was exactly what she wanted him to think.

Because if it were his idea, there would be no cause for suspicion on his part.

The affair was a torrid one, and soon they were spending nearly every free moment together, often drinking, more often making love. He spilled his guts to her on a regular basis about his estranged wife and his financial difficulties, but never did he mention his job and she didn't ask.

For awhile.

Eventually it would have been more suspicious to continue avoiding the subject than to inquire how Mr. David Goodell earned a paycheck, so she did.

"Bloodless bureaucrat," he had answered. "I'm nothing but a nameless, faceless entity, an anonymous cog in the cumbersome machine that is the United States government."

Even drunk, he never said a word about the Central Intelligence Agency.

And that was fine, too. Lisa continued to cultivate the relationship, using sex and a sympathetic manner to convince this poor, lost man that someone in the world gave a damn about him, that at least one person would listen to him, and sympathize, and allow him to cry on her shoulder and then screw her silly.

All of it had led to tonight.

She could not have helped but notice the fact that even when he was drinking, he was very careful not to misplace his briefcase, nor to leave it unattended in public, nor to toss it casually onto his living room couch even when his apartment was locked up tight. No matter how drunk he might be, or how depressed, or even how amorous, he was always careful to stow the case in his hallway closet.

He was more likely to forget his name than to misplace or mishandle his briefcase.

But one thing Lisa had noticed he was *not* careful to do was spin the tiny wheels that served as a mechanism to activate the briefcase's pair of brass locks when he was at home. He'd rummaged through the case on three different occasions in front of her, and not once had he spun the little brass wheels when he was finished.

The briefcase had been the prime focus of Lisa's interest almost from the moment she "met" David Goodell. Thus, it had been critical he not become aware of her interest in it.

She was careful never to mention it or ask questions about it.

She pretended not even to notice it.

All of that would end tonight.

Tonight she would search it.

*   *   *

March 17, 1984
9:20 p.m.
Washington, D.C.

"Nightcap, baby?" They hadn't been inside David's apartment more than three minutes and already Lisa had stripped down to her bra and panties.

Normally she would have waited the few minutes it took her horny "boyfriend" to get around to undressing her, to let him think, as always, that he was making the first move. But now that she had decided to make a play for the briefcase it was all she could think about. She wanted to get down to business.

Immediately, if not sooner.

"I don't know," he slurred. "I've had a lot to drink already and I wanna be able to…perform…"

"Please, baby?" she purred. "I've only had one drink and I want to have at least one more before we start. You know how alcohol makes it easier for me to get naughty."

A pleased smile slid across his face. She had known he wouldn't be able to resist the offer of a drink when she phrased it in terms that were so dear to his heart.

"Fair enough," he said, and began to rise unsteadily from the couch.

"No, baby, I'll make the drinks. You just relax, it'll only take me a minute."

He sighed gratefully and dropped back onto the couch. "Good. I love watching you walk around when you're…undressed."

She flashed him a lascivious smile and padded to the small bar in the corner of the living room. Grabbed the whiskey bottle and a tumbler of water. Dropped ice cubes into two glasses. Poured the whiskey and then mixed in the water.

Her back was to David and she glanced over her shoulder to see him watching intently, features slack, eyes glazed. She grinned at him while reaching into her bra and removing a tiny plastic bag filled with two even tinier white tablets.

She dropped the tablets into the drink on the right and they began fizzing quietly. By the time she'd finished stirring both drinks the tablets had fully absorbed into the liquid.

Lisa wasn't into drugs—in her line of work, altered states of consciousness did not lend themselves to long careers, or long lives—but she considered Rohypnol almost magical. She'd used it before to render targets unconscious and she knew she would use it again, once David Goodell had faded into the past, nothing more than another career success.

David's eyes were drooping as she carried the drinks to the couch. The drug was probably unnecessary, given how much he'd had to drink. Once he passed out—and he looked like he was almost at that point now—she doubted anything short of a nuclear blast would rouse him.

And even then, he'd be too damned hung over to worry much about what his "girlfriend" might be up to.

She didn't care.

Better safe than sorry.

* * *

March 17, 1984
9:50 p.m.
Washington, D.C.

It took maybe twenty minutes for the Rohypnol to take effect. Lisa—whose real name was Anna Tarenko—could tell immediately when it did. David went from drunk and wobbly and slack to unconscious. Out cold.

He would remain that way for far longer than Lisa needed him to, but that was fine with her. And when he awoke, what would have been a painful hangover to begin with would be almost unbearable.

Again, fine with her. She had nothing against David Goodell per se, but felt no particular fondness for him, either. He was a means to an end, nothing more and nothing less.

She lifted his feet onto the couch so he was prone and then covered him with a blanket. That was the best she could do for him; she wasn't about to try to wrestle his unconscious bulk into the bedroom.

She dressed quickly and moved to the living room closet where Goodell always stored his briefcase. She hadn't touched the drink she'd made for herself a couple of minutes ago, and her slight buzz from the one she'd consumed at the bar was by now almost completely gone.

The briefcase was leather, scuffed and cracked in spots, and approaching the end of its life span. She guessed it had been given to David as a graduation present somewhere along the line, which would explain why he hadn't replaced it yet.

She set it on top of the coffee table and knelt next to it, pulse racing. She hadn't been able to get close enough the few times he'd opened and closed the case in her presence to see the combination that would unlock the clasps, so if he'd gone against his history and spun the numbers when he last locked it, she would be out of luck. Everything she'd done to get to this point would be nothing more than wasted effort.

The Soviet State had outlawed organized religion decades ago, but many Russians had a history of faith going back much longer than the Union of Soviet Socialist Republics. As dedicated as she was to the advancement of the Soviet cause, Anna's family was one of those, and she said a quick prayer before reaching up with both hands and placing a thumb on each of the locking mechanisms.

Then she slid them smoothly away from each other and the clasps sprang open with a pair of identical rich "clicks."

She was in.

3

April 12, 1984
6:20 p.m.
Washington, D.C.

"We need to talk, David."

Lisa stood, hands on her hips, and waited for a response from the older man. He had lessened his drinking since beginning his "relationship" with her, which made him much more dangerous as a foe. She had plied him with a couple of very strong drinks tonight, though. Ensuring he was loose and suggestible would make him much easier to control.

He stumbled backward a step, surprised at the commanding tone in her voice. It was unlike anything he had come to expect from her, which was exactly the point.

After drugging David Goodell and breaking into his briefcase nearly a month ago, Lisa had maintained the fiction of a romantic interest in the CIA bigwig.

For a while.

Most of the stuff she'd found inside the case was worthless. Pens, pencils, writing paper, a calculator, bar napkins. The detritus of a life spent sitting behind a desk, attending staff meetings, and pretending to matter. But one item had more than made up for everything else.

One item had been worth its weight in gold. Worth more than its weight in gold.

One item had been so explosive and valuable it took Lisa a moment to fully comprehend how lucky she had gotten.

It was a single sheet of computer paper, slipped into one of the briefcase's file folder divisions. David had obviously stuffed the paper into the case at some point in the last couple of months and then forgotten about it.

Printed on the paper were a date and a list of names under the heading "Russia."

These were not just any names. The list contained one row of names next to a corresponding row of names, the significance of which was immediately obvious, even to Lisa, who as a KGB field operative had never seen anything like it.

The names on the left side of the paper were aliases, and the names on the right side were the actual identities of CIA covert operatives working in Russia. Or maybe it was vice-versa, the real names on the left side and the aliases on the right.

It was a minor detail that was irrelevant to Lisa. The type of detail that would be resolved by someone much higher in the intelligence chain of command than she.

She had smiled and secured the list as David lay unconscious on his couch a few feet away. Then she'd transmitted the information to Moscow at her first available opportunity.

To say her handler had been impressed would have been a massive understatement. Within days, her orders had come through: continue to move slowly with Mr. David Goodell, Assistant CIA Director for Eurasian Operations, but when the moment was right, turn him.

And that was exactly what Anna had decided to do tonight.

So when she told him they needed to talk, she barked at him, her voice clipped and angry, copying exactly the manner one of her KGB instructors had taken with her years ago during training.

It had succeeded in focusing her completely, and she hadn't been half drunk at the time like Goodell was now. She was certain her gruff manner would command—and retain—his attention. The attitude was utterly unlike anything she had exhibited toward him in the nearly three months they had known each other.

His brows knitted together in confusion. "What...what are you talking about? What's going on, honey?"

"What's going on is that the situation has changed. You will no longer refer to me as 'baby' or 'honey,' and I will no longer utilize those terms with you."

"I…I don't understand."

"You will understand soon enough."

His face flushed. "Is that so? Enlighten me then."

It was time to bring the hammer down, to reveal to David Goodell the new dynamic in no uncertain terms.

"The nature of our relationship has changed. We are no longer lovers, we are now employer and employee."

"Employer and employee? What are you talking about, Lisa?"

"What we are talking about is this: I own you. The vast majority of the time, you will go about your business as Assistant CIA Director for Eurasian Operations as you always have. You will—"

"How do you know about—"

"I know plenty, David. I know much more than you realize. As I was saying, most of the time nothing will change for you. However, on occasion you will be expected to gather intelligence regarding certain CIA activities in the Soviet Union. You will gather that intelligence and supply it to me on demand. Do I make myself clear?"

"I most certainly will not." He was making a show of resistance, as she had known he would. But all the blood had drained from his face and he looked as though he might be sick. "Who are you? More importantly, whom are you working for?"

"Your first question does not matter. As you have probably deduced by now, my name is not Lisa Porter. You will never learn my real identity, and it is irrelevant to our purposes, anyway.

"As for your second question, well, I think you already know the answer. You should, at least. You're not much of an Assistant Director for Eurasian Operations if you cannot by now make that very basic connection."

He sank to his knees. She could see the synapses firing, could see all the pieces falling into place in his head. Suddenly it made perfect sense why a beautiful younger woman would show such an interest in a middle-aged alcoholic bureaucrat with a broken marriage. His thought process was pathetically transparent.

"You're KGB," he mumbled quietly.

"What did you say, David?" She'd heard him perfectly well, but wanted to force him to say the words again. They were music to her ears, and after months of listening to his pathetic whining, day after day, and constantly having to prop him up psychologically—not to mention having to sleep with him and pretend she was enjoying it—she felt she had earned the right to a little gloating.

"I said you're KGB. Well I've got news for you, Lisa Porter. Or whatever your name is. I'm calling the authorities. I've given you nothing of value, so I have nothing to fear from you."

"Are you certain about that? What makes you think I've gotten nothing of value from you?"

"I couldn't have given away any secrets because I've told you nothing about my job. You know I work for the CIA, so what? That information by itself is of no value whatsoever."

"You don't believe there is any chance you may have left something damaging in your briefcase? The briefcase I have become adept at breaking into?"

She didn't think it would be possible for him to turn any paler, but she was wrong. Still, he gamely attempted to maintain resistance. "I would never have brought anything damaging home from the office."

Lisa smiled evilly. "Does *this* look familiar to you, Mr. Assistant CIA Director for Eurasian Operations?"

She removed a photograph from the back pocket of her jeans and unfolded it with a flourish. Set it down on the coffee table and smoothed it out.

Depicted in the photo was the list of CIA operatives working in Russia. Next to the list—which Anna had photographed on this very table—was a copy of the *Washington Post* front page, dated March 17.

It was the day Lisa had changed David Goodell's life forever, although he could not have known it at the time.

"Oh, God," Goodell muttered. "How did you get ahold of that? Where did you find it?"

"I already told you. You really should be more careful what you put into your briefcase."

He crumpled at the waist, his body folding in on itself until his forehead crashed down on the living room carpet with a loud *thunk*.

Lisa let him suffer a little longer. She'd waited a long time for this moment and was determined to enjoy every last second of it. The satisfaction was exquisite. She hadn't thought anything could top the feeling of great sex—not that she'd experienced any of *that* in the last three months—but she realized now she'd been wrong.

This was the best sensation ever.

But all good things must come to an end, and eventually it was time to move on. "I know this comes as a tremendous shock, David. But there is an upside for you."

"Upside?"

She realized he'd begun crying and the thought sent a thrill like a lightning bolt through her body. Great sex, indeed.

"What possible upside could there be? My career is over and I'll spend the rest of my life in prison. That's assuming I'm not executed for treason."

"You are not looking at the big picture, David. Stop feeling sorry for yourself and consider this situation for what it truly represents: an opportunity."

"Are you insane? What kind of opportunity could this possibly represent?"

"No one in the CIA knows you took that list of operatives' identities out of Langley, correct?"

"Of course not. *I* didn't even know. What difference does that make?"

"It makes all the difference in the world, David. Because as long as you do as instructed, *I'm* not going to tell anyone about this little slip-up."

"That's the upside? You won't rat me out?"

"You didn't let me finish. I am well aware of your financial difficulties. You've done nothing but cry on my shoulder about your free-spending wife and all the college tuition you owe, as well as the fact you have no idea how you're going to pay off those debts."

"Yeah. My life sucked before and it's even worse now. Thanks for the reminder."

"No, David. Your life doesn't have to suck. I've already told you what I expect from you. Now let me tell you what you will receive in return. Not only will your career continue largely unchanged, with the exception of those relatively rare times I need you to provide intel to me, but Moscow is willing to offer compensation for your continued cooperation."

"Compensation?" Now she had his attention. His face remained a ghostly white, but his eyes locked onto hers as he waited for her to continue.

"That's right. My superiors wish to be very fair to you, David. The opportunity to avoid a firing squad should be sufficient motivation for you to work with us—" he winced and she had to suppress a smile—"but as long as you continue to provide valuable and actionable intelligence on those occasions we request it, you will earn a salary paid in tax-free American dollars that will dwarf your current CIA paycheck."

He stared at her in stunned silence. His lips moved but no words came out.

"So, what do you say, David? It seems like a very simple decision to me. A no-brainer."

She'd tightened the noose expertly around Goodell's neck until he truly had no legitimate options.

He sat for a moment, a broken man, on his hands and knees on the living room floor of his cheap apartment. Then he nodded slowly, as Lisa had known he would.

After all, the decision really was a no-brainer.

PART TWO
LATE 1987

1

December 31, 1987
11:35 p.m.
Georgievsky Hall, Grand Kremlin Palace
Moscow

Evgeni Domashev stood in the shadows of the Grand Kremlin Palace's Georgievsky Hall. Standing in the shadows was nothing new for Evgeni. He had spent a lifetime in the shadows. Tonight he watched revelers ringing in the New Year, a scowl of distaste etched onto his face.

Evgeni was a hard man who had lived a hard life, and as such, the scowl of distaste was his more-or-less default expression.

Tonight, however, he had more reason than usual to feel grim.

Because a traitor was in attendance.

Here, on the banks of the Mockba River, a stone's throw—and not even a long throw, at that—from the Kremlin, sat men working actively to destroy Mother Russia and the grand Soviet alliance.

The temerity was enough to make his blood boil. He wanted to reach out and strangle the traitor and his American accomplice, to march across the ballroom and choke the life out of both tuxedo-wearing menaces. He would start with the American, of course, but would save his greatest wrath for the Russian, who as a fellow countryman should know better than to do business with the sworn enemy of the Russian state.

Evgeni realized he had wrapped his hands into tight fists,

knuckles white, tendons stretched to their limit, and he forced himself to relax. He closed his eyes and stretched. Took a deep, calming breath. He was not a man accustomed to subtlety. His handlers *were*, however, and they had chosen a punishment less straightforward than what Evgeni would have selected, but ultimately every bit as severe.

And every bit as justified.

The ballroom at Georgievsky Hall was opulent and, to Evgeni, more than a bit intimidating. It featured soaring columns and a vaulted ceiling from which hung the most massive gold chandeliers he had ever seen. Banquet tables covered in brilliant white linens dazzled the eyes, and the artificial light spilling from the chandeliers reflected off the heavily varnished wooden floor like noontime on a cloudless summer day.

It was an awe-inspiring sight and one, he knew, he was likely never to see again. Men like Evgeni were not often invited to gather in places like this. In fact he had not been invited tonight, at least not officially. His name was included on no guest list, and although he wore the sharpest-looking tuxedo he'd ever seen, the nametag fastened to the breast pocket was not his.

It was not anyone's.

But the suit matched perfectly the suits of the men serving tonight's guests, and that was what mattered. Because when the time came to act—and that time was rapidly approaching—he should not cause an eyebrow to be raised in concern. Not from the men whose lives he was charged with ending, and not from anyone else in attendance.

If humor had been part of Evgeni's psychological makeup, he would have been amused at the transformation the majority of the evening's guests had undergone over the course of the last several hours. Vodka flowed freely all night, seemingly enough vodka to fill the banks of the Mockba, and guests who had begun the evening stoic and stiff with formality, were now loosey-goosey, flushed and drunk, laughing heartily and dancing the night away as they toasted the arrival of 1988.

There were only a few exceptions to the near-universal revelry.

Those exceptions were Evgeni's targets. The targets were not so foolish as to allow themselves the loss of control that copious amounts of alcohol provided. Tonight's business was rife with risks for them, and even the most foolhardy of men knew better than to tempt fate by drinking to excess. The targets nursed their drinks carefully, smiling and maintaining a façade of carefree enjoyment while their eyes never stopped scanning for danger.

Not that it would matter.

Evgeni wondered what state secrets the Russian thought he was sharing with the American, and how many *real* Soviet secrets he'd shared in the past, before his malfeasance had come to the attention of the KGB. Evgeni knew his superiors had discussed long and hard—and heatedly—what action to take regarding Gennadiy Alenin's treachery, with a significant number of men arguing for using Alenin to feed false information to the Americans.

Intellectually the argument made a lot of sense. But the KGB had other dupes feeding false information to other Americans. They had no use for one more. Eventually it had been determined that sending a message to Russians handling sensitive information was important, too. A harsh reminder was in order, a reminder that disloyalty would not be tolerated.

Rather, it would be dealt with severely.

Permanently.

The band situated at one end of the long ballroom played on as the clock ticked toward midnight. The noise and chaos had increased steadily over the course of the evening, and Evgeni knew his decision to wait, rather than acting immediately, had been a good one. The frenetic activity inside the massive banquet hall would provide the perfect cover for what he was about to do.

The targets had finally finished their first drink, several hours after being served.

Evgeni snorted his contempt. If the men were trying to blend in with their surroundings, they had failed miserably by staying sober while all around them people were getting blessedly, mind-numbingly drunk.

Keeping their wits about them was one thing, looking ridiculously out of place was another thing entirely.

He knew they would have to order a second drink, if only to maintain their cover.

A moment later they did. The Russian traitor waved over a

waiter and placed the drink order, and when the tuxedoed server disappeared along the service corridor toward the bar—which had been set up in the kitchen for the evening—Evgeni followed. He waited just outside the kitchen for the man to return.

A moment later he did. The waiter stepped through the swinging door, moving quickly, a pair of vodka glasses balanced on his tray. He stepped nimbly to the side to pass Evgeni and his surprise was evident when Evgeni stepped to the side to block him.

"Excuse me," the waiter said, his irritation clear. "Coming through."

"I don't think so, Comrade," Evgeni said. He rabbit-punched the waiter in the throat with his right hand as he smoothly inserted his left under the drink tray.

The waiter crumpled to the floor, gagging and coughing, the noise of the attack drowned out by the band and the general mayhem echoing through Georgievsky Hall.

At that moment, the swinging door opened again and Evgeni's partner for tonight's assignment stepped into the service corridor. He slipped his forearms under the still-sputtering waiter's armpits and dragged the man through the doors and out of sight.

Evgeni glanced down the hallway in the direction of the ballroom and cursed. The confrontation had taken just seconds but had not gone unobserved. Another waiter had entered the hallway and was even now approaching. He had slowed his pace at the sight of the brief confrontation but continued walking.

Evgeni prepared to take him down quickly, before the man could sound an alarm, but his concern turned out to be unwarranted. In true stoic Russian fashion—and showing the experience and sound judgment of a longtime Kremlin employee—the waiter said nothing.

He didn't even register surprise.

He simply stepped around Evgeni as the other waiter had attempted to do and disappeared through the doors, where he would cease to be a problem. Evgeni's partner would detain him in the kitchen for the next few minutes.

After that it wouldn't matter.

Evgeni reached into the breast pocket of his tuxedo and withdrew what appeared at first glance to be a small plastic spray bottle. It was slightly larger than the size and shape of a spritzer of eyeglass cleaning fluid.

But it was not a spritzer of eyeglass cleaning fluid.

He peered down in the murky lighting, trying to determine the direction in which the spray nozzle pointed. Then he rotated the nozzle, opening the head, and aimed it directly away from him. Once he was certain he had gotten it right he double-checked his work. His actions were a matter of life and death, and if he got them wrong, well, his death would be…unpleasant.

Finally satisfied, Evgeni tilted the little plastic spray bottle toward the two vodka glasses on his tray. He delicately spritzed a thin film of liquid into the first glass, pumping three times, determined to expend enough of the bottle's contents to ensure success.

Then he repeated the procedure with the second glass.

Then he twisted the spray nozzle tightly closed. He double-checked his work—again—and then slipped the spray bottle back into his breast pocket, realizing only now that his hands were shaking slightly and his heart was racing.

Evgeni sighed softly and straightened his bow tie. He calmed himself and then placed what he hoped was a look of bored subservience on his dour face.

Then he walked down the poorly lit service hallway and entered the Georgievsky Hall ballroom. He moved smoothly, mimicking the real waiters, navigating tables and sidestepping drunken partiers. In seconds he found himself at his targets' table.

"Comrades," he said in a tone he hoped was sufficiently deferential as he placed a glass in front of each man.

The American was immediately suspicious. "You are not our waiter," he said in nearly perfect Russian. If Evgeni had not known the man to be a foreigner he might not have guessed.

Evgeni smiled. It was not easy, and probably not convincing. Still, the smile was genuine, because he had elected to tell the truth. Sort of. "Your waiter fell and injured himself. He needed someone to take his place and I was available."

Evgeni folded a hand under his tray and bowed slightly at the waist. "Enjoy, gentlemen. Toast the incoming year!"

He walked away and felt the heavy stares of the two men boring holes into his back as they wrestled their uncertainties. Evgeni didn't care. He had completed his mission as assigned and he was relatively certain the targets would relax and drink their vodka.

If not it would be no great loss as far as Evgeni Domashev was concerned. He could always move on to Plan B if the targets left their drinks untouched. Two bullets to the skull of each man as they exited the Grand Kremlin Palace would be less subtle than the KGB's preferred method but equally effective.

And from Evgeni's perspective, much more satisfying.

He walked up the service hallway far enough to disappear from sight of the targets, then pivoted and peered into the ballroom. The band had stopped playing as the clock ticked toward midnight, and the revelers were counting down drunkenly, a ragged, atonal serenade to the final seconds of 1987.

"Ten! Nine! Eight! Seven!..."

The targets stared at each other, heads together, as they held an impromptu discussion Evgeni knew had nothing to do with the dawn of a new year.

"Six! Five! Four!..."

The Russian traitor, Gennadiy Alenin, was gesturing decisively at his glass as he spoke. It was an obvious attempt to reassure the American. Evgeni could imagine the monologue: "There is nothing to worry about, Comrade. No one is aware of our... arrangement...I promise you."

"Three! Two! One!"

Georgievsky Hall erupted in cheers. The sound of glasses clinking together was nearly deafening. At the targets' table, Alenin lifted his glass high and nodded at the American, smiling from ear to ear.

The reluctant American gazed back at Alenin unblinkingly.

And unsmilingly.

The grimness in his features reminded Evgeni of his own reflection in the mirror every morning when he shaved.

A couple of seconds passed and the din inside the ballroom began to fade when the American finally sealed his fate. He lifted his glass, still without a trace of a smile, and toasted 1988. Then both men drank down their vodka in one long swallow.

Evgeni turned away for the final time. He exited the Grand Kremlin Palace with his partner and never looked back.

2

Riding in a chauffeured limousine with her boss was even more uncomfortable for Tracie Tanner than being summoned to his home. She wouldn't have thought anything could be worse than that, but it turned out she had been wrong.

Technically, she *was* summoned to his sprawling McLean property this morning, but there hadn't been time to go inside. She'd no sooner pulled to a stop in the driveway than CIA Director Aaron Stallings burst out his front door and marched to the rear of an idling black car that had been shined to a mirror finish.

In typical fashion, Stallings hadn't told her what to expect upon arrival. In the past she'd always been forced to wait, once at the front door and then usually a second time at his closed office door.

She'd never driven anywhere with him.

Tracie's surprise was so great that she stood for a moment beside her car, unsure whether she was supposed to join Stallings or if maybe he'd been called away on some national security emergency during the time it had taken her to drive here.

He turned in her direction and spread his hands, making his impatience clear. *Why are you not right behind me?*

"Good Lord," Tracie muttered to herself. "This could be a very long day."

She sighed and joined Stallings at his limo, flexing her still-healing left hand compulsively. She'd broken several small bones in it back in November during the ill-fated attempt to recover three hundred million dollars worth of buried Nazi treasure—the fabled Amber Room—in Wuppertal, West Germany, and her efforts at speeding recovery time from the injury had been so single-minded she now found herself working the bones, tendons and muscles in the hand constantly and without conscious thought.

But not without lingering pain.

Stallings opened the door and clambered into the back seat. Then he slid to the other side to allow Tracie room to enter. The moment she closed the door, the car began accelerating down Stallings's long driveway.

"How's the hand?" he asked, bypassing chitchat as he always did.

"Never better."

He bent and examined the scars on the back of her hand, delicate lines, still raw and red, where surgeons had sliced open the skin to access the damaged bones. It was a surprising gesture of concern from a man to whom sensitivity was a mostly foreign concept, but the intensity of his stare made Tracie uncomfortable.

She felt naked and exposed, and after a moment she folded her hands together in her lap, covering the scars and removing them from his penetrating gaze.

"So," she said.

"So," he agreed.

"Why am I here?" she asked, already annoyed after spending maybe thirty seconds with the man. "And where are we going?"

"What do you know about Polonium-210?" His answer was disingenuous, as usual. And confusing, also as usual.

She looked up into his face and said nothing.

"Well?" he challenged. "Did you not understand the question?"

"I understood the question. I just *told* you everything I know about Polonium-210, which is absolutely nothing. It sounds like something that might power the Millenium Falcon."

"The what?"

"Never mind. I've never heard of Polonium-210, or Polonium with any other number attached. I assume that's about to change."

"You assume correctly." For the second time this morning, Tracie's boss surprised her. He fell silent.

Since her dismissal from the CIA and then her rehiring by the legendary spymaster as his own personal one-woman black ops team, their meetings had always followed a certain predictable, if uncomfortable, protocol: hostility from Stallings, followed by defensiveness from Tracie, culminating in the boss laying out an assignment and then Tracie stomping away in anger.

While the hostility and defensiveness were still present, this meeting had deviated from the script, leaving Tracie feeling off-kilter. She elected to sit back and let things play out. She had little choice in the matter, in any event. Aaron Stallings had spent close to a half-century in the spy game and wasn't about to reveal anything to an underling—especially her—unless and until he had decided the time was right.

The route taken by the limo driver felt familiar, and after just a couple of minutes, Tracie was almost certain they were headed someplace she had not expected—CIA headquarters. She'd been inside the complex several times since her firing last spring, but always on an unofficial basis and never accompanied by the head man himself.

Stallings seemed to be getting impatient. He cleared his throat and shifted uncomfortably in the seat next to her and Tracie smiled to herself. He had expected her to press him for details of the meeting and when she sat back quietly she'd thrown *him* off his game.

It was a good feeling.

Without preamble, he said, "Polonium-210 is a radioactive element."

"I thought it sounded nuclear."

"It is. There have been rumors through the years of the Soviets—and others, most notably the East Germans—using Polonium-210 as a poison. I assume you're familiar with hydrogen cyanide?"

"Of course. It's what Adolph Hitler and Eva Braun supposedly used to commit suicide in their bunker at the end of World War II. We know now nothing of the sort ever happened, but that's the story the world has accepted for nearly the last half-century."

"Correct. Well, for purposes of comparison, Polonium-210 is around two-hundred-fifty thousand times *more deadly* than hydrogen cyanide."

Tracie whistled softly. The comparison was hard to imagine.

Then she tilted her head, concentrating. "Wait a second. If this Polonium-210 is so deadly and so radioactive, how the hell could any assassin use it without being contaminated with radiation and suffering the same fate as the victim?"

"That was my exact first question as well." Stallings nodded his approval. "The actual science is complicated and hard to understand. And for our purposes, it's also irrelevant. But basically, Polonium-210 emits Alpha radiation, which, due to the large size of the particles, is unable to penetrate human skin. It can't even pass through something as flimsy as a piece of paper. To be deadly, it must be ingested—swallowed or breathed in—by the victim."

"So as long as the assassin is extremely careful, he should be okay."

"Theoretically," Stallings said. "At least that's what the science people tell me."

The limo pulled up to a gate at Langley that Tracie had never noticed before. It was unobtrusive, in an area not easily accessible. The driver flashed a badge at a sentry and the fortified gate swung open.

"I assume you're telling me all this because one of our people has been poisoned with Polonium-210."

"No. That's not why I'm telling you."

"Then...?"

"I'm telling you because I have reason to believe *several* of our people have been poisoned in that manner."

A sick feeling rolled through Tracie's belly. "How many?"

"A half-dozen that we know of, maybe more. We've lost several people, good men and women, over the last few years to a mysterious illness. The indications are always the same: flu-like symptoms, vomiting and extreme weakness followed by hair loss and death in less than a month. Sometimes a lot less."

Tracie whistled again. She wondered if any of the victims were operatives she'd worked with over the years.

"Obviously," Stallings continued, "we suspected poison. We

even thought we might have narrowed the possibilities down to thallium poisoning. But the doctors assure me that that thallium contains certain radiation signatures that were not present in any of the victims. And Polonium poisoning is rare. Almost unheard-of, in fact, not to mention extremely difficult to diagnose, since the radioactivity is invisible to typical testing."

"Invisible? Then how did you make the connection?"

The car pulled to a stop in front of a glass door. Tracie wasn't sure but she thought they might be near the CIA's in-house infirmary.

"It doesn't matter," Stallings said. "I'll tell you later if you really want to know. His voice was subdued and his manner restrained in a way Tracie had never seen before out of the CIA's top man.

"Right now, there's someone I want you to meet."

3

Tracie walked wordlessly with the subdued Stallings through Langley's infirmary, which was small but well staffed with medical personnel and stocked with supplies sufficient to operate a mid-sized city hospital.

The CIA chief stopped in front of a closed door. Despite her near certainty that they were here to visit a case officer who had suffered radiation poisoning, the bright red and white warning placard affixed to the door caused Tracie a moment's hesitation and a spike of uneasiness.

Stallings smiled grimly. "Don't worry. He's under quarantine but it's precautionary only. We can safely enter."

Tracie followed him into the room and blinked in surprise. She almost could not prevent herself from gasping aloud at the sight of the man prone in the hospital bed. His skin was pale and translucent, with the delicate wrinkled appearance of a man in his nineties. Any hair he'd had before the poisoning was long gone, and tubes ran from various machines and monitors into both of his arms and both wrists, with others disappearing under the thin blanket covering the patient.

Stallings moved to the foot of the bed and said, "Agent Tanner, I'd like you to meet Agent Fowler. Agent Fowler, Agent Tanner."

The man's eyes had been closed since their entrance despite the fact Stallings had made no attempt at stealth. Now they fluttered open. They were bright and piercing blue, and they locked onto Tracie like laser beams.

He tried to smile and almost succeeded, but his lips were cracked and scabbed over and covered in dried blood.

"It's my pleasure," he said, the voice wafer-thin and reedy. "And please, call me Charles. Let's not stand on formalities, shall we?"

Tracie stepped forward and took the agent's left hand in both of hers. She maintained a gentle grip, worried about causing more pain than he was clearly already suffering. Stallings's use of her real name had jarred her—she rarely used it unless among family or friends—but the reason was obvious: there was no risk because Fowler wouldn't be going back to work.

Or even getting out of bed.

Ever.

"I'll call you Charles if you call me Tracie. Deal?"

"Deal."

Stallings watched the exchange quietly, his eyes never leaving Tracie. She felt the steady gaze on her even as she smiled at the dying man in the hospital bed.

The CIA director waited a moment and then said, "Up until two weeks ago, Agent Fowler was in Moscow on assignment. You'd been feeling well, correct, Fowler?"

"Yes sir, that's correct."

"When did that change?"

"After my meeting with a Soviet informant on New Year's Eve. I took possession of classified documents, left the rendezvous point and was in bed shortly after one a.m. Moscow time. By five in the morning I was vomiting, heaving so badly I thought I might break a rib."

"Were you concerned about your illness?"

"Not particularly. I assumed I'd either caught a flu bug or maybe was suffering food poisoning from something I'd eaten that day. But from there things only got worse. I spent all that day in bed and by the next day I was still vomiting—not that anything was left in my stomach—and could barely walk. That's when I knew I'd been poisoned."

Stallings rested a hand lightly on the man's blanket, a paternal gesture surprisingly—and touchingly—out of character. He said, "Agent Fowler notified his handler of his concerns, and we had him on a plane out of the Soviet Union the next day."

Tracie grimaced. "That must have been horrible, having to fly halfway around the world when you were so sick."

"The flying wasn't the hard part. The hard part was getting from the safe house to the airfield. It's not easy trying to remain inconspicuous when you can barely walk and can't eat without puking everything back up."

Fowler again attempted to smile and again mostly failed. "I wasn't this bad off back then, though. At least I could get out of bed. That capability deserted me over a week ago. They tell me it won't be coming back."

Tracie's heart broke for the man. She had worked extensively in the Soviet Union and East Germany prior to her dismissal from official CIA duty, and the thought that it could have been her lying in that bed was impossible to ignore. "Do you think your informant poisoned you?"

He shook his head, the motion slow and careful. Then he closed his eyes, as if that small act had caused severe pain.

Probably it had.

"It wasn't my informant. He had no reason to kill me. And even if he wanted me dead, he wouldn't have been as subtle as radiation poisoning. Two 9mm slugs to the skull would have been more his style."

He shook his head again, despite the obvious discomfort it caused. "I know exactly when I got poisoned. The waiter who'd been serving us all night disappeared just before midnight and was replaced by a different man. The guy gave off a very bad vibe, like he was trouble. There was no way he was a waiter. I can't explain how I knew, I just did. Work in the field long enough and you become very good at judging people."

Tracie nodded. She'd discovered the same thing after eight years of nearly continuous service in hot spots around the globe.

And yet Fowler had been victimized anyway.

"I know what exactly you're thinking," he said. He may have been physically wasted, but his eyes were fine and his mind clearly still sharp. In a way, it magnified the tragedy. "You're wondering why I drank the vodka when I was so concerned about the waiter-who-wasn't."

"Why did you?" Tracie's voice was almost a whisper.

"I wish I could give you a good answer. I guess I was so concerned about maintaining my cover while working *inside* the Kremlin, that I allowed my desire to blend in to override my sense of caution."

He looked up at Tracie and Stallings, his sunken eyes red and haunted. "I imagine my contact is in the same boat as me. He drank a glass of vodka from the fake waiter, just as I did. Hell, maybe he's dead by now. Lucky bastard."

Tracie dropped her eyes and then glanced across the room at Stallings. "It's obviously the KBG's doing. But why go to all the trouble, with all the attendant risks, of radiation poisoning, when they could simply have taken Agent Fowler, interrogated him and then executed him? No one would ever have been able to prove what happened, even if we knew."

"They're sending a message," Stallings said, "in a way that making someone disappear—or even putting two bullets in his head—doesn't do. They're telling us they know exactly who Agent Fowler is and exactly whom he works for. And they're telling us they can get to our people whenever they want."

"They're sending a message," he repeated. "And it's costing a good man his life."

"I'm not in the ground yet," Fowler said. "I'm going to keep fighting until I take my last breath. You can count on that."

"I know you will," Stalling said. He reached for Fowler's hand and squeezed gently. "I would expect no less."

The CIA director cleared his throat violently and Tracie knew it was to cover the fact that he was nearly in tears. "We're going to leave now and let you rest. It will take all you've got to recover and get back to work, and we need people like you in the field."

Stallings stalked to the door and opened it, and Tracie turned to follow. Fowler had closed his eyes again and already looked as lifeless as he had when they first entered the room.

Before they could leave, though, Fowler said, "Director Stallings?"

"Yes, Charles?"

"I have a wife and two young children."

"I know."

"Please make sure they're taken care of."

"Of course, Charles. I'll personally make sure your sons never forget their father was a hero." He pulled the door closed, and through her tears Tracie noticed Stallings was crying as well.

4

January 17, 1988
8:45 a.m.
CIA Director's limousine
McLean, VA

The limousine was quiet for a long time during the ride from Langley back to Aaron Stallings's home. Tracie was a little surprised the director hadn't stayed at the facility to begin his workday and simply instructed the driver to bring Tracie back to her car.

Finally she said, "Why did you bring me to meet Fowler?"

"Isn't it obvious? He had intel to share."

"I didn't learn anything from him you hadn't already told me, or at least nothing you *could* have told me."

Stallings had been shuffling through a sheaf of papers he'd pulled out of his briefcase, and now he slid the paperwork back into the case. He snapped it shut and gazed at Tracie levelly.

The silence stretched out. It was different from the previous quiet, which had been shocked and sad.

This felt electric.

"I brought you," he said, "because I wanted you to know what's at stake when you go to Moscow."

"I thought that might be it. And don't worry, the message has been received loud and clear."

"Good."

"Is there any chance Fowler could recover? I mean, now that

the doctors know what's wrong, they must have some course of treatment they can try."

"Fowler's a dead man," Stallings said after a moment's hesitation. "He knows it, his family knows it and the doctors know it. He's been a dead man since the moment he drank that vodka in the shadow of the Kremlin. There is no cure for Polonium-210 poisoning. There is no treatment. Fowler's almost at the end now. The doctors say it's a little surprising he's lasted this long, but his organs have started shutting down. He'll be gone soon. Tonight, tomorrow, maybe the next day at the latest."

"What's my assignment?" she asked, her voice hard and cold.

"I think I told you back in my office that we suspect Fowler is not the only operative who's been a victim of Polonium-210 poisoning."

"You told me. And now that you know what to look for, you can exhume the dead agents and have their bodies tested to be sure, correct?"

"No. That's not correct."

"Why not? Don't you want to be certain?"

"Of course I want to be certain, Tanner, but it's simply not feasible."

"Not feasible? What do you mean? Can't the doctors test for radiation?"

"No, Tanner, they cannot," Stallings snapped. Whatever trace of humanity he'd inadvertently allowed himself to display back inside Agent Fowler's infirmary room had vanished, replaced by the short-tempered irascibility Tracie had become accustomed to.

"Here's how it was explained to me," he said, speaking only slightly less aggressively. "Polonium-210, in addition to being deadly, is also nearly impossible to uncover unless the coroner knows what to look for and the autopsy is performed almost immediately."

"I don't understand."

"The element has a very short half-life, meaning all traces of it disappear from the victim's body quickly. We could dig up the bodies of the operatives and, with the exception of the most recent victim who was buried only a few months ago, all traces of the Polonium would likely be gone. Even the exception I mentioned would be hit-or-miss. It's possible too much time has passed in his case as well."

"But you feel certain all six of these men were poisoned in a similar manner by the KGB."

"Yes I do."

"And they all suffered the way Fowler has suffered, and continues to suffer."

"Yes they did."

"Back at your office, you said you'd tell me how the doctors discovered Fowler had been poisoned by Polonium if I really wanted to know. I really want to know."

Stallings sighed. "It was a lucky coincidence. By all rights, we still should have no idea."

"I don't understand."

"The medical people were discussing Fowler's symptoms in the cafeteria while one of the United States' leading nuclear scientists was getting a cup of coffee on a break from a meeting he was attending. The man's a genius and an expert on Polonium radiation, and his ears perked up at what he overheard. After his meeting ended, he mentioned his suspicions regarding Polonium to the case officer escorting him out of the facility. That person contacted the doctors. The scientist was right on the money."

"Lucky break," Trace said.

"Not for the dead operatives."

She nodded grimly. "Good point."

A moment of silence passed and Tracie said, "I'm going to ask again. What's my assignment?"

"I think you know."

"I want to hear you say it."

"You will fly to Russia. You will hunt down the man responsible for murdering our people. When you do, you will execute him."

5

Finding a secure location from which to maintain surveillance would be Tracie's first challenge. It wouldn't be easy. She was dog-tired and jet-lagged, and Moscow's average January high temperature of approximately twenty degrees Fahrenheit more or less eliminated any outdoor position as a realistic possibility.

With Charles Fowler on his deathbed back in the states—hell, given his condition when Tracie visited, by now he was probably gone—the CIA had been left with a gigantic hole in their Moscow-area operations.

There were other assets in the region, and Tracie had memorized aliases and contact numbers should it become necessary to utilize one. But she was extremely reluctant to do so, for obvious reasons: if the KGB had infiltrated CIA operations to the point they were able to assassinate six agents in the past three years, it would be impossible to know who she could trust and who might turn her into the next victim.

Further complicating things was the fact that the CIA safe house Fowler had been using as a base of operations was almost certainly compromised. If the KGB knew Fowler was CIA, Tracie had to assume they had learned *everything* about his Moscow

45

operation, meaning the safe house had been bugged, rendering it off-limits.

Nuclear, so to speak.

But redundancy was the key to covert operations, and the more hostile the territory, the more critical redundancy became. In the case of the Central Intelligence Agency's USSR operations, redundancy meant always maintaining more than one safe house in any particular region, the locations of those safe houses being made available to their operators on a need-to-know basis only.

Fowler hadn't needed to know the location of the backup safe house in Moscow, so he hadn't known.

Which meant Tracie should have a safe place to rest her head while here.

Theoretically, at least.

Because, theoretically, Charles Fowler should have been safe here as well. Unless and until Tracie could determine how Fowler had been outed to the KGB, she was willing to take nothing on faith.

The good news was that she had a place to stay. The bad news was that it was a dump. She dropped her travel bag on the floor of a tiny, cold and dirty little ground floor apartment in what she hoped was one of Moscow's least desirable neighborhoods. If it wasn't, things were worse behind the rapidly crumbling Iron Curtain than she'd realized.

Calling the safe house an "apartment" would be to do a grave injustice to the term. Wedged between two massive, sagging brick-walled structures—factories or warehouses, from the looks of them—that appeared to have been empty since Nikita Kruschev's time as Soviet Secretary General, the place was two rooms plus a kitchen Tracie wouldn't have considered eating in without first updating her tetanus vaccination.

But the condition of the place was irrelevant to her. She'd dealt with worse in the past and undoubtedly would again in the future. Always assuming she survived her current assignment, of course.

She craved sleep but wasn't going to get any. She splashed water on her face—cold water, naturally; it appeared a hot water heater hadn't been included in the lease agreement—and then changed into her darkest and warmest clothes.

Then she walked alone into the brutally cold Russian night.

* * *

Among the intel Stallings had supplied was the Moscow address of Gennadiy Alenin, Charles Fowler's Soviet contact and the man from whom Fowler had been receiving Russian secrets for more than two years. Fowler had met with Alenin at the Grand Kremlin Palace on the night of the poisoning.

It seemed the obvious place to start.

At 1:00 a.m. Moscow time the only people braving the cold were down on their luck—the hookers, the homeless, and assorted other have-nots. Tracie ignored them and they ignored her. Lowering their fur-lined hoods and pulling off their woolen facemasks for the sole purpose of sticking their noses into other people's business apparently became less desirable the lower the temperature plunged.

Small favors.

Despite Moscow's huge size, by chance Alenin's apartment building was located relatively close to Tracie's safe house. Holding a high enough clearance at the Kremlin to access classified Soviet information was evidently no guarantee of a salary sufficient to afford high-end accommodations.

Tracie elected to ignore the near-zero temperatures and proceed on foot. Even in the dark of night, she could gain a much better feel for her surroundings by walking than would be possible from a bus or a train, even if she could catch one at this hour.

Plus, she guessed the CIA-generated identification documents she'd been issued should be sufficient to fool anyone who might challenge her in this part of town and at this time of night, but why take chances? Freezing-cold toes were far preferable to the prospect of fighting her way out of a Russian jail or facing a firing squad—or Polonium-210 poisoning, for that matter—so not even the slap-in-the-face of the bitter cold as she stepped outside caused her to question her decision.

Twenty minutes of brisk walking got her within sight of Alenin's building. Like most of the surrounding structures, the high-rise was drab and utilitarian, concrete block construction that appeared to offer the bare minimum in terms of comfort and livability.

Maybe the interior was nicer than the exterior, but Tracie had spent enough time in Soviet-bloc countries to know that was almost certainly not the case.

Shivering slightly but warmer than she would have expected thanks to her brisk pace, Tracie circled the building. She slowed down and took her time, keeping sufficient distance between herself and the apartment house to avoid arousing suspicion in the unlikely event anyone was paying attention.

As she had expected, there were two entrances. The rear doorway opened onto a trash-filled alleyway filled with broken glass and vagrants, some drinking and some sleeping in doorways, covered in mountains of blankets.

At least, she hoped they were sleeping and not dead.

By the time she'd completed her circuit, it became clear which doorway would have to be kept under surveillance. Nobody with an ounce of common sense would risk using the rear entrance in anything other than an emergency, least of all a worried—or quite possibly by now grieving—young wife.

Tracie turned her attention away from Alenin's building and began moving slowly along the cracked sidewalk, scanning the area opposite it. She wasn't sure exactly what she was looking for, but she *was* sure she'd recognize it when she saw it.

And she did.

Abandoned buildings were not typically lacking in a neighborhood gone to seed. It was true in the United States and it was especially true here. Even in the dirty half-light of the few operating streetlamps, Tracie could see several surveillance possibilities.

She made a couple of passes along the sidewalk adjacent to the two most likely locations, settling on the one that would allow her the best view of the front entrance to Alenin's apartment while also—hopefully—concealing her from passersby.

She committed the location to memory, by now shivering badly.

Then she turned back toward the safe house, once again moving quickly. This time it wasn't just to stay warm. She wanted to catch a few hours of sleep before returning in the morning.

6

January 19, 1988
6:40 a.m.
Moscow, Russia, USSR

Tracie slept better than she would have anticipated, probably because she'd been so damned tired by the time she got back to the tiny safe house she was practically asleep on her feet. The temperature inside was chilly but still much warmer than outside, and she took her cue from the vagrants in the alley, piling as many blankets as she could find atop the lone single bed and then crawling under, still fully dressed.

By six in the morning she was up and feeling refreshed, relatively speaking. She bundled up and then retraced her steps to Gennadiy Alenin's neighborhood. The morning was overcast and raw, the skies as dark and bleak as the city itself, and along the way she grabbed breakfast and the largest coffee she could find at a streetside diner.

The food was overpriced and bland, but the CIA was paying and the coffee was hot and strong, so Tracie considered it a net gain.

Upon her arrival outside Alenin's apartment building, she again circled the structure, looking for anything she might have missed last night. Sunrise wouldn't occur for nearly another ninety minutes, so the visibility wasn't much better it had been a few hours ago. Still, nothing she saw changed her previous assessment that

49

Alenin's wife—her name was Ekaterina, according to Stallings's intel—would exit the building via the front door rather than the rear.

Satisfied, Tracie returned to the rear of the building and hiked a block north before crossing the busy street and turning back south. It was early enough that the heaviest rush of commuters, traveling by car, bus, or on foot, wouldn't begin to clog the streets for another thirty minutes or so.

The city was coming to life, however, and ducking into the abandoned building she had selected last night to conduct her surveillance without raising any eyebrows would present a challenge.

She slowed her pace, ambling along the sidewalk, hoping to give the impression of a young woman who had left her apartment a few minutes early and was taking her time getting to her destination. She wasn't sure how believable the ruse would be, given the extreme cold, but it was worth a try. Her aim was to arrive in front of the abandoned building accompanied by as few pedestrians—and thus potential witnesses—as possible.

The first trip past the building didn't work. The sidewalk wasn't exactly clogged with people, but she wasn't comfortable slipping sideways and into the recessed doorway. She continued past, taking the opportunity to examine the structure close-up on her way by.

It looked as though it had once housed offices. The large picture windows fronting the street had been smashed out years ago and then boarded up with plywood. Years of Russian winters had taken a toll on the wood, with small sections rotted entirely away, giving the boards the pockmarked look of a severe acne sufferer.

The front entrance had been a set of double glass doors. The doors were chained together and padlocked, but the glass was gone, only a few jagged shards remaining as a potential challenge to anyone who might want to enter. Plywood had been used to seal the entrance, but rot had taken its toll here, too, and a gaping hole provided what Tracie thought might allow sufficient room to slip inside.

She pictured the vagrants sleeping in a freezing Moscow alleyway last night and wondered how many other homeless had spent the night inside this ancient office.

And how many might still be inside.

She would have to deal with that situation when and if it arose, but right now the challenge was simply to enter without being seen. She strolled past the building and continued another block, then feigned checking her pockets frantically. *Oh! I've forgotten something I need!*

She shook her head in disgust for the benefit of anyone who might be paying attention—it didn't appear as though anyone was—and then reversed course, just another forgetful young woman returning to her apartment to retrieve whatever she'd forgotten.

She approached the crumbling entryway again and decided now was the time. Pedestrian traffic was minimal and she could discern no police presence in the area. She was dressed all in black, and the early-morning gloom should make her difficult to see.

When she reached a point directly in front of the entrance, she lifted her left wrist and glanced down as if checking the time. She slipped left, into the recessed doorway and out of sight of any pedestrians not standing within a few feet of her.

She idled in the doorway, pantomiming reaching into her breast pocket for a pack of cigarettes, and for a brief moment the sidewalk was empty for maybe twenty feet in each direction.

That was when she crouched down and slipped through the rotted-out plywood covering the doorway and into the abandoned building.

* * *

Tracie had expected the building to be hollowed-out and empty, but it wasn't. Abandoned desks, chairs and other office furniture littered the interior, forcing her to move slowly. What little ambient light there was faded away a few feet inside the smashed doorway, and she didn't want to alert a passerby to her presence by bumping into a desk, or worse, injure herself on a sharp object she couldn't see.

She had expected to be tripping over sleeping vagrants, but as far as she could tell she was alone. Perhaps the homeless residents had burrowed deeper into the structure, farther away from the bitter cold seeping into the building through the openings in the doorway and missing windows.

Tracie was relieved not to have to deal with a challenge from someone worried she was encroaching on his territory. She didn't want to have to hurt an innocent person already beaten down by life, and it was critical she avoid any altercation that might draw the wrong kind of attention—the official kind.

The doorway seemed to give onto a large foyer that at one time had probably been a receptionist's area. She felt her way along the north wall, moving in the direction of Gennadiy Alenin's apartment building. Eventually she reached a wide hallway. A short distance along the hallway a door opened into what at one time had been a doctor's office. Or dentist. Or tailor. Whatever.

The office door was long gone, and Tracie entered the room. Unlike the reception area, this space was completely empty. A ghostly ring of half-light to her right revealed the presence of one of the rotted-out sections of plywood she'd seen covering the windows on her reconnaissance mission.

She moved to the window and bent down. Pressed her face to the plywood and peered out the hole. Bitter cold air whistling through the opening caused her eyes to water, and she blinked rapidly to clear them.

Then she smiled.

She had a near-perfect, unobstructed view of the front entrance to Alenin's apartment building.

Now all she could do was wait.

* * *

Tracie had given a lot of thought to how she might pick up the trail of Charles Fowler's assassin, and her working theory was that a young woman living in an inner city Moscow apartment would likely shop for groceries every day. Over the course of Tracie's career working in Russia, she'd spent time in numerous apartments, one or two of them in Moscow, and they had invariably been small, dank and depressing, with little room to store extra food.

Perhaps more to the point, shortages in Communist bloc countries were commonplace. Buying anything from fresh fruit to meats to toilet paper was a hit-or-miss proposition, so the savvy Russian consumer was forced to shop nearly every day or risk missing out on an item that might not become available again for weeks.

That was her theory. And she was banking on it being proven correct, even in the case of a woman whose husband was either on the verge of death or already gone.

* * *

For several hours there was nothing. People came and went across the street, obviously; it could hardly be otherwise in any decent-sized apartment complex. But none of the people remotely resembled the woman whose photograph she'd been given by Aaron Stallings.

The CIA had done extensive research into Gennadiy Alenin's background upon his recruitment by Charles Fowler two years ago. The Alenins had been married a little over ten years and were childless. Ekaterina was a small woman, slender and often sickly. To the agency's knowledge there was no history of infidelity on either side of the marriage.

In keeping with her straightforward personality, Tracie's initial instinct had been to act boldly—to march into the apartment building, make her way to the Alenin's apartment, and talk her way inside. Time was critically important if the KGB planned on continuing to eliminate American assets, and sitting on her heels on a cold concrete floor when lives were at risk chafed badly.

However, boldness was one thing. Stupidity was something else entirely. Stupidity would get her killed. And the notion that the KGB would poison a Kremlin staff member for sharing Soviet secrets with their bitter enemies, the Americans, and then *not* bug the offending man's apartment was impossible to accept.

They probably would not waste the manpower it would take to maintain twenty-four hour live surveillance on the wife. At least

Tracie assumed they wouldn't, since Fowler had never approached, nor had any contact with, Ekaterina Alenin.

But the Soviets would almost certainly have installed listening devices in the apartment, probably since well before the assassination attempt on New Year's Eve.

All of which meant Tracie needed to corner the woman alone, outside her apartment.

The surveillance was exhausting. Daybreak had brought little relief from the bitter temperatures, and the opening in the rotted plywood was in a difficult spot—too close to the floor to allow Tracie to stand upright, too high up to allow her to sit.

She bent at the waist like a shortstop getting ready to field a ground ball.

She perched on her knees.

She squatted on her haunches.

Every position she tried became unbearable after a short time, and she didn't dare take her eyes off the entrance to Gennadiy Alenin's building long enough to stand up and stretch, or to walk around and loosen her cramping muscles.

Finally she spotted her target.

Small and frail-looking, dark glasses covering her eyes, heavy winter parka zipped all the way to the scarf at her throat, Ekaterina Alenin stepped out the front door of the building across the street. Only a small portion of the woman's face was visible, but it didn't matter.

Tracie knew it was her Alenin.

Now she had to catch her.

7

Exiting the abandoned building would involve a certain amount of risk; there would be no way to avoid it. Tracie couldn't afford to wait until she was certain there were no pedestrians clogging the area, as she had done while breaking in. If she delayed even a few seconds, Ekaterina Alenin would disappear and Tracie would have to waste more time waiting for her to return.

Tracie raced through the darkened building, relying on the half-light and her recollection of the obstructions to avoid tripping and breaking her neck. She crouched as low as possible while approaching the front entrance and hit the ragged hole at nearly a dead run.

She burst through the plywood and stumbled onto the sidewalk, dropping to her hands and knees before immediately leaping to her feet. A heavyset woman in a thick ushanka sprang back, surprised at the sudden appearance of a woman where there previously had been only empty space. She glared at Tracie and then waddled away at full speed, arms wrapped protectively around her body.

If she'd had time to think about it Tracie might have been amused by the woman's reaction, but her attention lingered on the old lady only long enough to eliminate her as a potential threat.

Then she disregarded her entirely and focused on the crowded sidewalk in front of Gennadiy and Ekaterina Alenin's apartment building.

Her pulse raced and she began walking quickly south, scanning the crowd on the other side of the street. *Dammit. Where the hell could she have—*

Then she saw her.

Alenin was moving slowly, like a woman with the weight of the world on her shoulders. She'd barely gotten thirty feet in the time it had taken Tracie to scramble out of her surveillance location. Ironically, Tracie had given the woman too much credit and had been focusing her search too far away from the apartment.

She moved along the sidewalk in rhythm with the young woman on the other side of the street. It was tempting to keep the traffic between them; doing so meant alleviating risk because there was virtually no possibility of being spotted by her target.

But it also increased the likelihood of Tracie losing her. Traffic was heavy and if Ekaterina were to suddenly dart down a side street or alley, Tracie might not be able to cross the busy thoroughfare in time to reestablish contact.

The first opportunity she got, she crossed over, sprinting through traffic and then disappearing into the crowd at least fifty feet behind her target.

So far, so good.

Ekaterina was entirely focused on moving forward. Tracie guessed she could have stopped traffic by dancing a jig in the middle of the street and the woman wouldn't have noticed. *I guess having a husband hovering on the brink of death will do that to you.*

Alenin had gone two blocks when Tracie decided to make her move. If the woman was going grocery shopping, as Tracie suspected, it seemed likely she must be close to her destination by now, since she would have to carry her groceries all the way back to her apartment on foot when she was finished.

Tracie closed the distance between them. It didn't take long. Alenin was still moving slowly.

Tracie reached out and touched her lightly on the elbow.

Said, "Excuse me, Mrs. Alenin." She hoped her Russian hadn't gotten too rusty since being yanked out of the field eight months ago.

The woman jumped noticeably, every bit as startled as the old woman had been when Tracie barreled out of the abandoned building.

"Yes? What do you want?" Her eyes were red and puffy from crying, and under the fur-lined hood of her heavy winter coat she wore what looked like a black kerchief over her hair.

And Tracie knew. Gennadiy Alenin was already dead. Ekaterina Alenin was a widow. No wonder she seemed preoccupied.

"May I please have a moment of your time, Mrs. Alenin?"

"Who are you?" Now the woman's eyes were not just sad, they were filled with suspicion as well.

"I'm very sorry about Gennadiy," Tracie said, maintaining eye contact.

"If you know Gennadiy is dead, I'm sure you understand I just want to be left alone."

"Of course I do, but we have much to discuss regarding your husband. May I buy you a cup of tea, Mrs. Alenin?" Thanks to her years spent operating in the USSR, Tracie knew tea in Russia was as ubiquitous as coffee in the United States. Next to vodka, it was probably the most popular drink among Russians.

"How do you know my husband?"

This was taking too long. Tracie felt the weight of eyes on them. Pedestrians would begin to get annoyed by people clogging the sidewalk after thirty seconds or so of non-movement. This would make them memorable. If Ekaterina began causing a scene, they would become even more memorable, and Tracie would have no choice but to abandon her plan and leave before the arrival of the authorities.

Assuming they hadn't already been spotted by police.

Last chance. "I don't actually know your husband, Mrs. Alenin, but I know someone who suffered the same fate as Gennadiy. Please, sit down with me over tea and if you wish to leave after we've begun talking, I'll walk away in the other direction and you will never see me again."

Despite her suspicion, Ekaterina had never pulled away. Tracie still had a light hold on her elbow, and she began steering the woman along the sidewalk.

Finally the young widow heaved a sigh that was half sob and nodded. "I would love a cup of tea."

8

The café was crowded, but Tracie hoped the bustle of customers and buzz of conversation would work to her advantage. As likely as it was that listening devices had been installed inside the Alenin's apartment, it was that *un*likely they were present here.

But, of course, in Soviet Russia you could never be too sure.

If nothing else, the cacophony of voices and the rattling of servings and utensils filling the small tearoom would render it nearly impossible for anyone to overhear their conversation. The last thing Tracie wanted was to add to this young woman's misery, and if the KGB thought in any way Ekaterina Alenin had been involved in her husband's treason against the Soviet state, misery would be exactly what she would get. And plenty of it.

After a short wait, the women were seated at a table for two in an alcove between two windows facing the street. Black tea was most popular with native Russians, so Tracie ordered it for both of them.

Moments later their server placed an ornate silver samovar in the middle of the table. Next to the samovar, the man set down a matching silver carafe filled with not-quite boiling water. He then placed a pair of gilded glass holders—made of gold and silver and every bit as ornate as the rest of the tea set—containing clean drinking glasses in front of each of them. He completed the service by removing a basket of freshly baked bread from his tray and setting it on the table next to the samovar.

He did all of this without speaking or making eye contact with either Tracie or Ekaterina, and then he turned on his heel and whisked away without a word.

Inside the samovar, which stood on a small four-footed base and featured an ivory-handled spigot, loose tealeaves were steeping in a small amount of water. Age-old tradition Russian tradition called for the samovar to be filled with extremely strong tea, which the drinker would add to her glass via the spigot. The mixture would then be diluted with the hot water to arrive at a glass of tea as weak or as strong as desired.

Tracie busied herself preparing her tea as Ekaterina did the same. Ekaterina's movements were fluid and practiced, Tracie's less so. Sugar and cream were available, but Russians typically drank their tea black, and since the point of this exercise was to put the young Russian widow at ease, Tracie passed on both.

Finally Ekaterina lifted her glass to her lips and sipped delicately.

Then she raised her eyes to Tracie's and said, "You told me someone you know suffered the same fate as my Gennadiy. Explain what you mean, please. Gennadiy died from a severe flu. It is not surprising you might know someone who has had the flu."

Tracie shook her head slightly as she sipped her own tea. Ekaterina's face was pale and her eyes still puffy from grief, but her statement seemed utterly guileless. Either Ekaterina Alenin was one of the finest actresses she had ever met, or she knew nothing about her husband's involvement with the CIA.

Had she been aware of it, even the most trusting person in the world wouldn't have been able to avoid...suspicions...regarding the nature of her husband's passing.

"Mrs. Alenin, your husband did not die from the flu."

"Of course he did. What else could it be? Moscow winters are harsh. It happens. Of course he died from the flu."

She does suspect. Her response had been too quick, and too rote, and delivered too flatly. Tracie guessed the circumstances of her husband's sudden violent illness and death had been on

Ekaterina's mind almost constantly. Her face was set in an iron mask, her features as bland as their waiter's had been.

"Mrs. Alenin, your husband suffered radiation poisoning. He was assassinated. Murdered."

"That is ridiculous. Gennadiy died from the flu." She turned her head toward the street and watched impassively as pedestrians hurried by, bundled up against the bitter chill. Despite her best efforts, though, tears filled her eyes and threatened to spill down her cheeks.

"Were you aware of your husband's…extracurricular activities? Did you know he was meeting on a semi-regular basis with a man representing a government whose interests are not aligned with the Union of Soviet Socialist Republics?"

Ekaterina's eyes hardened.

Her gaze narrowed.

She turned back toward Tracie. "Are you poisoning me, too? Is that it? Was it not enough to murder my husband, now you must finish me off as well?"

"I am not here from the KGB, Mrs. Alenin. I'm not here to murder you. You asked me to explain what I meant when I said I knew someone who had suffered the same fate as Gennadiy. May I do that?"

Ekaterina's eyes remained flinty, but she held Tracie's gaze without blinking or flinching. After a moment she nodded slightly.

"Thank you," Tracie said softly. She thought about the circumstances of a clandestine meeting scheduled for a bureaucrat on December 31, and realized no wife would agree to watch her husband walk out the door on that night of all nights without a decent explanation of where he was going and what he was doing. Ekaterina may not have known how deeply Gennadiy was involved in espionage, but of course she had some idea.

Tracie took another sip of tea and continued. "The man I know who suffered the same fate is the man with whom Gennadiy met on New Year's Eve at the Grand Kremlin Palace."

Ekaterina's eyes widened. "Then you are…"

"Yes." Tracie nodded. "I represent those…competing interests."

"That man. Is he…?"

"The last I knew, he was still alive," Tracie said. "But he was fading rapidly. By now he is certainly gone."

"Why are you here? What do you want with me? Haven't you people ruined my life enough already?"

"I am not here to ruin your life, Mrs. Alenin. I'm here to investigate and understand the circumstances of your husband's death. I'm here to ensure something similar is never repeated."

Ekaterina stared, saying nothing.

Tracie could feel her pulse pounding. The tension was palpable. If this didn't work, she would be back to square one, and without a single idea where to go from here.

"What do you want to know?" the woman whispered.

She wasted no time getting started. "Had anything changed for Gennadiy in the days leading up to the New Year's Eve meeting?"

"Changed? In what way?"

"Did he seem worried or nervous? Preoccupied in ways he had not been before?"

"Gennadiy was always nervous. Always preoccupied. From the moment he started meeting with your friend, he knew he was making himself a target."

"Then why…?"

"My husband's family has a long history of dissatisfaction with Soviet rule in our country. Gennadiy was no different. But until the last few years, that dissatisfaction never advanced beyond dinner-table grumbling and unhappy discussions during family gatherings. Once he began working at the Kremlin, though, he had the opportunity to observe first-hand the inequity of our political system, a system where peasants are forced to endure long hours standing in line just for the possibility of receiving essential goods and services, while the chosen few are literally showered with riches."

The woman's face flushed with anger, and Tracie realized Gennadiy wasn't the only member of the Alenin family who had chafed against Soviet rule. His wife seemed to share his feelings on the subject.

Or course, discovering the powers-that-be had assassinated your spouse might serve to crystallize previously unheld beliefs in a way that nothing else could.

"So," Tracie said, "you didn't notice any changes in your husband's mood or behavior. No new concerns."

Ekaterina shook her head. "No. Nothing. As I said, he was always concerned and always worried. If he was *more* concerned or worried recently, he kept it to himself."

"Did anyone unexpected come to visit Gennadiy during the course of his illness? Anybody who wasn't a family member? Anyone you didn't know?"

She shook her head again, and Tracie's spirits sank. This was going nowhere fast. "No one visited Gennadiy besides family and friends, either at home or in the hospital as far as I know."

"How much time did Gennadiy spend in the hospital?"

"A couple of weeks. His illness advanced so quickly that after the first few days I was unable to care for him. From that point he did not leave the hospital until the doctors decided there was nothing more they could do. He returned home at the end and was dead within two days. That was three days ago." The widow's lips trembled but she maintained her composure.

"So Gennadiy passed away at home?"

"That was his desire. He did not want to die in an antiseptic hospital room, surrounded by concrete block walls and uncaring strangers. I am glad I was at least able to fulfill that final wish."

Gennadiy died at home.

A dawning realization began to creep through Tracie, the realization that the link she needed was about to be revealed.

The KGB had poisoned Gennadiy Alenin.

The KGB would want to dispose of Alenin's radiation-soaked corpse, if only to protect their secret.

"Where is Gennadiy's body now?"

"At the funeral home. I...I haven't been allowed to see him since he died. He is being prepared for burial, but the funeral director says it may be another couple of days before he is ready."

Bingo.

The "funeral director" was KGB. He had to be. Soviet intelligence operatives were probably removing Alenin's organs and scrubbing the body of radiation as best they could.

"I am not happy with the funeral home," Ekaterina continued. "I have made that clear to the director."

Tracie perked up. "Unhappy? Why?"

"When they removed my husband's body from my home, the

63

crew was impudent and disrespectful. They even made an inappro-
priate joke about the 'flu' that killed Gennadiy."

"What kind of joke?"

"They asked me if I knew what strain of flu had killed my
husband."

"What strain of flu? What did you say?"

"I said of course I did not know."

"And what did they say?"

"One of them said he had fallen victim to 'The Kremlyov
Infection.' Then the other chuckled as if sharing an inside joke. It
was rude and disrespectful and I told them so."

Tracie knew she had what she needed.

9

January 21, 1988
12:35 a.m.
Kremlyov, Russia, USSR

The Russian-made ZiL-157 delivery truck was big and old and loud. It was also uncomfortable, and not just because Tracie guessed the thing had rolled off the assembly line sometime around the year she was born.

The truck had been modified from its original configuration in a small but critical way: CIA engineers had lowered the cargo box's original floor four inches. It was now asymmetrical, with cutouts that allowed it to sit low on the vehicle's frame, while still permitting clearance for drive shaft operation.

A new floor had then been constructed four inches *above* the location of the original floor, its wood worn and aged perfectly to match what one would expect to see in a work truck that had been in more or less continuous use for better than a quarter-century.

The result was a wafer-thin, eight-inch hideaway running the length of the ZiL's cargo box.

It would soon house Tracie Tanner.

The truck rumbled along the pitted, pothole-strewn road toward the city of Kremlyov, one of the most secretive, highly secure locations in a country legendary for its secretiveness and high security.

From the moment Ekaterina Alenin uttered the words,

"Kremlyov Infection," over tea two days ago in Moscow, Tracie had known she would find herself in this situation or a similar one.

Kremlyov was a closed city, also known as a ZATO, home to a key Soviet nuclear plant. Many Russians, even lifelong residents of Moscow, located just a few hundred kilometers to Kremlyov's northwest, were unaware of the city's existence unless they had reason to know of it.

But Tracie knew.

Tracie was aware of the existence and location of every Russian nuclear plant, as well as every military base, airport, power plant, and other important element of Soviet infrastructure. It had been information critical to the performance of her duties as a CIA covert operative working in Soviet-bloc countries.

Following her dismissal from active CIA duty last year, she'd doubted she would ever again have use for that knowledge. But now, less than nine months later, here she was.

Back in Russia. Back in danger.

Her initial instinct had been to hike into Kremlyov, to slip into the city unnoticed. It was located in a remote area, surrounded by a harsh wilderness unusual for a city of more than eighty thousand people. There would be no shortage of places where she could enter unobserved, had Kremlyov been an ordinary city.

Hiking would represent the easiest and quickest way in.

But there were two problems with her initial plan.

One, Kremlyov was surrounded by prison-style dual parallel barbed-wire fences, two-hundred-thirty-two square kilometers worth. That configuration in itself would offer little challenge to her. It would barely serve to slow her down.

But in the area *between* the fences, all trees had been removed and all the soil overturned. This allowed suspicious Soviet officials to know immediately if an intruder had broken or cut his—or her—way through the fences and entered the city.

The second problem was that the Russians had buried sophisticated listening devices under the no-man's-land ringing the city. Any attempt to breach the exterior fence and hike to the interior, even by someone as small as Tracie, even in the remotest part of the forest, would be immediately flagged and brought to the KGB's attention.

She would most likely be apprehended before ever setting foot inside Kremlyov.

She also considered walking into the city atop the frozen Mockba River. This time of year the ice was probably at least three feet thick. But even if she could do so without setting off the underground sensors—a possibility that was by no means certain—there would be nowhere to hide. Police or KGB would see her approaching for hundreds of yards, even if she kept to the edge of the river.

Again, she would be arrested before ever getting close to her objective.

It became obvious very quickly that she would need help.

She had hoped to get in and out of Russia without ever making use of the CIA contact information Aaron Stallings had provided, given the current lethal uncertainty regarding security. Still, the mission came first, and there would be no getting into Kremlyov, which was a close to a medieval fortress as was possible in 1988, without assistance.

So, very reluctantly, she had contacted the most recent agency operative—besides herself—to arrive in country, calling him via encrypted satellite phone. Her reasoning was that the newest operative would have the least covert experience, but would also have had the least opportunity to be outed to the KGB.

It wasn't much to bank her life on but it was the best she could manage.

That operative had then coordinated for use of the specially modified delivery truck. He was the man now driving Tracie into the lion's den.

When Director Stallings had shared the intel regarding other agency operatives currently working in Russia, he had assured her this man had only been in country a few weeks, meaning the odds of him being compromised were minimal.

Stallings's information hadn't eased Tracie's mind much then, and it didn't now, either.

She had worked with Aaron Stallings enough to know the director was not above telling the occasional little white lie—or the occasional whopper, for that matter—if he felt it necessary to advance a mission. Stallings saying Tracie's contact had recently arrived in Russia didn't necessarily mean Tracie's contact had recently arrived to Russia.

* * *

Tracie rode with her fellow CIA case officer in the truck's cab for most of the trip from Moscow to Kremlyov. Her agency-produced identification would be more than sufficient to protect her in the event of a routine traffic stop, thus there was no reason to spend four hundred miles wedged into what felt like a mail slot.

Conversation was kept to a minimum. The other operative was a young man, curly-haired, slim and with a studious appearance. He looked to Tracie like he should be holed up inside a university library writing a doctoral thesis on some obscure historical event, not driving across the Soviet Union on an espionage assignment that could get him executed.

She supposed that was the point.

While he seemed pleasant enough, both operatives knew better than to attempt anything other than the most basic of pleasantries. Getting to know someone in this situation on anything more than an operational level would be a mistake. When the mission was complete, they would likely never see each other again. The alternative was far too risky.

Besides, she'd learned her lesson about getting close to another agent months ago in an underground tunnel beneath Wuppertal, West Germany. Working with a young man she'd initially detested, she had begun to feel a certain closeness to him as he revealed himself to be both resourceful and brave.

That young man had died a sudden and shocking death, a death for which Tracie blamed herself. The bitter regret she felt for her actions—and inactions—on that day lingered and probably always would.

It was the second time in less than a year she'd lost someone for which she'd felt the tug of attraction during a mission, and she had vowed it would be the last. She would never make that mistake again.

So the conversation was pleasant enough as the kilometers rolled past, if stilted and awkward. But it had done nothing to prevent a look of mild astonishment on the man's face when out of nowhere, Tracie said, "Stop the truck."

The two-lane country road was deserted, the early morning pitch-black and bitterly cold, and for a moment the agent—he had introduced himself as "Ryan Smith," which meant that his real name was most certainly not Ryan Smith—looked quizzically across the front seat without taking his foot off the accelerator.

"Now, Ryan. Stop the truck now."

He shook his head and pulled to the side of the road.

"Thank you. Now back up until I tell you to stop."

"What's this about?"

"It's about saving our asses. Just do it."

He shook his head but shifted into reverse and the ZiL-157 chugged back along the empty road.

"That's far enough," Tracie said, concentrating her attention on the side mirror.

"Okay. What now?"

"Now you pull the release on the rear bumper. I'll be right back."

The hidden crawl space beneath the modified delivery truck was accessible only through a removable metal bumper installed on the rear of the vehicle and crafted to look identical to the ZiL-157's factory-installed bumper. One release handle, similar to a standard vehicle's hood release, was located in the front of the truck under the steering wheel. A second release handle had been built into the crawl space itself.

"Whatever you say," Smith answered. "You're the boss."

Tracie opened her door and climbed down out of the cab. She trotted behind the truck and into the middle of the road. A squirrel that had been run down by a passing vehicle sometime in the last few hours lay in the road, its lifeless corpse frozen to the pavement.

Wrinkling her nose in disgust, Tracie prodded the squirrel with the toe of her boot to dislodge it, then picked it up and held it away from her body. She walked to the rear of the truck and motioned for Smith to pull the release.

A moment later he did, and the bumper clunked open, dropping off the frame and hanging from the rear of the truck by a pair of heavy cables. Tracie tossed the dead animal into the crawl space and then fastened the fake bumper back into position.

A moment later she had climbed back into the truck. Smith stared at her unblinkingly. It was clear he thought she'd lost her mind. Tracie pulled a package of wet naps out of her backpack and cleaned her hands thoroughly, then smiled at her companion.

"Just another day at the office," she said sweetly.

"You want to tell me what that was all about?"

"I told you before. It's about saving our asses."

"How is a dead animal going to…? Ah, never mind. Any other wildlife corpses you'd like to collect before we continue on to Kremlyov?"

"Nope. One should do it."

"And you're actually going to crawl back there in the dark with a dead animal."

"For a while."

"A while? Then what?"

"I told you. I'm—"

"I know, I know. You're saving our asses."

He shook his head again and shifted the big delivery truck back into first gear. It rumbled on toward the fenced-in ZATO.

They drove on in silence for a few minutes, and then Smith said, "I'm sure you'll understand if I don't shake your hand when this is all over."

Tracie couldn't help but laugh.

*　*　*

The modified truck was slightly more than ten miles from Kremlyov when Tracie said, "It's time."

They probably could safely have driven much closer before she slid into the claustrophobic space under the truck, but she couldn't see taking any chances. There was far too much at risk.

No one had spoken for a long time, both operatives lost in thought. What they were about to attempt was risky, more so for Tracie, but for Smith as well. To Tracie's knowledge, even the CIA had never attempted to breach the heavy security of any closed Russian city, much less the most fortified ZATO of them all.

If they were caught, they would be interrogated extensively, subjected to some of the most extreme methods of torture ever devised. Then they would be executed. No one in the United States would come to save them. No one would ever even know what had happened. They would simply disappear as if they had never existed at all.

At her words, Smith eased the truck to the side of the road and stopped. He flipped on his hazard lights and prepared to act as though he was changing a flat tire in the event of another motorist's approach.

It would be an unlikely occurrence. Sunrise was still more than an hour away, and the roads had gotten progressively bumpier and more pothole-strewn the closer they came to Kremlyov. It was as if the Soviets were using any and all methods to discourage visitors.

Tracie slipped on a pair of gloves, then climbed down to the road and padded to the rear of the truck, backpack slung over her shoulder. Smith pulled the release and the rear bumper clunked down once again. Tracie pulled a flashlight and aimed it into the crawl space.

She reached inside and removed the dead squirrel, thankful for her gloves but wrinkling her nose exactly as she had done before. She couldn't help it. She'd done plenty of distasteful things in service to her country. Some of them had been downright unsettling; a few would haunt her nightmares for the rest of her life. But in terms of sheer, stomach-turning disgust, she didn't think anything she had ever done could match this moment.

She dropped to her hands and knees and then crawled beneath the idling truck, careful to avoid scalding herself on the exhaust system. She'd done *that* before, a few months before in West Germany, and once was enough.

Inside the right wheel well, she shoved the animal's still frozen corpse into the gap where the fender had been bolted to the frame. It was a tight squeeze, and she had to use her gloved hands as a hammer to seat the squirrel securely. If it fell out onto the road between here and Kremlyov, this would all be for nothing.

She pounded and pushed and prodded and eventually decided

the animal was positioned as well as she could manage. She would have to hope for the best.

She crawled back out from under the ZiL-157 and grinned in the murky darkness at Ryan Smith, who was once again looking at her like she'd lost her marbles. Hell, maybe she had.

She stuck her hand out. "It's been a pleasure, Smith. Get us inside that city and then drop me off somewhere near the address I gave you. After that, get the hell out. With luck you'll never have to take on an assignment this suicidal again."

Her temporary partner stared at her outstretched hand in horror and she laughed. "Just kidding about the handshake," she said. "Don't worry, I'll burn these gloves as soon as I can."

Ryan Smith—or whatever his real name was—chuckled uneasily.

Tracie had introduced herself to him using her preferred alias of Fiona Quinn, and after a moment, he answered. "You're one of a kind, Quinn, you know that?"

"So I've been told. Best of luck, Smith, and be careful out there. Maybe we'll meet again someday." She trudged to the removable rear bumper and slid inside the opening.

A moment later, the false bumper clunked back into place.

A moment after that, the gears grinded and then the truck lurched forward.

Twenty minutes later, air brakes squealed and the ZiL-157 rumbled to a stop. They had arrived at the armed checkpoint to Kremlyov.

In the dark, suspended under the false floor of the delivery truck, Tracie crossed her fingers. *Here goes nothing.*

10

January 21, 1988
6:25 a.m.
Kremlyov, Russia, USSR

Tracie knew there would be armed Soviet soldiers at the checkpoint. There were armed Soviet soldiers at *every* break in the dual fences surrounding Kremlyov. Each entrance and exit to the city featured a small guardhouse, staffed twenty-four hours a day by men whose job it was to be suspicious of everyone and everything.

The men with guns didn't particularly concern Tracie. The false bottom built into the ZiL-157 was a marvel, virtually invisible to the naked eye. No one would notice the four fewer inches of clearance in the cargo box unless they loaded or unloaded identical delivery trucks every day, and even then she doubted most people possessed the powers of observation necessary to pick up on the alteration.

The only real possibility of detection lay in the size of the removable bumper, which by necessity was slightly larger than typical for this type of vehicle. It had to be, in order to fit over the entrance to the "mail slot," as Tracie thought of it.

But the bumper's size difference was relatively minor. Smith told her longtime operatives in the area said this truck had been used hundreds of times over the past decade-plus, ferrying everything from Soviet dissidents to escaped political prisoners to classified documents around and out of the Soviet Union.

The likelihood of the slightly too-large bumper being spotted by Red Army soldiers unfamiliar with this type of truck was slim, especially in the predawn darkness and the bitter cold.

So she felt reasonably confident of a smooth entry into the city.

Unless there were dogs.

If the Soviets used dogs trained to employ their superior sense of smell in order to sniff out the scent of hidden humans, the whole plan could fall apart before she ever got inside Kremlyov. It was a possibility that had gnawed at her almost from the moment Smith offered the use of the CIA-modified truck.

She lay motionless inside her hiding place as boots crunched across the pavement. A moment later the gate guards requested a bill of lading from Smith up front in the cab. The situation was eerily similar to one she had faced just months ago, when she'd hidden inside a delivery truck to gain access to a secret Nazi training camp in West Germany.

That ruse had worked. Maybe her luck would hold.

The guards didn't seem particularly suspicious, and that was a good sign. This situation was one they faced hundreds of times a day, as the goods and services necessary to keep a fenced-in city of more than eighty thousand residents running smoothly came and went in a near-constant flow.

But then everything changed in an instant.

The scrabble of paws on the frozen ground announced the arrival of exactly what Tracie had feared most—dogs.

Dammit.

She forced herself to breathe slowly and steadily.

In and out.

It was critical she remain perfectly still.

The dog became more active as it approached the truck. Tracie could hear it straining and whining, pulling on its lead. Its handler grunted as he fought against the excited animal, and the conversation at the front of the truck that had been casual and perfunctory suddenly took on a wholly different tone.

Tracie couldn't quite make out the words, but the guard's voice became clipped and guttural. Officious.

The man raised his voice and now Tracie *could* make out the words. He was telling Smith in Russian to get out of the truck.

Outside the dog was jumping around and whining, obviously excited, and Tracie could picture the scene perfectly.

The guards were now on edge.

The dog had detected a scent.

Tracie concentrated on breathing quietly as she said a quick prayer. Her eyes were wide open and they strained against the darkness even though she knew seeing anything would be impossible.

She followed the progress of the dog as it circled the truck. Listened to one sentry trying to control his excited animal as the other grilled Smith next to the cab. To his credit, Smith was playing his part perfectly, insisting he had no idea what was happening, that his vehicle contained nothing but a delivery of bread and bread products to Kremlyov restaurants and bakeries.

"Goddammit," the dog handler swore. His voice seemed to be coming from roughly Tracie's level, rather than from above, where it would be if he were standing. She guessed—hoped—he was shining a flashlight under the rear of the vehicle.

Keeping still was one of the hardest things she'd ever tried to do. Tracie Tanner was hard charging, straightforward, some would say bullheaded. To lie motionless under this kind of extreme stress was more of a challenge than she would ever have imagined.

Without warning, the truck rocked on its frame. The motion wasn't violent or excessive, just a slight movement she might have missed entirely if her senses hadn't been on high alert.

Tracie smiled. They might get through this.

"Pasha," the dog's handler said in a loud voice. It once again came from above Tracie. She guessed the man had climbed to his feet and was calling to his partner on the other side of the truck.

"What is it?"

"Marx is on top of his game today. He sniffed out a dead squirrel." The voice faded as the dog handler walked around the front of the truck.

"He is keeping Kremlyov safe from road kill." The sound of laughter floated through the walls of the truck as the dog continued to strain against its leash.

Come on, come on. If it took too long to wrap this up, the men might begin to wonder about the dog's continued excitement, or about why a frozen squirrel would be emitting a scent at all.

Now the guards were teasing Smith. "What did you do, come here through the forest? Drive one hundred kilometers per hour? That animal was jammed so tightly under your truck, I doubt it will fall out until it decomposes."

Smith said something Tracie couldn't make out, and the men shared a laugh. Then the truck rocked again from what she assumed—and hoped—was Smith climbing back behind the wheel.

The engine revved and then the ZiL-157 began creeping forward. The last thing Tracie heard as they entered the city was the dog handler ridiculing his animal for hunting down a dead squirrel.

*   *   *

Tracie wasn't sure how long they drove around after entering Kremlyov, but it was at least thirty minutes. To the best of her knowledge, no westerner had ever entered the city, and although surveillance satellites and aircraft had mapped it as thoroughly as possible from above, finding the correct street address would present a challenge.

They drove up and down inclines and around corners, stopping at traffic lights, the idling engines of other vehicles wafting through the walls of the truck. The sounds of the ZATO were no different than Tracie imagined they would be in D.C. or any other city. There was nothing to indicate she and Smith were interlopers inside one of the most secure and secretive enclaves in the world.

Eventually the air brakes squealed again and the truck pulled to a stop. A moment later Smith shut down the growling engine. Silence descended and then footsteps crunched along the side of the truck.

Smith pounded his fist twice on the side of the cargo box, their agreed-upon "all clear" signal.

Tracie took a deep breath and pulled the handle to release the rear bumper.

The now-familiar CLUNK indicated the bumper had dropped

and was hanging by its dual cables. Tracie pushed herself backward in the narrow space, crawling into the dirty gray light of a Russian winter morning.

She dropped to the ground. Refastened the bumper and shrugged her backpack onto her shoulder. Smith was nowhere to be seen but she'd told him to make himself scarce the moment he gave her the signal to exit the truck. If something went wrong, there was no reason to offer the Soviets a two-for-one special on captured operatives. Tracie was determined not to make life that easy for the KGB.

She glanced as much as possible at her surroundings without drawing attention to herself as she walked casually away from the delivery truck. The direction didn't matter. The goal was to put distance between herself and Ryan Smith, whose assignment now was to make his way out of the city and back to his Moscow safe house.

He had chosen a good location in which to drop off his cargo. The distant sound of traffic told Tracie they weren't far from the populated portions of Kremlyov, but this spot was quiet and, as far as she could tell, empty. She guessed she wasn't far from the Mockba River but wasn't quite sure why she thought that. There would be no sound of running water at this time of year since the river would be frozen solid.

She walked at a rapid pace, but not so fast that it would arouse suspicion, and after fifteen minutes had left the ZiL-157 and Ryan Smith—wherever he was—far behind. Hopefully by now he had returned to the truck and was well on his way out of the ZATO and on to safety.

Kremlyov was just beginning to come to early-morning life. Cars zipped past, most of them old, all of them, unsurprisingly, Soviet-made. The sun had risen but was fighting a losing battle against a low overcast that threatened snow.

Tracie found herself in a semi-residential area, with maybe a dozen nearly identical tiny homes clustered in a small neighborhood far to her south and a series of shops and businesses located where she now stood, near a main highway playing host to most of the traffic.

She wandered into a combination deli/pastry shop and sat at a table. She craved coffee but ordered tea and a biscuit, since Russians were far less enamored of coffee than Americans. Nothing would be more ridiculous than getting caught because she couldn't forego a cup of coffee and had made herself stand out.

Her order arrived and she sipped her tea while crunching on her biscuit. At the moment she wanted to warm up and get her bearings. The plan was a simple one, at least for now: wait for her target to leave for work and then break into his home. She would search his house from top to bottom. With any luck, she would find what she needed and slip out of the city undetected.

The odds of that happening were slim, but a girl could dream, and that was Tracie's at the moment.

If it didn't work out, she would do what she'd always done—figure something else out. She had a backup plan in mind, but it would be risky as hell, and she hoped she wouldn't be forced to execute it.

Either way, that was a worry for later. One of the first things she'd learned with field work was that there was absolutely no point in worrying what might happen at some point down the line. Things were always changing, variables constantly being introduced, and the only certainty for an operative was that things *would* change and she *would* have to adapt.

She sipped her tea and ate her biscuit and allowed the warmth to seep back into her extremities. She'd worn her winter parka, but the crawl space under the truck had been unheated and un-insulated. Even though she'd only been inside it for about an hour, she had been shivering badly by the time she exited. The opportunity to banish the chill was not something to take lightly.

Too soon the tea was gone and the biscuit reduced to a few crumbs on the plate. She pushed herself to her feet and pulled on her coat. It was time to find a quiet spot—the place Smith had chosen to drop her off should work quite nicely—to consult her map and figure out how far she would have to hike to get to her target's home.

Hopefully the CIA's sources were at least somewhat accurate, because although Kremlyov was a relatively small city, it was still far too big and Tracie far too exposed to go door-to-door searching for the man she needed to find.

11

January 21, 1988
9:20 a.m.
Kremlyov, Russia, USSR

According to Tracie's intel, the manager of Kremlyov's Arzamas-16 nuclear plant was a nuclear physicist and administrator named Yuri Ryakhin. An accomplished scientist, Ryakhin had been the facility's manager for nearly a decade, and had been rewarded for his loyalty to the Soviet cause—and presumably also for his accomplishments—with a private home in a relatively secluded part of the city.

Ryakhin's housing situation factored prominently into Tracie's plan, as did the fact that he was an older man and lived alone.

The CIA's intel on Yuri Ryakhin had been collected almost exclusively through intercepted communications: bugged telephone calls, wiretaps, intercepted mail and the like. The information was as thorough as it could be under the circumstances, but since no one had yet managed what Tracie attempted this morning—entering Kremlyov and getting eyeballs inside the ZATO—everything they had on Ryakhin was all necessarily second or third-hand.

But the home address she had been given was rock-solid. After leaving the pastry shop she looked Ryakhin's supposed address up on her partial map of Kremlyov and started walking. Ninety minutes later she entered his neighborhood and ten minutes after that she was inside his house.

Perhaps the crime rate was low in Kremlyov, or maybe because he lived inside a city that was hermetically sealed, Yuri Ryakhin felt shielded from the possibility of compromise by a foreign government. But his home was unprotected by any kind of security system, and while he had locked his doors this morning before leaving for work, the locks themselves were almost embarrassingly easy to pick.

Tracie stepped into his small living room and shook her head. He should have known better than to make a break-in so damned easy. The director of a nuclear facility presented a juicy target to foreign intelligence services, especially during a decades-long Cold War.

Apparently he hadn't gotten the memo, though, and while it was foolish of him, it was fortunate for Tracie. There was no way to avoid exposing herself to the prying eyes of neighbors while picking Ryakhin's lock, and that exposure had been minimal thanks to the man's unknowing cooperation.

Tracie felt fairly certain no one had seen her enter. The neighborhood appeared deserted and the thick forest surrounding it had allowed her to maintain concealment while observing the home for any sign of movement.

When thirty minutes passed with no activity, she strode out of the underbrush, consulted a phony work order as if checking the address—the neighborhood appeared empty but why take chances?—and crossed to the front door in seconds. She climbed the steps, defeated the lock and was in.

The first three things she did upon entry were to clear the house, to ascertain the location of the rear door, and then to open a rear window. The structure was empty, as she had been almost certain it would be, and the rear door and window would allow at least the potential for escape in the event she was wrong about the break-in not being observed.

Having protected herself as best she could, it was time to get down to work. The clock was ticking, and while she doubted Ryakhin would return home before the end of the workday, there could be no accounting for the prospect of the man coming down with an illness, or having taken the day off, or for any one of a thousand other possibilities that could lead to a negative operational outcome.

Ryakhin had a home office and it seemed like the logical place to start, so she did. After the ease with which she had accessed the man's home she was entirely unsurprised to find his desk drawers unlocked. The desk itself was huge, a shiny walnut L-shaped behemoth featuring six drawers and probably thirty square feet of desktop space.

None of the drawers contained anything close to what she was looking for. A quick check convinced Tracie that if Ryakhin had taken any work materials home he hadn't stored them in his desk.

She conducted a through search of it anyway. This would be her only opportunity inside the home of one of the highest-ranking members of the Soviet Union's nuclear program, and even if Tracie couldn't find the specific item she was looking for, there was always the possibility she might stumble across something completely unrelated that could be beneficial to the U.S. intelligence community.

It quickly became apparent that wouldn't be the case, either.

One drawer was stuffed full of purchase receipts, some going back twenty years, none for anything interesting.

Another contained pens and writing paper and envelopes and Russian stamps. There was a calculator and a telephone book.

One of the larger drawers was stuffed full of pornographic magazines. Some were Russian, some were Czechoslovakian, a few were East German, but the vast majority had been published in the United States.

Tracie raised her eyebrows in surprise and muttered, "Well, well, well, Yuri. Aren't you a horny little bastard?"

Yuri Ryakhin may have been a staunch Communist, committed to the spread of the Soviet state, but his choice in reading material demonstrated an obvious weakness for big-breasted, blonde American women.

Tracie filed this information away in her mind even as she slid the overstuffed drawer closed. This was the sort of thing that could potentially be exploited in the future. A "random" meeting in Comrade Ryakhin's favorite drinking establishment with a scantily-clad, amply endowed blonde, a drunken dalliance where

Ryakhin spilled a state secret or two, just to impress his new fan, and just like that the CIA might have a new blackmail target, a source of potentially game-changing intelligence.

Of course, if Tracie's plan came together the way she hoped it would, in all probability Comrade Ryakhin would soon be out of a job. Maybe he would find himself in front of a Russian firing squad. But you never knew how the ball was going to bounce in the world of covert operations, and a potential weakness in the opponent was an opportunity not to be taken lightly.

She finished searching the desk and found nothing further of interest. Glanced around the office. A bookshelf covered the rear wall, filled with what looked like roughly an even split between technical manuals on the subject of nuclear power generation, classical Russian literature, and modern thriller novels.

There wouldn't be time to rifle through each book, which was what really should be done, so Tracie picked a couple dozen at random, flipped through the pages, and found nothing unusual.

The remainder of the office was a wasteland as far as potential intelligence was concerned. An ancient television sat on a table in the corner, topped by a VCR machine. A rotary-dial telephone had been placed within Ryakhin's reach on the desk. A few pictures hung on the wall, featuring people Tracie did not recognize. Presumably they were Ryakhin's relatives and friends.

The office was a washout.

She moved to the man's bedroom and searched his dresser drawers. Besides uncovering another porn stash—*these must be his favorites*—sharing space with his socks and underwear, she found nothing of interest.

She rifled through the drawers of his nightstand.

Nothing.

She was rapidly reaching the conclusion that Plan B was going to be necessary, regardless of how much she might want to avoid it.

She moved to his closet and checked through the clothing, searching pockets and looking for anything unusual.

Found nothing.

Spent a couple of minutes tapping on walls and searching for a hidden compartment, feeling ridiculous. This was real-life, not a goddamned spy movie. The notion that a Soviet nuclear expert would hide actionable intelligence inside a secret compartment in his bedroom wall was just silly, and after a short time she stopped, thankful none of her contemporaries were here to see her. If Ryan Smith had looked at her funny after she scraped a frozen squirrel off the pavement, she could only imagine what his reaction would be to this.

She closed the closet door and dropped to her hands and knees, peering under Ryakhin's bed.

She searched his bathroom.

Performed a perfunctory search of his kitchen.

The man's house was useless, exactly as she had expected. But she'd had to wait for Ryakhin to return home from work anyway, so at least she'd spent her time productively even if she hadn't found anything.

That was what she told herself, anyway.

She checked her watch. Nearly five p.m., Moscow time. Ryakhin should either be preparing to leave work or—if Tracie was lucky—maybe he was even now on his way home.

All she could do was wait for him to arrive.

She didn't have to wait long.

12

January 21, 1988
5:20 p.m.
Yuri Ryakhin's home
Kremlyov, Russia, USSR

Tracie was ready when he walked into the house.

A key rattled in the useless lock and then the front door swung open. A burst of bitterly cold air presaged Ryakhin's arrival by half a second and then the man stepped into his living room.

And Tracie stepped out from behind the door and placed her gun lightly against the side of his head.

"Step forward, please, Comrade," she said in Russian. She spoke quietly but forcefully.

To his credit, Ryakhin didn't scream. He didn't freeze up in terror or drop to his knees and begin babbling for mercy. He simply moved clear of the front door and then Tracie kicked it closed.

"What is this about?" he asked. "If it is money you want, you are welcome to what is in my wallet, but I assure you it will not be anywhere near enough to make this assault worth the legal difficulties you will have when you are apprehended."

"I don't want your money, Comrade."

"Then what?"

"It's very simple. I want information."

"Information? What kind of information? What are you talking about?" He raised his hands in frustration and began to

85

turn to face Tracie but stopped in mid-pivot as she shoved the gun much harder against his skull.

"Do not test me, Comrade Ryakhin. I will not hesitate to execute you."

"What kind of information do you want?" he asked again, although he seemed to begin to realize how much trouble he was in. His voice had lost most of its initial bluster and Tracie thought she could hear the trace of a quiver.

Good.

"I want the kind of information that can only be accessed in your office."

He sighed. "Fine."

He turned to begin trudging down the short hallway.

"Not your home office, Comrade."

"Then what...?" His voice trailed away as her implication struck home. "You mean you want to access my office inside the plant?"

"That is exactly what I mean."

"But...you expect to march me into the facility at gunpoint and not immediately be apprehended by security? Do you not understand the plant is protected by armed guards?"

"I do understand that, Comrade. I understand exactly what I am asking you to do. It is you who does not understand. Let me tell you exactly what is going to happen. We will drive to the plant. We will enter exactly as you just said, with you at gunpoint. But my gun will be hidden. No one will know I have it except you, and you need only remember one important fact: if you do not get us inside the building, you will die. You will never see or hear the bullet coming, but you will die. Do you understand me, Comrade Ryakhin?"

"But...but...if you shoot me you will never escape. You will die, too!"

Tracie nodded. "Probably. But you will still be dead. Is that a trade-off you wish to make?"

He stood silently.

Tracie said, "I didn't think so. Now, are you ready to march back out to that Lada sitting in your driveway and be on our way?"

This time, Tracie took his silence as assent.

*   *   *

The drive across the city was a short one, less than fifteen minutes. But the tension hanging in the air made it feel much longer.

Darkness came early this time of year in western Russia and the twinkling lights of Kremlyov made the city look like any other. Ryakhin drove in silence, still maintaining his composure better than Tracie would have expected.

They followed the Mockba River for a few minutes and when Tracie suspected they might be getting close, she said, "How much further?"

"We are almost there."

"Good. Don't forget what I told you before. I don't care what you have to say to get us past security, but whatever you tell them, make it good. Make it believable. Otherwise you will be dead before you even know what's happening."

"I understand," he said gruffly.

Despite his status as a pornography-obsessed Communist nuclear bigwig, Tracie couldn't help liking the guy. He had more guts than a lot of professionals she'd met in this line of work, including many Americans.

But it wouldn't make a damned bit of difference if she had to kill him.

*   *   *

To say the guard seemed suspicious would be to shortchange the word. Tracie could tell immediately that Yuri Ryakhin returning to work after he'd gone home for the day was extremely unusual.

They drove up to a security checkpoint at the front gate that she guessed was only slightly less sophisticated than the one they'd snuck through to enter the ZATO. As the guard approached the little car, his eyes were narrowed and his body language screamed apprehension. He relaxed a little when he got close enough to make out the identity of the driver, but then he stiffened again when he spotted Tracie in the passenger seat.

Ryakhin cranked down his window and the guard said, "Good evening, Comrade. What brings you back here when you should be sitting down to dinner?"

"It will be a late dinner tonight, my friend. My niece is visiting from Moscow where she is attending school. Nuclear physics. We are all very proud of her." He turned to offer a quick smile at Tracie before returning his attention to the guard.

She was amazed at how relaxed he seemed. She'd placed her gun in the pocket of her parka, but her hand remained on the grip and Ryakhin knew full well the business end was trained on him.

"But…Comrade." The security guard was visibly uncomfortable and Tracie knew exactly why. This was a secure nuclear facility and strict procedures undoubtedly covered visits like this one.

Procedures that obviously had not been followed.

Her suspicions were confirmed when he continued. "Comrade Ryakhin, all visitors are required to obtain pre-approval in writing prior to their tour."

"Yes they are. That is correct. And I admire your diligence, Comrade. But do you know whose job it is to approve or disapprove those tours?"

"Of course, sir. It is your job."

"Exactly. And you may consider this my approval notice."

"Uhhh…" The man was perplexed. And he seemed to be regaining some of his initial suspicion. The longer they sat here the more dangerous this little excursion became.

The worst part was that none of this was within Tracie's power to control. Anything she tried to do, any move she made or words she said, would serve only to destabilize the situation. She was a college student visiting her uncle. As such, she would have absolutely nothing to say at a moment like this.

"Comrade." Ryakhin spoke with stern disapproval. "This is *my* facility and I just told you my niece is approved to visit. We will of course remain clear of all classified areas, but she *will* enter with me and she *will* tour the plant. Am I making myself clear?"

The young man cleared his throat and shuffled his feet. He dropped his eyes. "Of course, Comrade. Of course."

"Good. Feel free to make a notation on the security log, and I will be sure to clarify the visitor policy at the next staff meeting. Right now, though, it is cold and I am getting tired, and I would like to show my niece through the facility and get home. So if you don't mind stepping aside…"

The security guard nodded and stepped back.

Reluctantly.

Ryakhin cranked his window closed and eased down on the gas pedal and the little Lada sputtered forward.

The guard bent and gazed intently at Tracie as they passed, and she arranged her features in what she hoped was an innocent expression, willing herself to look like a Russian college student. She'd always been petite and looked younger than her age, but she guessed she must rapidly be approaching the point in her life where "college student" would cease to be a believable disguise.

Then the man was behind them and Tracie felt herself relaxing.

Ryakhin shook his head. "You are very fortunate, young lady. I did not think that was going to work. I will have some serious explaining to do Monday, probably to Moscow, if that young man does what I suspect he will do and informs my superiors."

"No," Tracie said. This old guy was getting a little too comfortable and it was time to reestablish her dominance.

"No," she repeated. "*You* are very fortunate. If that hadn't worked you would be lying in a pool of your own blood right now."

"I am aware of the stakes, believe me. If I did not fully understand that my life was hanging by a thread, we would not be inside these fences right now."

"Just keep that in mind and you'll have no problems."

Ryakhin nodded tiredly and pulled the Lada into a spot near the plant's front entrance. "Where are we going, specifically?"

"Where are your most sensitive records kept?"

He hesitated and Tracie removed her gun from her pocket. She held it below the dash and out of sight in the event anyone were to pass by, but the place seemed more or less deserted.

"*Where?*" she hissed.

"My office."

"Then we're going to your office. Lead the way, Uncle."

13

January 21, 1988
6:05 p.m.
Arzamas-16 Nuclear Plant
Kremlyov, Russia, USSR

The interior of the plant was dingy and poorly lit. Like seemingly everything else constructed in Soviet Russia over the last seventy years, the plant was utilitarian in nature, a blocky concrete mass devoid of anything resembling artistic creativity. Of course, a nuclear plant wasn't the sort of building that lent itself to flights of architectural fancy, but Tracie had thought the administrative wing might at least be dressed up a little.

She was wrong. They moved through narrow corridors, encountering few workers along the way, a factor that puzzled her at first. Then it occurred to her that Russia was identical to the United States in at least one way: administrative personnel worked administrative hours, and once the workday was over the admin wing turned into a ghost town until the beginning of the next workday.

Yuri Ryakhin stopped outside a closed wooden door. It was equipped with a frosted pebbled glass window designed to prevent passersby from seeing inside the office when the door was closed. He fumbled with a set of keys and Tracie could see his hands shaking.

She didn't know whether it was from nerves or age.

Didn't care much, either. He *should* be nervous. It meant he hadn't forgotten the revised command structure.

Ryakhin selected a key and unlocked the door and a moment later the pair entered what was clearly a reception area. The receptionist's desk—currently unmanned, of course—stood sentry outside a door that opened into Ryakhin's office. A bank of grey metal filing cabinets filled the wall to Tracie's left.

The plant manager crossed the office, selecting a second key as he did so. He stopped in front of his own door and unlocked it, Tracie right on his heels in case he got the bright idea to try and slam the door in her face and lock himself inside.

He didn't try it.

They stepped into an office that was every bit as dismal as the rest of the building. It was a decent size but featured the ubiquitous concrete block walls and olive-green linoleum floors that seemed to grow like bacteria inside every Soviet-built structure. The desk was decades old, its metal finish scarred and dented.

Tracie tried to imagine a big-shot nuclear facility manager back in the States working in this office and couldn't do it.

Ryakhin turned and spread his hands. "What now?"

She realized she'd allowed her mind to wander, a situation that could have proven deadly in other circumstances. *Get your act together, dammit.*

Her expression revealed none of her inner turmoil. She narrowed her eyes and said, "Where do you keep the classified material? I'm sure it's not in the outer office."

"No," he agreed. "The classified records are stored in the filing cabinets behind my desk."

"Get back there," Tracie said, gesturing with her weapon. Her tension was rising, her respiration coming in abbreviated breaths that might be more accurately described as quiet pants. She'd risked her life sneaking into the closed ZATO to reach this point. If what she needed was not here, she would have to go back to Square One, with a major additional stumbling block: after tonight it would be next to impossible to hide her presence in Kremlyov from the Soviet authorities.

She might already be past that point. The security guard had seen her in Ryakhin's car and even the plant manager had admitted that the guard might well notify the breach in security protocols to his superiors.

Plus, Ryakhin was now a major loose end. The "visiting niece" routine would only work once. She would never get inside this building again. And whether she killed Ryakhin after they left here or merely secured him inside his home, his absence would not go unnoticed. It was a Friday night, which meant she probably had until Monday, but eventually someone would come looking for a bigshot like Yuri Ryakhin when he didn't show up at work.

And when they did, Tracie had better be far away from here or she would never escape alive.

Now that the time had come to access classified information, Ryakhin was becoming less cooperative. He moved slowly, pretending to search for the key to the locked filing cabinet. He shook his head and muttered something Tracie missed, but his act was transparently obvious: *I'm trying, I really am, but I can't seem to find my key. We might not be able to access this material, after all.*

"You have three seconds." Tracie spoke quietly, almost in a whisper. She'd learned a long time ago that if you truly wanted to command someone's attention, you should lower your voice. "If that cabinet is not open by the time I count to three, I will put a bullet in your back, Comrade."

He froze for a moment and then moved more quickly once again.

"One."

Ryakhin selected a key and bent over the cabinet.

"Two."

He slid the key into the locked and turned it, and then swiveled to face Tracie. "All right, the cabinet is open."

"Tell me what you know about Polonium-210."

Ryakhin's face went sheet-white and he stumbled backward into the filing cabinets as if Tracie had shoved him.

"Sit down," she said, "before you fall down."

"Thank you." He dropped into his desk chair and wiped a palm across his face. He'd begun sweating heavily. "May I remove my coat?"

She nodded, keeping her weapon trained on him. When he'd pulled off his parka and dropped it onto the floor she said, "No more stalling, Comrade Ryakhin. Polonium-210."

He cleared his throat as if preparing to launch into a symposium speech. "Polonium-210 is a radioactive element. It is naturally occurring, and in small amounts is harmless to humans. There are approximately thirty Polonium isotopes, each differing from the other only in their number of neutrons. Polonium is quick to decay and decompose, so it changes rapidly—"

"That's enough, Comrade."

The nuclear expert continued speak for several seconds after being interrupted, then blinked in surprise as if only now understanding Tracie's words. "I'm sorry. I thought you wanted to know about Polonium-210."

"Do you honestly believe I kidnapped you at gunpoint and forced you to smuggle me inside this secret nuclear facility so you could give me a scholarly treatise on Polonium?"

"But I thought you said—"

"I told you once to stop stalling and I'm not going to say it again. You nearly passed out from fear when I mentioned Polonium-210 a moment ago. I think you know exactly why I'm here. I don't even think you're particularly surprised that I—or someone like me—have finally shown up.

"But just in case I'm giving you too much credit, let me spell it out: your facility has been producing small quantities of Polonium-210, a radioactive substance far deadlier than cyanide, for the last several years. I want to know the name of your KGB contact, the man who is receiving the Polonium, and I want to know where I can find him. You're going to tell me."

Ryakhin started shaking his head as if perplexed. Tracie still thought he was a cool customer for a civilian, but his acting skills suddenly left a lot to be desired.

She said, "I'm not asking whether the Polonium was produced here, Comrade. I *know* that it was. That radioactive material has killed several good men, men who suffered agonizing deaths no one deserves to go through. So do not bury your head in the sand and hope this all goes away. It's *not* going away until I get what I came for."

Ryakhin dropped his head and sighed deeply. "I can tell you the name of my Polonium-210 contact. But I do not know how to find him. He finds me. He tells me what he needs and when he needs it, and then he takes delivery of the product here at the facility."

"Get the name."

The physicist/administrator turned in his chair and bent over the filing cabinet. He mumbled to himself again but this time Tracie got the impression it was in concentration and not a delaying tactic. He pulled open a drawer with a screech and began thumbing through the contents.

A moment later he lifted a file out of the drawer and placed it on his desk. "Here we are," he said.

"Hand the file to me."

"But it's…" His voice trailed away and he smiled sheepishly. It was trembling and nervous but seemed genuine. "I was about to say—"

"I know. You were going to remind me the information is classified. But we both know that already, don't we, Comrade?"

He passed the file across his desk. Tracie took it from him with her left hand while holding the gun on him with her right. She seriously doubted the old man had a weapon hidden inside his desk, but she'd been wrong before and this wasn't the time or the place to find out she was wrong again.

"Sit back in your chair, Comrade Ryakhin, and get comfortable. I have some reading to do and you're not going to move one muscle until I've finished. Do we understand each other?"

He nodded, and Tracie got down to business.

14

January 21, 1987
7:20 p.m.
Arzamas-16 Nuclear Plant
Kremlyov, Russia, USSR

The KGB operative's name—or at least his alias—was Piotr Speransky.

According to Ryakhin's records, there had been seven instances since July 1984 when the Arzamas-16 nuclear plant had produced a tiny amount of Poloium-210 per KGB instructions, and in every instance the receiving party had been Speransky.

Further intelligence on the agent was minimal. The file was thin and conspicuously short on specifics regarding Arzamas-16's most secretive customer. Tracie wasn't surprised. The notion that the Soviet Union's ruthless intelligence service would offer more than the bare minimum information necessary to complete the transactions was laughable.

But even inside the KGB there was clearly at least a modicum of concern that the radioactive poison—lethal and nearly untraceable as it was—not end up in the wrong hands. Were that scenario to occur, the resulting disaster could be dramatic. Hundreds of Russians—or more—could conceivably suffer the agonizing deaths the KGB had reserved for American intelligence operatives and at least one Soviet citizen deemed a traitor.

But the file did contain a photograph of Speransky. Tracie

studied it closely while glancing up every few seconds. She wanted to ensure Yuri Ryakhin didn't become emboldened by her lack of attention to him and do something foolish, like scream for help or reach for the telephone on his desk.

Her immediate instinct upon entering Ryakhin's office had been to yank the phone's cord out of the wall, disabling it. But she hadn't done so, because she hadn't been convinced she wouldn't need it. Besides, it would take the old man several precious seconds to pick up the handset and activate even one number using the telephone's old rotary dial, and that would be more time than she would need to convince him of the error of his ways.

She examined Piotr Speransky's photo carefully. It was a head-shot and thus included nothing below his shoulders. This factor, and the lack of anything in the photo's background to provide perspective, made estimating the man's size difficult. He appeared middle-aged and big-boned but lean, a large man whose chiseled face and hard expression radiated toughness.

Brutality.

The willingness to carry out orders, even if doing so meant sentencing other men to a vicious and brutal death.

It was the face of an executioner.

Tracie committed every aspect of the photo to memory. If all went according to plan, she would soon find herself face-to-face with the KGB killer who was calling himself Piotr Speransky, and she wanted to take no chances of misidentifying him. No one else, not even another KGB operative, deserved the fate she had planned for Speransky.

Other than the name and photo, the file contained little of use. Pen-and-ink initials—Ryakhin's own, Tracie assumed—jotted down next to each entry in a descending column of dates indicated exactly when delivery of the Polonium had taken place in each instance.

The latest dose had been manufactured and then handed over just a few weeks ago.

December 26, 1987.

Five days before the CIA covert operative known as Charles Fowler and his Russian informant, Gennadiy Alenin, had been dosed with Polonium-210, effectively ending their lives.

Tracie focused on the date and thought back to her first and only meeting with Fowler, sick in his hospital bed, tubes running into and out of his body, unable to keep food down, unable to walk, unable to care for himself, now almost certainly dead. Charles Fowler, with a now-widowed spouse and two now-fatherless young children.

The smoldering sense of fury she had felt walking out of Fowler's quarantined room inside the Langley infirmary began to return and she relished it. She allowed the anger to seep through every pore in her body, to settle in her bones and fuel her determination, to spur her forward. She would need every last ounce of resolve she could muster if she were to complete her mission.

Tracie Tanner had done much in service to her country that many would not understand. That more than a few would condemn. And she had always done it with the certainty she was advancing her nation's agenda, an agenda of freedom and democracy.

But she had never done what this mission required.

She felt Ryakhin watching her, his curiosity evident. He, of course, knew the file contained little information that would be useful to an American spy, and he was clearly wondering what in the hell she was doing staring at the same page in the thin file for so long.

Fine. Let him wonder. Yuri Ryakhin was nothing but a link in a chain, and if he were to escape this encounter with his life he should consider himself supremely fortunate.

Tracie continued to monitor Ryakhin while she allowed her mind to wander, considering options moving forward. She had hoped for more usable intel from this file, but would have been lying to herself if she said she'd actually *expected* it. Her hopes had been based on the fact that the information was housed inside a security-protected facility, which was itself inside a closed city protected by Red Army soldiers armed with automatic weapons.

Still, she had learned enough to puzzle out a next move. It was risky and dangerous, but what about this mission hadn't been? For that matter, what about her nearly eight-year CIA career hadn't been risky and dangerous?

Yuri Ryakhin decided to speak. "I told you we had no address for Comrade Speransky. He has taken delivery of the Polonium inside the gates of this facility without exception. I have no idea where he goes when he leaves here and frankly, I do not want to know."

"I believe you," Tracie said. "I believed you when you said it the first time. But that doesn't matter."

"It doesn't matter that you can't find him? You said yourself you've gone to a lot of trouble and considerable risk to occupy a seat inside this office, and now you find yourself at a dead end. I, of course, do not mind, but—"

"That's where you're wrong," Tracie interrupted.

"Excuse me?"

"I'm not at a dead end."

"I do not understand. All you have is a name, which is undoubtedly an alias. You have no idea where Speransky is, nor how to find him."

"It doesn't matter where he is. And I don't have to find him, because he's going to come to me."

"How are you going to get him to come to you?"

"I'm not going to. You are."

* * *

There was only one other useable piece of intel inside the file, but it was as valuable to Tracie as gold: a telephone number.

For a covert KGB operative to provide a method by which a civilian—even a civilian as powerful and influential as Yuri Ryakhin—to initiate contact was extremely unusual. From an operational perspective, it would have made much more sense for Speransky to contact Ryakhin at the times and in the places he deemed appropriate. After all, the KGB had become a semi-regular customer at the Arzamas-16 plant.

But years of working with lethal radioactive poisons undoubtedly changed things from Speransky's perspective. He had been walking around with instruments of death far more powerful than the plague in his pocket for well over three years, blunt instruments that, if released accidentally or in the wrong circumstance, would be just as deadly to him or to those around him as they would be to the KGB's intended targets.

So Speransky was trying to protect himself. By giving Yuri Ryakhin a means of contact, he was hoping to provide himself with at least the possibility of an out—a chance for survival should the Arzamas-16 plant manager determine Speransky had been exposed to radiation during one of the transfers of the deadly material.

And that perfectly natural desire for self-preservation would prove to be his undoing.

Tracie plopped the file onto the desk in front of Ryakhin. She placed her index finger over the telephone number and said, "You're going to call this number."

"You want me to telephone the KGB? You'll be signing your own death warrant, young lady, not that the prospect particularly concerns me."

"You let me worry about that. Just do as you're told."

Tracie was almost certain the number would go to Speransky himself, not to a KGB station somewhere. The KGB wouldn't have allowed Speransky to provide a contact number to Yuri Ryakhin, because the KGB wouldn't be the least bit concerned about the possibility of the accidental exposure of one of their operatives to lethal radiation. They would be entirely mission-oriented.

If Speransky went down, they would replace him with another operative.

If that operative went down, they would replace him with a third.

It was a brutal business. It was brutal on the CIA end, and Tracie guessed it was even more so on the KGB end.

She would use knowledge that to her advantage.

Ryakhin sputtered and shook his head. "What am I supposed to say on the off chance I am even able to get in touch with Comrade Speransky?"

"We'll go over all that, don't worry. We will go over it and over it until you are prepared to say exactly what I tell you to say. Exactly."

15

January 21, 1988
8:15 p.m.
Moscow, Russia, USSR

Evgeny Domashev had just finished pouring his third glass of vodka and was settling back down on the couch when the telephone rang.

This was unusual. He wasn't due back at work for days, although it was always possible his KGB handler had an assignment for him that would not wait.

It certainly wasn't a friend calling. Evgeny had no friends. He had partners during working hours, and lovers on occasion, but there was not one person in the world he would consider a "friend" in the commonly accepted usage of the word.

That was how Evgeny wanted it. He had been killing and maiming men and women in the name of Soviet intelligence for as long as he could remember, and when he wasn't busy killing and maiming, he wanted his time to be his own.

He telephone continued to ring and Evgeny stared it, glass halfway to his lips, as though perhaps the damned thing would come to life and explain itself.

It didn't, so after a moment Evgeny placed his glass carefully on the table and lifted the receiver from its cradle.

"Da?" It was a rude way to answer, but he didn't care. In fact, he *wanted* to convey his displeasure with whoever had been foolish enough to call. He spit the word curtly into the phone.

"Comrade Speransky?"

The voice sounded vaguely familiar but Evgeny couldn't place it. Maybe if he hadn't already polished off two tall glasses of premium vodka it wouldn't have been such a mystery.

He cleared his throat and said, "Who is this?"

"Comrade Speransky, this is Yuri Ryakhin."

Everything clicked. Ryakhin was head man at the Arzamas-16 nuclear plant, where Evgeny had taken delivery of the goddamn radioactive poison the KGB had seen fit to use as their newfound favorite assassination tool. No wonder he'd had trouble recognizing the voice. They'd spoken less than two dozen times in the last four years.

A telephone call from Ryakhin could not be a positive development.

"You should not be calling here, Comrade Ryakhin. Not ever. Not unless there is some kind of emergency."

"That's just it. This *is* an emergency." Ryakhin sounded tense, upset.

Perhaps the man's tension had something to do with the emergency. Considering the type of emergency the director of the Arzamas-16 Nuclear Plant was likely calling about, perhaps Evgeny would soon be tense and upset as well.

"What is the matter, Comrade Ryakhin?"

"There was a problem with one of the lead-lined bottles we use to transfer the Polonium to you."

A sick feeling wormed its way through Evgeny's belly. The vodka he'd drunk felt as though it might be planning a revolution. A violent one. "What kind of problem?"

"A crack. It was a very small crack, a hairline crack, not nearly large enough to allow the suspension to leak out of the bottle."

"But large enough to allow radiation to escape? Is that what you are telling me, Comrade Ryakhin?" He realized his voice was increasing in volume and he worked to moderate it. The vodka revolution in his belly gained momentum.

"I am afraid that is correct."

Unreasoning panic ripped through Evgeny. His extremities

turned cold and suddenly he felt a strong need for the toilet. He could barely think, could barely—

Wait a second. Get ahold of yourself. "That shipment of Polonium was transferred nearly a month ago. Why are you only now realizing there was a radiation leak? How would you even know?"

A short pause. "Our in-house radiation sensors picked up the leak. It took some time to narrow down the source of the radiation, but our nuclear engineers assure me—and I believe them—that the radiation came from your shipment."

"But I feel fine. Not ill at all. I've never felt better or stronger. Why am I not sick if the bottle leaked radiation? Alenin is in the grave, as I am sure the American is as well. Why have I not fallen ill?"

"You will, Comrade. The dosage you received was small enough that it will take the Polonium some time to achieve lethality. But it will. If you are not feeling sick now, you will begin to soon. Very soon."

Evgeny realized he was shaking. He tried to stop but could not. In his stomach, the vodka revolution seemed to be nearing critical mass.

Maybe the illness was setting in now. He had tried to banish what he knew about the effects of Polonium-210 poisoning to a remote corner of his mind in order to allow him to best perform his duties, but there was only so much banishing a man could manage. He knew it was a brutal and vicious way to die.

He realized Ryakhin was still talking. "Excuse me? I missed that. Say it again."

"I said there may still be time to reverse the effects of the radiation, but it must begin *immediately.*"

"Reverse the effects?"

"There is a possibility, yes."

"What must begin immediately?"

"The treatment, of course."

A ray of hope. "So I must get to a hospital, then."

"No. Not a hospital. No hospital in Moscow—or anywhere in Russia, for that matter—will be equipped to deal with this type of radiation."

"Then where do I go?" Evgeny felt his anger rising. This was

Ryakhin's fault. Ryakhin and the goddamned Arzamas-16 plant. The old bastard had better start providing some answers, right now, or Evgeny would make it his mission with whatever life he had left to send the old man straight to Hell before he died.

"You must come here, Comrade Domashev."

"What do you mean, 'here'?"

"Arzamas-16. The facility. You must come here. Right away. First thing in the morning. Our infirmary is equipped to deal with exactly this type of medical situation. We may be able to cleanse the radiation from your system before you suffer too much internal damage."

Evgeny shook his head. This was all happening too fast. His stomach continued to roil, but so far the revolution remained contained. "Why wait until tomorrow? If I leave now, I can be in Kremlyov by—" he glanced at his watch, which seemed to be dancing a samba on his wrist—"three a.m. Maybe sooner."

"No, Comrade Speransky. There is nothing we can do for you until tomorrow. It will take me that much time to set up the infirmary with the equipment and medications your treatment will require."

"Tomorrow."

"That is correct. If you can, plan to arrive at the facility around nine a.m. That should permit thorough preparation while still allowing treatment to begin in a timely manner."

"Nine a.m.," Evgeny repeated. "I'll be there."

"Very good."

"And Comrade?" Evgeny's voice was cold and hard.

"Yes?"

"This treatment had better work, or I won't be the only one facing an untimely death."

16

January 21, 1988
9:05 p.m.
Arzamas-16 Nuclear Plant
Kremlyov, Russia, USSR

Yuri Ryakhin was drenched in sweat when he hung up the telephone. He looked pale and his hands were shaking and Tracie almost—but not quite—felt sorry for him.

He ran the back of his hand across his forehead and said, "I don't think you have any idea what you have gotten yourself into."

"I would say, from the looks of things, you're more concerned about what I've gotten *you* into."

"Perhaps, young lady, perhaps. But Piotr Speransky is no ordinary man. Not even close. He is a dangerous man, a killer, the kind of man who would end your life without a second thought. He is *not* someone to be trifled with."

"Is that so? Well, neither am I." Her voice was flat. "Did you ever once consider what Speransky was doing with that death cocktail you've been manufacturing for him? Just once?"

He stiffened in his chair. "That is not my concern. It has never been my concern. We all have our jobs to do, and as director of a nuclear facility, mine is to provide Polonium-210 if my government requests Polonium-210. It is not my position to question its purpose."

"How convenient for you. Well, I've given it plenty of thought.

I've seen first-hand the kind of damage you and the Soviet government have done with the Polonium you're only too happy to provide."

Ryakhin gazed at her impassively.

"And I'll tell you something else," she continued. "Piotr Speransky might well be every bit as dangerous as you claim. After all, we know he's a killer. But he is *not* the most dangerous person you've ever met. That person is sitting right in front of you. And she's angry. And that does not bode well for you."

The room fell deathly silent, Ryakhin dropping his head and goggling at his desk blotter as if suddenly becoming aware of its existence for the first time. "I am just an ordinary man, trying to do his job the best I can."

"There's one problem with that. People are getting killed because you're doing your job."

"What happens now?" Ryakhin's previous cool composure had vanished. In its place was the dread certainty that Tracie was going to execute him where he sat. His hands were shaking and all the color had drained from his sweaty face.

Tracie ignored him. She sat motionless as she considered her next steps. Then a thought occurred to her and she gazed at Ryakhin in intense concentration. "You told Speransky the container of Polonium must have contained a hairline crack."

"You told me to say whatever it took to get the man here as soon as possible. I thought that would accomplish your goal most effectively."

"And it did," Tracie said, "which is one reason why you're still breathing. Do you always transfer the Polonium in the same type of container?"

"Da," the old man answered. "We fabricated special spray bottles that allow Comrade Speransky to disperse the liquid suspension when he is ready, but which contain a thin lining of lead to protect him, and those around him, from radiation while the mixture is in his possession. I believed a crack in that lead lining would sound perfectly plausible, and as you observed, Comrade Speransky seems to have accepted my words, God help us."

Tracie shook her head. "But the bottles are always the same? Every time you transfer Polonium-210 to Speransky you use an identical one?"

"Da. We contracted for several dozen bottles when the project began almost four years ago. It seemed the wisest thing to do."

Several dozen.

"And these custom-manufactured bottles have just one purpose? To carry around this deadly radioactive poison?" The Soviets had used Polonium-210 on a half-dozen U.S. covert operatives and at least one Soviet citizen over the last three-and-a-half years. Tracie pictured Charles Fowler lying in his hospital bed, wasted away and suffering immeasurably before finally—mercifully—dying. Then she envisioned at least eighteen to twenty-four more lead-lined spray bottles stored somewhere inside the Arzamas-16 plant, ready and waiting to cause more suffering and death.

Ryakhin nodded slowly. He wasn't sure where this conversation was heading but it was obvious he didn't like it much.

"Show me," Tracie said suddenly, pushing to her feet and flicking her Beretta toward the closed office door.

"Show you?" Ryakhin shook his head in confusion. "Show you what?"

"The special spray bottles. The containers you've been using to allow a murderer to transport lethal radioactivity before using that radioactivity to execute good people. Show me. I want to see them."

* * *

Ryakhin was moving much more slowly now than he had when Tracie first ambushed him inside his home. The telephone conversation with KGB operative Piotr Speransky seemed to have taken more out of him than had the experience of being threatened with a loaded gun. But he seemed to be doing as he was told, and until she began to suspect he had stopped cooperating she decided not to push it.

Leaving the manager's office to do anything other than exit the Arzamas-16 plant and drive away was risky, probably more so than Tracie could justify. But she wanted to see the delivery method the Soviets had chosen for their poison.

It was more than just idle curiosity.

Perhaps she could gain an operational advantage.

The corridors remained dimly lit and mostly empty. She wasn't familiar with the operation of a nuclear plant, especially one inside a Russian ZATO, but she assumed a facility this size and this valuable to the Soviets would require at least a skeleton crew of workers during off-hours to keep things running smoothly.

And if that were the case, the lack of people roaming the corridors led her to believe Ryakhin was leading her away from the operational areas of the plant and deeper into the administrative wing. It was a little surprising.

Eventually Ryakhin stopped in front of another locked door. He fumbled through his keys until selecting the proper one, and a moment later Tracie found herself inside what amounted to a massive storage closet. Row after row of metal shelving stretched into the distance, covered with everything from reams of paper and other office supplies to electrical servos, tools, hardhats and hundreds of motors and replacement mechanical parts, the purposes for which Tracie could not even guess at.

Ryakhin moved to the right and then wandered down a row, rubbing his jaw and muttering softly to himself.

A third of the way down the aisle he said, "Aha!" He stopped in front of three sturdy crates placed side-by-side on a shelf. He reached for one of them and Tracie was beside him in an instant, her weapon trained on Ryakhin's midsection. It seemed unlikely in the extreme that the plant manager had hidden a gun in here, but there was no reason to take chances, and Tracie wasn't about to.

"Slow and easy, Comrade," she muttered. "Slow and easy."

He had begun to regain a little color, but now it once again drained from his face as the Beretta's barrel nudged him gently in the side.

"I am only giving you what you wanted," he whispered.

"Fine. Just be sure you remain focused on what matters to you right now."

"Do not worry. There is little danger of me forgetting."

"Open the crate."

Ryakhin pulled the cover off the top. Lined up inside were small spray bottles, exactly as the plant manager had described back in his office. They were slightly larger than the size bottle of eyeglass-cleaner someone might buy at the pharmacy, but still plenty small enough to slip into a pocket.

And then use to poison someone.

Tracie leaned forward and peered into the box. This storage area was just as poorly lit as the rest of the plant, but she could see empty spaces where the bottles used to murder half a dozen American operatives had once sat.

"Hand me one of them," she said.

Ryakhin seemed to have anticipated her request. Almost immediately he reached in and withdrew one of the bottles and then dropped it into her open palm. It was heavier than it appeared, which made sense. The lead lining would add considerable weight.

Given the purpose of the lead, though, she doubted Speransky would have complained.

"I'm going to keep this," she said. She slipped her hand under a flap in her backpack and dropped the little spray bottle into one of the pockets.

Ryakhin watched, his expression one of confusion. And, of course, fear.

"Souvenir," she said, smiling sweetly. "I want to keep a memento of how much fun this has been."

That was when the door swung open behind them and a Russian voice said, "Stop right where you are!"

17

January 21, 1988
9:15 p.m.
Moscow, Russia, USSR

It took a few minutes for Evgeny Domashev to regain his bearings after the disturbing—*okay, terrifying*—phone call from the Arzamas-16 plant manager.

He slammed the telephone handset down on its cradle and sprang to his feet.

Paced his apartment aimlessly.

Attempted to take a slug of vodka and slopped the precious liquid down his shirt, betrayed by his shaking hands.

On his second attempt he held the glass in both hands, and although they were still shaking he was at least able to get some into his belly this time. The liquor slid down his throat with that familiar pleasant burn, and somewhat surprisingly Evgeni found his nerves calming just a bit.

This situation was nothing new, not really. He had been in tight spots before and gotten out of them just fine. Maybe not as tight as this one, maybe none of those spots had threatened the kind of agonizing death sentence he now faced, but still, adversity had a way of hardening a man and Evgeny Domashev had faced plenty.

He paced some more and forced himself to think. There was much to do. The egghead scientist/plant manager Ryakhin had told him to travel immediately to Kremlyov for treatment, which of course meant that Evgeny would have to take a leave of absence from the KGB.

He was not due back to work for a couple of days, but while Ryakhin had not specified how long the radiation-eradication treatment would take—and Evegny had been too shaken up by the unexpected phone call to ask—he had to assume it would be a longer process than that.

This presented a problem.

Evgeny could not simply advise his superiors that he'd been dosed with radiation and must now take time off to (hopefully) be cured. Their first question to him in response to that notification would be a good one: how had he become aware of this radiation poisoning when he hadn't even begun to feel ill yet?

That was not a question he would be able to answer, at least not to the KGB's satisfaction. By providing Yuri Ryakhin with his unsecured home telephone number, Evgeny had violated strict Soviet intelligence policies designed to protect his identity.

Not to mention state secrets.

If he admitted to violating those policies, Evgeny would not have to worry about becoming ill. Dying from exposure to Polonium-210 would be the least of his concerns. He would likely be executed behind the KGB's Moscow headquarters building and buried in a shallow grave before he ever began exhibiting symptoms of radiation poisoning.

He continued to ponder the issue as he moved into his bedroom and began tossing clothing into a small travel bag. The problem of how to handle his handlers was not an insurmountable one. He would figure out something to tell them that would be believable. One didn't spend the majority of one's adult life in the field of covert intelligence operations without becoming a practiced and proficient liar.

Another sip of vodka.

Another warm burn in his throat.

Another calming splashdown in his belly.

Evgeny pushed the KGB problem to the back of his mind as he stopped his manic packing for a moment. He dropped the half-filled bag onto the floor and sat on the edge of his bed.

Thinking.

Now that he had absorbed the first terrifying shock of Ryakhin's phone call and begun considering what the nuke-plant operator had said over the phone, Evgeny felt an uneasiness settling over him. He couldn't quite put his finger on what that uneasiness represented, but it *wasn't* related to his fear of dying from Polonium-210.

It was more amorphous than that.

Less tangible.

Something about this situation didn't smell right.

An intelligence specialist learned early on in his career to trust his instincts. It was an important lesson. If it wasn't learned, and quickly, one of two things happened: either the specialist trusted the wrong people and gathered faulty intelligence, thereby eventually losing his job, or he trusted the wrong people and eventually lost his life.

Evgeny could not deny there was every possibility Yuri Ryakhin was telling the truth. Evgeny was no nuclear physicist, not by a long shot. Studying had not been his strong suit while in school, and he would be the first to admit scientific theories and concepts were mostly beyond his ability to comprehend.

But he wasn't stupid, either, and Moscow boasted some of the finest libraries in the world. One of the first things Evgeny had done four years ago after being selected for the Polonium-210 Project— also known as Project Kremlyov Infection—was to research the effects of radiation sickness in general and Polonium-210 in particular.

Much of what he read was technical, beyond not just his ability to understand, but the scope of his research as well. However, he'd learned plenty about nuclear radiation and its effects on the human body.

And it was without exception ugly.

And frightening.

Another sip of vodka, another nice burn. Oddly, the alcohol seemed to be focusing Evgeny and allowing him to think clearly when it should be having the opposite effect.

Evgeny had accepted his mission even after conducting his research into the effects of radiation poisoning. He did so partly out of a sense of duty to Mother Russia, but also because once selected for a KGB mission, an operative did not decline to participate. It simply was not done. The operative who made the decision to turn down an assignment from his superiors would disappear in short order, sent to a work camp in Siberia or worse.

But his research had stayed with Evgeny Domashev ever since. He'd thought about it often, especially during those periods when his mission was active, when he was carrying the deadly radiation in his pocket, tucked away next to his internal organs before being used to end the life of another enemy of the Soviet State.

Just because he was an assassin didn't mean he had no feelings.

But the point was that radiation poisoning—especially the amount of radiation produced by that damned Yuri Ryakhin in his damned Arzamas-16 plant—was not subtle. It did not come on slowly. It did not sneak up on the victim.

It was like a hammer striking the victim in the head.

In fact, Evgeny had always thought of Polonium in terms of the Soviet Union's iconic hammer and sickle flag when used to eliminate American assets: The hammer was used to stagger the enemy, and then the sickle cut that enemy off at the knees.

But here was the problem, and perhaps the reason for Evgeny's unease. He did not feel like a man being struck on the head with a hammer, and he did not feel like a man whose legs were being sliced off by a sickle.

He felt fine.

He did not feel weak, or ill, or even the slightest bit tired.

He simply did not feel like a man who had been dosed with nuclear radiation.

He fully admitted to himself that he could be wrong. Ryakhin might be—and probably was—telling the truth about the radiation, that a hairline crack had opened up in the last lead-lined bottle and that even now, poison was attacking Evgeny's organs.

It was the most likely scenario. He could not imagine a single reason why Ryakhin would lie.

But still, that sense of unease would not go away. It was there, and it was real, and Evgeny trusted in it every bit as much as he trusted in Ryakhin's superior scientific knowledge and his nuclear acumen.

Maybe more.

And an intelligence officer who wanted to stay alive always developed a backup plan. It was second nature to a man who had worked in the field as long as Evgeny had.

He pushed to his feet and picked up his drink.

Exited his bedroom, the half-filled travel bag forgotten for the moment.

Walked into his tiny living room and plopped down on the couch.

For a long time he stared at the telephone, lost in thought. Then he picked up the handset and dialed a number from memory.

When the call was answered he said, "Hello, Comrade Mineyev, this is Evgeny Domashev. It has been a long time, eh?"

The man on the other end of the line was suspicious, Evgeny could tell. This call to another KGB operative was as unusual as Ryakhin's call to Evgeny had been. But it could not be avoided.

Evgeny waited, holding his breath, hoping he had chosen the recipient of his call wisely.

After a moment Nikolay Mineyev said, "*Da*, Comrade, it has been too long. I believe it has been since…what…1983? Ukraine? Am I remembering correctly?"

Evgeny breathed a sigh of relief. He wasn't out of the woods yet, but at least Mineyev hadn't hung up on him or threatened to notify KGB headquarters about the violation of protocol the telephone call represented.

He chuckled. "You are indeed remembering correctly. After the conclusion of the mission, we must have closed a dozen bars. I am still hung over!"

The men shared a laugh and Mineyev said, "I appreciate the memory, Comrade, but something tells me you did not call out of the blue just to relive old times. What can I do for you, my friend?"

Evgeny took a deep breath. *Here goes nothing.* "I have a bit of a problem, old friend, one that requires the kind of assistance only a fellow operative can provide."

"The fact that you are contacting me personally tells me this is not an officially sanctioned operation."

Another deep breath. Evgeny prayed neither man's phone was being monitored. If one of them were, he had just condemned himself and his old friend to death, probably preceded by an extensive period of torture.

It was too late to worry about that now. "You are correct, Comrade. But the good news is that your assistance would most likely involve only a few hours of your time and a car ride to Kremlyov and back."

"What is happening, Comrade?"

Evgeny briefed his fellow KGB operative on what he needed, including in his narrative only the barest outline of *why* it would be necessary to travel to the ZATO. And, more importantly, why he thought he might need backup.

He spoke for several minutes, and Mineyev asked a few questions, but after those first few tension-filled seconds, Evgeny felt himself beginning to relax.

Mineyev was going to do it, he could tell.

When he hung up the phone, Evgeny felt much calmer than he had since before Yuri Ryakhin's surprise telephone call. He now had his backup plan. It was probably utterly unnecessary, but he would have felt naked and exposed without one.

He sat for a long time on his couch, quietly sipping his vodka and thinking.

Eventually he returned to his bedroom and finished packing.

18

January 21, 1988
9:20 p.m.
Arzamas-16 Nuclear Plant
Kremlyov, Russia

Tracie froze at the command to stop. The voice came from behind her and Ryakhin and was filled with tension.

It was immediately obvious what had happened. Ryakhin hadn't fully closed the door when he and Tracie entered the storage area a few minutes ago. A patrolling member of the Arzamas-16 security team spotted the partially open door and decided to investigate. It only made sense. No doors should be open in the administrative wing of the plant after business hours.

Perhaps Ryakhin had left the door ajar intentionally, to draw the attention of security. Perhaps not.

The question was moot at this point. Tracie should have ensured the damned door was closed and she hadn't.

Now she had problems. It remained to be seen how serious those problems were.

For a long moment nothing happened. The silence was complete. Tracie and Ryakhin stood completely still and the guard seemed uncertain how to proceed. He couldn't see them from his position just inside the door, but he knew someone was here.

"Walk toward me," he finally said. "I am armed, so proceed slowly. One move I don't like and I'll shoot."

Well, that's reassuring. Tracie jammed her gun into the waistband of her trousers at the small of her back. She un-tucked her blouse and allowed it to flutter over her waist. Hopefully that would be enough to hide the damned thing. She'd left her parka in Ryakhin's office, so it wasn't like she had many options.

Ryakhin had turned and begun trudging toward the sound of the security guard's voice, and Tracie grabbed his sleeve.

"Remember our cover," she hissed. "If you don't get us out of this, the first bullet is going in that guard's forehead, and the second in your back."

He paused but didn't acknowledge her words.

"Comrade Ryakhin, do not doubt my ability with this gun. I'll kill both of you before that man has time to squeeze off a shot."

"Move toward me, now!" The security guard's voice had risen an octave. His stress was obvious. If they waited any longer, Tracie feared he might begin randomly peppering the storage area with bullets.

Ryakhin sighed shakily and nodded, and together they retraced their steps. Ryakhin turned the corner at the end of the narrow row between shelves, Tracie right on his heels.

The security guard stood just inside the open doorway, weapon held in both hands. It was currently pointed at the floor. His eyes widened in a disbelief that was almost comical at the recognition of his boss. Yuri Ryakhin was clearly the last person he had expected to see in this location at this time of night.

"Comrade Ryakhin," he said. "What…what are you…?"

Then he saw Tracie and his eyes narrowed. His reaction was very similar to the one the gate guard had shown upon their arrival at the plant. "What is going on here, Comrade?"

Tracie placed her hands on her hips, waiting for Ryakhin's response. She hoped the motion wouldn't appear too unnatural or suspicious but she wanted her right hand as close as possible to her Beretta should she need to slip it out of her waistband and take down the guard.

Her hanging blouse worried her. It served to hide the weapon from view but offered the very real possibility of a snag should she need to move quickly.

Her threat to kill Ryakhin had been a bluff, but she hoped that with all the stress he wouldn't recognize that fact. She would shoot this security officer if she had to, but she needed the scientist/administrator alive in order to avoid raising the suspicions of the guard at the front gate on their way out. He already suspected something was wrong. Leaving without her "uncle" would only serve to crystallize those suspicions.

Ryakhin said, "Comrade, thank you for your sharp eyes and quick action. I apologize for any concern I may have caused with this unexpected visit."

"It is no problem. But…Comrade Ryakhin…who is the young lady? What are you doing here at this time of night?"

The Soviet nuclear scientist launched into his "visiting niece" spiel as Tracie stood demurely behind him and slightly to the side. She wanted a clear shot at the guard in the event things started to go south. Bitter experience had taught her that events had a tendency to change quickly, especially when they were changing for the worse.

The guard was skeptical. "But…why bring her here after hours? And why did we not receive notification that a visitor would be inside the facility this evening?"

"Comrade, I am far too busy to take time out of my day to give facility tours. But since the visitor in this case is my niece, I wanted to be the one to show her around. Thus, the reasoning for the nighttime visit."

"And the lack of notification?"

"I apologize for that. I simply forgot to advise the security team of tonight's visit." He chuckled softly and Tracie hoped the strain in his voice wasn't as clear to the guard as it was to her. "I had this very same conversation with Dmitri out at the guard shack just a couple of hours ago. Again, I apologize for the inconvenience. I'll not make this mistake again, I assure you."

Tracie's stomach sank at the mention of the timing. She hoped the guard wouldn't notice, but he was too sharp. "A couple of hours ago? How long does a facility tour take, Comrade? And why would the tour include the storage area?"

Dammit. Tracie's hand crept closer to her weapon as the guard began raising his gun. She though it was an unconscious maneuver on his part but it provided a good indication as to the level of his suspicion.

Her adrenaline level, already high, skyrocketed. She sensed things slipping away.

But Yurin Ryakhin, the old Soviet scientist and administrator, pulled things together. He smiled broadly and put the tone of a proud uncle into his voice.

"Ah," he said. "My niece here wants to follow in my footsteps! She is studying to be a nuclear engineer, working very hard. So I wanted this tour to be as in-depth as possible, which is another reason why I didn't wish to use up valuable time during business hours."

"But, Comrade, the storage area?" The guard shook his head in confusion but Tracie sensed that the danger had passed. He lowered his gun again and this time his question seemed to be one of genuine confusion rather than suspicion.

Ryakhin put a conspiratorial tone in his voice and said, "Studying nuclear physics requires notebooks and paper. A *lot* of notebooks and paper. These things are expensive, eh? No one will notice a notebook or two disappearing from storage at Arzamas-16, eh?"

The old man reached up and slapped the guard on the shoulder, a gesture of bonhomie the young man must never have expected. In the modern Soviet Union, important men like the director of a prestigious nuclear facility did not treat lowly security guards as their equal. Or anything approaching their equal.

The man started in surprise. He was uncomfortable, unsure how to react, but he said, "Of course, Comrade. I'm certain no one will notice."

He began edging backward and smiled briefly. Tracie could see he was still uneasy with the situation, but the combination of Ryakhin's status as plant manager and semi-plausible explanation was keeping him in line.

For the moment.

"I have taken up enough of your time, Comrade Ryakhin," he said. "I must resume my rounds. Have a pleasant evening." He spun on his heel and marched through the door, then turned and disappeared down the hallway toward the operational side of the plant.

For all his obvious suspicion, the guard had never once addressed Tracie directly. It was easy to be overlooked when you were a petite woman in a patriarchal, authoritarian society. In this instance that had been a lucky break.

For the guard.

The man's concern had been obvious, and he'd allowed himself to be influenced by Ryakhin. But that influence had clearly gone against his better judgment, and Tracie had a strong suspicion the man would begin to second-guess his actions—or inaction—soon. He might just decide to return and investigate further.

Tracie had always been impulsive and hotheaded, quick to action. But despite those character traits, she had long believed the best kind of conflict was a conflict avoided, particularly when in hostile territory and outnumbered by men with guns.

It was time to leave.

It was well past time to leave.

"Move it," Tracie said. They stepped through the door and she flicked off the light.

Ryakhin pulled the door closed and said wearily, "What now?"

"I'll be out of your hair soon, Comrade Ryakhin. Let's get back to your office so I can grab that file and my coat. Then all you have to do is get us out of this snake pit and you just might escape with your life."

He didn't say a word; he simply began trudging in the direction of his office.

They encountered no one along the way.

Ten minutes later they were back in Ryakhin's Lada. Tracie had the urge to wave at the glowering gate guard on the way out, but she stifled it.

Fifteen minutes after that, Ryakhin had turned into his small driveway.

He killed the engine and turned to Tracie. "I don't suppose you're ready to get out of my car and my life now, are you?"

19

January 21, 1988
10:10 p.m.
Yuri Ryakhin's home
Kremlyov, Russia

Tracie smiled. "Why, Uncle, if I didn't know better, I would think you were growing tired of my company."

"Young lady, I grew tired of your company the moment you out a gun to my head inside my own home. I grew more tired every time you threatened me or one of my people."

"Yeah, well, sorry about that, Comrade, but I'm not going to count tonight among my most pleasant memories, either. If your government hadn't insisted upon assassinating my countrymen with your radioactive poison, I would never have had to put a gun to your head in the first place."

The old man's face turned instantly red. Tracie could see it flush darkly even in the muted light cast by the single streetlamp next to Ryakhin's driveway. "Maybe if *your* government didn't insist on meddling in the affairs of—"

He snapped his jaws shut with great effort as it seemed to occur to him that provoking the woman holding a loaded gun was not the best way to prolong his life.

He breathed deeply. Then in a calm voice he said, "What do you want from me now? Will it ever be enough, or were you lying about allowing me to live?"

125

"Whether you live or die depends entirely upon your actions moving forward, Comrade, just as they have since you first walked through your front door. Nothing has changed. You've done well to this point. Don't change your fate now."

"Fine." He mumbled something else under his breath.

Tracie couldn't make out what he was saying but didn't bother pursuing the issue. She didn't really blame the man for being angry. Undoubtedly all he had wanted at the end of a long workweek was to pour a drink and browse his extensive collection of American porn magazines.

Instead, he'd been hijacked at gunpoint and forced to betray one of his nation's covert operatives. A man who, from his perspective, was helping protect his country and keep him safe.

"Now," she said, "let's go inside your home and make you comfortable."

"Make me comfortable? What is that supposed to mean?"

"Just get moving, and you'll find out." She waved her gun at the man's front door and he reluctantly climbed out of his little car and shuffled toward the house. He looked tired and defeated.

Good.

Inside, Tracie walked directly into Yuri Ryakhin's kitchen. She selected one of the two chairs nestled against his small round kitchen table and slid it to the middle of the floor. Its metal frame had been chromed, and must have been garish and shiny when new but over the years had become dull and smudged. Uncared-for. The seat and seatback consisted of worn padding covered by cracked vinyl.

The chairs looked like something that might have graced an American kitchen around the time Tracie was born. They were relatively sturdy, certainly heavy enough to handle a tired old scientist who had to be nearing eighty.

Tracie pointed to the chair and said, "Sit."

She would have preferred to move it to the living room, where the carpeting would serve to soak up any noise the old man would inevitably try to make, but doing so would place him only a few feet from the front door. Better to position him farther away from potential visitors, even if the area was acoustically deficient.

Ryakhin huffed angrily. "You are not going to tie me up and leave me here."

"I can't have you notifying the authorities. Would you prefer I put a bullet in your head instead?"

"But...but...no one will know I am trapped here! If you do this, you will be sentencing me to death just as surely as if you had pulled the trigger. It will be slower and more painful, but the end result will be the same."

"Come now, Comrade, don't be so dramatic. It will be uncomfortable, sure. Unpleasant. You'll get hungry and thirsty, and sitting in your own waste won't be too enjoyable. But when you don't show up at the plant Monday morning and don't call anyone to explain your absence, someone will come looking for you. My guess is a helpful security guard will be dispatched to check on you by noontime, midafternoon at the latest. They'll find you, and when they do you can tell your tale of woe."

Ryakhin glared at her and she shrugged. "But at least you won't be dead. Now come over here and sit in this chair or I'll force you into it. You won't like it if I do."

He grumbled and cursed under his breath but did as she asked. She slipped her roll of duct tape out of the backpack and began securing him. Ninety seconds later he was bound, arms and legs to chair arms and chair legs, unable to move.

Next she stuffed a clean dishtowel into his mouth and secured it with more tape.

She examined her handiwork.

It looked secure.

Take nothing for granted. She bent and pulled at Ryakhin's wrists, one after the other, then repeated the action with his bound feet.

She couldn't move any of his limbs, not even slightly.

Yuri Ryakhin wasn't going anywhere.

Next she rummaged around in the scientist's cabinets. Selected the largest bowl she could find and filled it with water. Dragged the kitchen table next to Ryakhin and placed the bowl on it, positioning it so the man could bend his head and drop his face into the bowl.

"Might not be ideal," she said, "but a large section of towel is hanging out of your mouth like a panting dog's tongue. When you get thirsty, soak that portion of towel in the bowl. The water will absorb into the cotton in your mouth and hydrate you. You'll be okay for a couple of days. You'll be damned tired and hungry by Monday, but you'll survive, which is more than can be said for the men you helped poison."

Tracie shrugged her backpack onto her shoulder and moved down the hallway to Ryakhin's home office. Closed the door and rummaged through her backpack until she found what she was looking for: her secure satellite phone.

She needed to make a call.

* * *

January 21, 1988
10:45 p.m.
Yuri Ryakhin's home
Kremlyov, Russia

Tracie packed her sat phone away and zipped her backpack. Her work here was complete, but there was still plenty to do before tomorrow morning.

She would have preferred more prep time—another day at the very least—but her plan had been set in motion, and building in more time wasn't an option. Piotr Speransky had to believe he'd been dosed with Polonium-210 in order to force him to come to Tracie, and the only way to convince him to buy the fiction was to make him think it was critical he get to the Arzamas-16 plant for his "treatment" immediately.

After all, who would consider waiting even twenty-four hours if they truly believed they faced the agonizing death awaiting a victim of Polonium-210 poisoning?

Making Ryakhin tell him to wait even a few hours before starting from Moscow to Kremlyov was risky, but it had to be done. Tracie at least needed that much time to prepare.

She reentered Ryakhin's kitchen to check on the Russian nuclear scientist. His bindings were rock-solid and she knew the prospect of him escaping on his own was virtually nil. The time was nearly eleven p.m., so it seemed highly unlikely a man his age would receive any visitors for the rest of tonight, certainly none who might have a key to his home.

The weekend would be a crapshoot. There was no way of knowing whether Yuri Ryakhin was expecting company tomorrow or Sunday, and asking him would be pointless since he would undoubtedly lie.

And then by Monday he would almost certainly be found.

That would complicate matters immeasurably.

The smart thing to do would be to eliminate him. Put him down, and even if his corpse were discovered, he would at least be unable to tell the authorities *why* he'd been killed.

It was the smartest and safest option for Tracie. The moment he was found alive, he would start talking. He would describe the young, red-haired CIA operative who'd kidnapped him and forced him to reveal the identity of Piotr Speransky. Once that information came out it would take little time for the KGB to piece together Tracie's mission.

Leaving Ryakhin alive would be a mistake.

It was exactly what Tracie was going to do.

She'd done plenty of things over the course of her career that could legitimately be second-guessed, but for the most part she was comfortable with the operational decisions she'd made. She could look herself in the mirror. She rarely had trouble sleeping at night, at least where her performance during CIA missions was concerned.

But that would all change if she were to place a gun to Yuri Ryakhin's skull and pull the trigger. The man was a foe in the decades-long geopolitical cat-and-mouse game the United States had been playing with the Soviet Union; that much could not be denied.

And his knowledge and skill set had been directly responsible for providing the KGB with Polonium-210, allowing them to carry out their horrifying and cowardly mission to dose American operatives with radiation, sentencing them to death.

But ultimately, the man was nothing more than a scientist who had done his job. Had he refused to do that job, the Soviets would have executed him and installed someone more pliable into his office. Everything else would have proceeded exactly as it had.

So Tracie simply did not have it in her to murder him in cold blood.

If she had to deal with the repercussions of that decision down the line, so be it.

She flashed a smile at the old man, who gazed back at her with cold contempt.

"It's been fun, Uncle," she said. "But all good things must come to an end. See ya in the bread line."

She picked up his keys and walked out the front door for the last time.

She locked the door and checked it, then checked it again.

Then she hurried to his little Lada, started the engine and drove into the Kremlyov night.

20

January 22, 1988
8:10 a.m.
Six kilometers northwest of Kremlyov, Russia

Tracie didn't know if she'd ever felt this unprepared before an op. Working in Soviet-bloc countries for most of her career as a CIA field operative had steeled her to the realities of dealing with minimal backup, and her assignments since being rehired as Aaron Stallings's personal one-woman Black Ops team had reinforced that sense of professional solitude.

But what she was about to attempt, on a public road in Russia during daylight hours, could be reasonably classified as nearly suicidal.

In fact, this entire mission—to infiltrate Soviet Russia, then determine from whom inside the KGB the Polonium-210 assassination plot had originated, and then eliminate that person— undoubtedly fit that description.

Still, here she sat, gun in hand, waiting, senses on high alert and nerves thrumming.

One minor blessing to this insanity was that thanks to its status as a ZATO—a secretive, closed city inside a secretive, closed Soviet society—access into and out of Kremlyov was extremely limited.

If Piotr Speransky had taken the bait dangled in front of him by Yuri Ryakhin's telephone call last night and was even now rushing toward the Arzamas-16 nuclear plant for "treatment" of his mysterious radiation poisoning, he would almost certainly come via this relatively isolated roadway.

To drive any other route from Moscow to Kremlyov would add hours to the trip when Speransky—hopefully—assumed time was of the essence if he was to survive beyond the next couple of weeks.

Also, the volume of traffic into and out of Kremlyov was much lower, thanks to its ZATO status, than would normally be expected for a city of more than eighty thousand. Tracie had angled Ryakhin's little Lada into its current position on the side of the road almost two hours ago in preparation for this op, and during that time the road had remained mostly deserted.

Tom Petty was right: the waiting was the hardest part.

The waiting was *always* the hardest part.

Once the action started, Tracie knew she would remain calm under fire, cool and collected, her mind clear and her reasoning sharp. It had always been that way and there was no reason to believe today would be any different.

But sitting here *before* the action started—alone on the side of a remote Russian road, trying to prepare for every possible eventuality while knowing that doing so was impossible—was a different story. She felt small and helpless, at the mercy of a thousand different random occurrences, any one of which could blow her plans to bits.

And leave her at the mercy of the KGB.

Breathe, goddammit.

Her still-healing hand throbbed and ached, and she flexed it obsessively while trying to remain warm inside the Russian-made car. She'd left the engine idling and cranked the heater all the way up with the fan on high, but still it was no match for the bitter cold of another overcast Russian winter morning.

She sucked in a deep breath and blew it out, watching the resulting fog condense on the windshield and then slowly fade away.

Speransky should have been here by now.

Ryakhin had told him to arrive at the Arzamas-16 plant by nine a.m, so it wasn't like he was late yet. The KGB assassin could pass by this location twenty minutes from now and still make it to the plant with time to spare, but Tracie had set up almost two hours ago because she feared an early arrival.

If he'd taken the bait and truly believed he was suffering from early-onset radiation poisoning, he should be impatient as hell to begin treatment. She had been concerned that he would show up at the gates of the plant at first light, demanding to be allowed in to see Ryakhin.

That's what she would have done in the same circumstance.

So she'd driven the lonely road hours ago, long before any hint of daybreak, searching for the best location from which to conduct an ambush, determined to be ready should he come by early.

And then she had sat.

And waited.

With no sign of Speransky.

Where the hell was he?

It wasn't like Tracie to doubt herself. Doubt meant hesitation, and hesitation would get an operative killed.

But now doubts began to creep in. It was inevitable. It was human nature.

Maybe Speransky had smelled a rat and was staying away.

Maybe he'd smelled a rat and really *had* taken the extra time to circle well north of Kremlyov and enter the ZATO from a different access point.

Maybe he—

Her secure satellite phone burped twice and fell silent.

This was the signal she'd been awaiting for two hours.

It was time.

Speransky was coming.

21

January 22, 1988
8:20 a.m.
Six kilometers northwest of Kremlyov, Russia

Tracie had selected a location just beyond a sweeping curve in the road. The thoroughfare had been hacked out of a steep hill in this area, with land rising up behind her and a steep drop—not quite a cliff, but close enough—directly across the pavement, just beyond a ramshackle guardrail constructed of wooden pylons and rusted cable.

She crouched next to the open driver's side door of the Lada, using the vehicle to shield her from view of Speransky's oncoming car.

Hopefully.

Once he cleared the curve off Tracie's right side, he would only have a couple of seconds response time, and from his perspective the Lada should appear to be nothing more than one more old Russian car that had broken down in the worst possible area at the worst possible time.

She hoped the exhaust curling out the Lada's tailpipe would be invisible to the KGB operative. She'd backed as far into the underbrush as she was comfortable doing, while still allowing herself time for what would come next.

She counted down in her head, and exactly as she reached "one," a Russian-made sedan rounded the curve, moving at a relatively high rate of speed for the narrow, icy road and the poor driving conditions.

Good. Speransky would have less reaction time.

Tracie peeked over the dashboard, watching the vehicle's approach.

Patience. She couldn't act too soon or this wouldn't work.

Maybe it won't work anyway.

She pushed the doubts to the back of her mind and concentrated on the oncoming car.

Speransky had to have seen the Lada by now, but if so he wasn't about to stop and inquire as to the wellbeing of the stranded car's driver.

Patience.

Patience.

Now!

Speransky was almost past the Lada when Tracie took a long screwdriver and jammed it onto the accelerator, wedging the tool between the gas pedal and the front seat. The wheels spun, gravel peppering the trees behind the car, and then the car lurched forward into the narrow road.

There was nowhere for Speransky to go. He jerked his car hard right in a reflex action to avoid the impending collision, but then almost immediately jerked it back to the left as he came to the obvious realization: the cars were going to hit, but a collision on the road would be far preferable to crashing through the guardrail and careening down the side of the steep hill.

A split-second later the two vehicles came together to the sound of screeching brakes from Speransky's car, a whining engine from Ryakhin's car, and then crumpling sheet metal from both.

Tracie was on her feet and moving forward even before the collision. She held her gun in a two-handed shooter's grip as she advanced, crouched slightly, moving cautiously. The impact had caused both engines to stall, and the sudden silence in the stark Russian forest after the cacophony of destruction was almost disorienting.

She stopped six feet from Speransky's car. The vehicles had come to a stop on the shoulder of the road's southbound side. Both cars had come within inches of striking the guardrail, but neither had quite reached it.

Inside his car, the driver—it was definitely Speransky; he looked identical to the photo she had taken from the file in Yuri Ryakhin's Arzamas-16 office—shook his head, apparently to clear the cobwebs from the accident.

He appeared unhurt.

It didn't look as though he had spotted Tracie yet, as she stood slightly behind and to the right of the driver's door.

Now she edged forward, into Speransky's peripheral vision. In a half-second he noticed the movement and swiveled his head.

And looked directly down the barrel of Tracie's Beretta.

His eyes widened and then narrowed. As a veteran KGB operative, he would deduce immediately what had happened. Undoubtedly he was kicking himself right now for letting his guard down and allowing the ambush to occur.

Tracie needed to move fast. Keep Speransky on the defensive.

And there was another factor in play. Even a remote road would have traffic eventually. This situation would take an immediate turn for the worse if another motorist came along at the wrong moment.

She waved the operative out of his car. His eyes narrowed further but after a moment he complied, opening the door and stepping onto the pavement. He had removed his heavy winter parka for the drive and had to be freezing in the bitter temperatures, but Tracie was happy to accept that additional advantage. A man shivering violently would be unlikely to hit what he was shooting at, even if he were able to access the gun Tracie knew he had hidden somewhere on his body.

Speransky stood next to his open door, hands held palms-out and shoulder height, eyebrows raised in the obvious question: *what now?*

"Close your door and turn around. Feet apart. Place your hands on the roof." Tracie's voice was clipped and authoritative, and although he moved sluggishly, the man complied with her instructions.

She approached with the utmost care, keeping the Beretta trained on her target. Glanced through the side window into Speransky's car. Saw a single travel bag placed on the back seat and a blanket tossed on the floor.

"What is this about?" Speransky asked innocently.

"Shut up."

"I am a businessman, an innocent victim of a traffic accident, as you can plainly see."

"Shut up." By now she within arm's reach of the KGB operative. He was much bigger and stronger than Tracie, and while she trusted fully in her extensive CIA self-defense training, there was also no doubt the man calling himself Piotr Speransky was equally well-trained.

Which meant this was the moment of greatest danger for Tracie.

She jammed the barrel of her gun into the middle of his back and pressed it directly against his spine.

"One squeeze of the trigger," she said softly, "and you will spend the rest of your life in a wheelchair. Assuming you survive. Do we understand each other?"

"Your point is crystal clear," he answered drily. "Don't worry. I am doing exactly as instructed, but my question stands. What is this about?"

"We have to talk." She began patting the man down with one hand while keeping the gun pressed firmly into Speransky's back with the other.

"Is that so? I'm almost positive I haven't slept with you, since I can't imagine forgetting someone as stunningly beautiful as you. That being the case, I haven't the slightest clue what we might have to discuss."

"Oh, we have plenty to talk about." The bulge under his sport coat revealed a shoulder holster configured for a right-hand draw, and Tracie removed a Russian-made Makarov pistol. She tossed it across the road, where it skittered on the frozen pavement.

"Well, what do you know?" he said. "I wonder how that got there."

"Still want to stick to the story that you're just a businessman?" Searching his lower legs was problematic, but it had to be done.

She slid the gun down Speransky's back until she was holding it about belt level. Kept it pressed firmly in place as a reminder of the price he would pay should he choose to attempt to kick Tracie in the head.

The results were impressive. The "traveling businessman" was sporting not one, but two ankle holsters, each with a backup gun that she removed and tossed behind her. They bounced across the road and joined the first weapon, well out of harm's way.

"Guns are a necessity for the savvy businessman," he said innocently. "Roadside bandits are always a threat in the more remote areas of the country. But of course I do not need to tell *you* that."

Tracie had to give him credit. The man seemed unflappable, completely at ease.

So far.

She climbed to her feet and flipped up the back of his sport coat. Lifted a combat knife out of its sheath at the small of Speransky's back. It glittered in the dull grey morning light, razor-sharp and deadly. A second later it joined the guns on the opposite side of the road.

"You just lost several pounds of unnecessary weight," she said.

He shrugged. "One cannot be too careful."

"At last, something we can agree on."

"What happens now?"

"Now you turn around and we walk away from this car. You move very slowly and unthreateningly, and maybe you survive beyond the next few seconds."

He shrugged again and moved to his left. He moved carefully, exactly as Tracie had instructed, and she pivoted to the left behind him, maintaining steady pressure against his spine with her gun.

That was when the rear door of Speransky's car opened and a man pressed a gun into the back of Tracie's head.

22

Tracie froze and a gravelly voice behind her commanded, "Remove your gun from my friend's back and get down on your knees."

She raised her eyebrows. "Really, Comrade? Get on my knees? We just met. Shouldn't you buy me dinner first? Or at least introduce yourself?"

Dead silence from behind her.

For a moment nobody moved. She figured the man's lack of response was half due to confusion and half due to stunned surprise that she hadn't immediately complied with the order. And didn't even seem all that shocked at receiving it.

Speransky responded, though. He turned to face Tracie, smiling evilly, and said, "I admire that you can make jokes at a time like this. But soon you will not be laughing. Soon you will wish my friend behind you had pulled the trigger the moment he exited my car. We have a lot to discuss, you and I, and you will find I have a tendency to get...intimate...with my discussion partners."

Tracie ignored the threat, forcing her face to remain a mask. "Having second thoughts about receiving your radiation treatment, Comrade? You seemed to be in quite a hurry a moment ago, considering your speed on this narrow road."

Speransky spat on the ground. "This is what I think of your

141

'radiation treatment.' I saw through your ruse immediately. You obviously were holding Comrade Ryakhin at gunpoint, forcing him to tell his lies, but they did not fool me. Not even for a second."

"And yet here you are."

"*Da*, here I am. And here *you* are, now in custody."

"Is that how you see it?"

"That is how it is."

"If you say so."

"Enough!" The angry operative behind Tracie had apparently regained his composure at least sufficiently to once again partici-pate in the discussion. "Carefully hand your weapon to Comrade Speransky now. Or continue holding it and die. The choice is yours. It makes no difference to me."

Tracie grasped her gun by the butt between her thumb and forefinger. She swiveled her arm to the side and held it there, waist-high, watching in her peripheral vision for the man holding her at gunpoint to reach out for the Beretta.

A split-second later he did, and just before his hand could grab the gun she dropped it onto the pavement.

"Oops," she said. "Slipped. Sorry about that."

The man behind her spat on the ground in response, exactly as Speransky had done. These two seemed to do a lot of spitting.

"Bitch," he said. "Now, get on your knees. This is the second time I've told you. There will not be a third."

Again Tracie ignored him. She could not afford to drop to her knees. She would soon need every bit of leverage she could muster.

If her plan were to work.

It seemed to be taking too long, but her only option at this point was to try to delay.

She said, "So, it was the blanket?"

"The blanket? What blanket? What are you talking about, bitch?"

"The blanket. You know, the one that was spread out on the floor of Speransky's car. I assume you were hiding from little old me under that blanket."

His silence formed his answer.

She smiled. "Not your finest career moment, was it? I guess you won't be telling the other spooks about *this* op at next year's KGB Christmas party."

Tracie still could not see the second operative, but the rapidly building anger in his tone came through loud and clear. "It was sufficient to fool *you*. And for what it is worth, at least I will be alive to attend a party at Christmas. You will be just another forgotten agent, long-dead and decomposing in a shallow grave, missed by no one."

She shrugged. "I wouldn't be so sure about that, Ivan. And, just to correct the record, I knew you were under that blanket, hiding like a frightened little girl from the moment I saw it."

The man exploded, shouting, "On your knees, now! My comrade wishes to take you alive, but one more word out of you and I will shoot you where you stand. Nothing would please me more than to—"

The man's head exploded at the exact instant the *crack* of a single gunshot sounded from the wooded hillside behind them. A fine spray of blood misted over Tracie's head and shoulders as a bone fragment from the man's shattered skull ricocheted off her back.

Piotr Speransky flinched and stumbled backward as the operative behind Tracie dropped like a felled tree, his words cutting off abruptly. Even Tracie, who had been expecting the blast, ducked reflexively.

To Speransky's credit, he recovered quickly from his shock.

But not as quickly as Tracie.

She stepped forward, closing the distance between herself and the much bigger KGB man, folded her right hand into a fist and rabbit-punched Speransky in the throat.

He dropped to the ground, sputtering and hacking, and immediately began scrambling to his feet to fight despite the fact he suddenly could not draw a breath. He was on his hands and knees, about to launch himself at her, when she kicked him in the head, a sidekick with one heavy boot that sent him sprawling to the pavement again.

This time he didn't rise. He lay on his side moaning, legs and arms twitching, blood trickling from a gash on the side of his head.

Tracie bent and picked up her weapon as Ryan Smith pushed through the underbrush on the far side of the road and trotted toward the bloody scene.

"What took you so long?" Tracie said. "I was beginning to think you had fallen asleep back there."

He grinned. "Sorry about that. I couldn't get a clear shot. I was afraid I might miss the target and hit you instead."

She nodded and said, "Chalk one up for the wise use of discretion."

Then she hesitated. "Wait a second. If you were worried about hitting me with the shot, what changed? None of us moved, did we?"

"Nothing changed."

"Nothing changed? You just decided to take the shot anyway? What about hitting me by accident?"

"I didn't think I had a choice. You were doing such a good job pissing off the guy behind you I figured if I waited any longer he was going to shoot you himself. So I fired."

Tracie laughed, the sound high-pitched and shaky from the adrenaline racing through her system. "I was a bit hard on him, wasn't I?"

"I haven't heard that kind of ridicule from a woman since my last date."

She laughed again. "You're alright, Smith. I wasn't sure about you, but you came through like a champ. That was a hell of a shot, even with a sniper rifle."

"Wanna know a secret?"

"Of course I want to know a secret, Smith. CIA, remember? We're all about secrets."

"I barely qualified on the range at Langley. Shooting is probably my weakest skill."

She stared at him and then shook her head. "I'm glad I didn't know that *before* we planned this little op."

"About that. I have a question for you."

She glanced at the dead KGB operative lying next to Speransky's car. Glanced over at Speransky, who was still unconscious on his side but making noises like he might be coming to. Glanced up and down the still-empty road.

"What is it?" she finally said. "Make it quick, we have to clean this mess up and get the hell out of here. This has already taken too long."

"Understood. But here's my question: how did you know Speransky would bring backup?"

"How long have you been working in the field, Smith?"

"Six months."

Oh my God, this kid's a baby. "One of the first things I learned about field work is to always have a backup plan. And if you haven't learned that yet, it's time you did, because that knowledge will keep you alive. Always assume the other guy has seen through your plan, and always proceed as though that were the case."

He nodded thoughtfully.

"*Always*, Smith. Do that, and maybe you'll make it home alive to see Mrs. Smith."

He grinned again. "There is no Mrs. Smith."

"Well, you want to get home someday and round one up, don't you?"

"Hell, yeah."

"Then my rule still applies. Now shut up and let's get to work before we both wind up on the wrong end of a firing squad."

23

The first car drove past before they'd finished cleaning up their mess. Tracie duct-taped Speransky's hands, feet and mouth and had just shoved him into the trunk of Yuri Ryakhin's Lada when the vehicle appeared around the sweeping curve and approached at a rapid pace.

Dammit.

She'd hoped for a couple more minutes of privacy but wasn't particularly surprised to learn their luck had run out.

She jammed her Beretta into her waistband at the small of her back and glanced at the spot next to Speransky's car where Smith had shot the KGB man. He'd alertly covered the body with the blanket the man had used to conceal himself before ambushing Tracie—*very appropriate,* she thought. *Hide under it while you're alive, hide under it while you're dead*—but the suspicious lump on the pavement perfectly resembled what it was.

A body.

She shared a worried glance with Smith as the vehicle braked hard. This could get ugly in a hurry. There weren't many good options.

There weren't *any* good options.

She couldn't execute an innocent Russian citizen, and while she

147

had no doubt she and Smith could easily subdue even two or three people, once they had done so, what then? They couldn't very well take several people prisoner and hope to elude Russian authorities for more than a few hours.

And even if they could, the whole scenario would sidetrack her from her mission, and with Yuri Ryakhin alive and waiting to spill his guts in Kremlyov, time was extremely limited.

Dammit, she thought again.

The car slowed to a snail's pace. The "accident" had left both vehicles angled far enough into the road that passing the disabled cars would be difficult but not impossible. So far, Tracie thought the positioning of Speransky's car had managed to hide the dead KGB operative's body from view of the oncoming vehicle.

She walked quickly toward the middle of the road as Smith lingered near the blanket. She prayed Speransky didn't pick this moment to fully regain consciousness and begin banging on the interior of Ryakhin's trunk.

The car slowed to a stop. A moment later the passenger-side window was cranked down and an elderly Russian woman with bluish-grey hair and kind eyes peered out at Tracie.

"Oh, my," the woman said. "Is everyone alright?"

Tracie nodded. "Yes, ma'am, everyone is fine. Thank you for stopping, but we're both okay."

The old woman nodded and attempted to look past Tracie at the scene. Tracie had tried to position herself so the occupant of the car would not be able to get a clear view of the blanket, and she wondered whether she'd been successful.

The old woman's forehead wrinkled in confusion. Whether it was because she had spotted the blanket and was wondering about its significance, or for some completely unrelated reason Tracie didn't know, but it was critical she regain control of the situation.

She stepped closer to the car. "Thanks again for stopping, that was very kind. We're all set, though."

"Alright, dear. Would you like me to call for help when I get to a telephone?"

Tracie shook her head. "That's not necessary, help is already on the way."

She feigned looking at her watch and prayed it didn't occur to the old woman to ask the obvious question: *how* could help be on the way when there wasn't a telephone in sight?

"Okay then." The woman shook her head, clearly concerned about driving away from the scene of a car accident on a bitterly cold January morning. "Good luck. I'm glad no one was injured."

"Thank you." Tracie smiled. "And have a nice day."

The woman cranked her window closed and slid back to the driver's side. A moment later she eased past the damaged vehicles and accelerated away.

"That was way too close for comfort," Tracie called to Smith. "Let's finish the cleanup and get the hell out of here while we still can. I have a feeling that old lady's going to call the authorities the first chance she gets."

She hurried to the body. "First things first. Let's get this stiff out of the road. He could still get us both killed, without ever pulling a trigger."

She yanked the blanket off the dead KGB operative and tossed it aside. They grabbed the man by his armpits, Tracie on one side and Smith on the other, and dragged him the short distance to Speransky's car. His shattered head lolled to the side, jagged bits of skull protruding from the bloody cranium like shark's teeth.

Tracie reached out and pulled open the driver's side door, and they pulled/shoved/twisted the dead man's body until it sat upright—more or less—behind the wheel. The moment they released their grip, the body began slumping onto its side. Tracie grabbed the dead man by his coat collar and yanked him upright again. Then she secured the body as well as she could using the vehicle's safety harness.

She stepped back and examined her handiwork. "That's going to have to do. If anyone comes along and takes more than a casual glance at this guy we're screwed either way, so it's time to move on."

They were both panting from exertion but there was no time to rest. Tracie said, "Go get the bolt cutters. I'll finish cleaning up what I can here."

Smith sprinted across the once-again deserted road as Tracie slammed the door to Speransky's car closed.

She moved to Ryakhin's vehicle, which had been T-boned

neatly along the passenger-side door, but which to Tracie's eye appeared drivable. She was no kind of car expert, but neither the front wheel nor the rear wheel had been sustained any damage, and the engine compartment looked untouched as well.

She hoped so. Being able to drive Ryakhin's car would lower the complication factor immensely when it came to getting Speransky out of here, although it wasn't strictly necessary for the hastily devised plan to succeed.

Smith had driven a car down from Moscow overnight, leaving his safe house immediately after taking the satellite phone call Tracie had made from Ryakhin's bedroom. In the meantime, Tracie had stolen a second car.

Upon Smith's arrival, they stashed both vehicles in the underbrush less than a quarter mile from their chosen ambush location. Hiking to the cars would be doable, even with an injured Speransky in tow, but Tracie now hoped such a hike would not be necessary.

She opened Ryakhin's driver's side door and shifted the car into neutral, then heaved her one hundred-ten pounds against the frame. The vehicle creaked and groaned but began rolling slowly forward.

Tracie said a silent thanks to whatever anonymous Russian engineer had designed the sparsely traveled road. Its construction featured a slight grade toward the cliff side of the hill, a slope that likely made for treacherous driving conditions during winter storms, but which at the moment allowed her to move the small vehicle without any help.

Once it had started rolling, momentum took over and her task became easier.

Slightly.

She reached inside the open car door and turned the wheel to the left, and the little car eased off the paved portion of road, ending up parallel to the rickety guardrail. She jumped into the driver's seat and hit the brake. Shifted back into gear and activated the emergency brake.

By the time she climbed out of Ryakhin's car, Ryan Smith was pushing through the underbrush in the same location he had appeared after shooting Speransky's backup. This time, instead of a sniper rifle he was carrying a pair of heavy bolt cutters.

He hurried across the road and joined Tracie next to Speransky's car. It had sustained more damage from the accident than had Ryakhin's, and on the left front corner of the vehicle. But even though the headlight was demolished and the fender crumpled badly inward, the tire still held air.

That was a good sign.

But would the left front wheel still turn? If not, Tracie's plan for an easy escape would be dead in the water.

She moved to the front of the car. Examined the angle of the wheels. Speransky had turned right initially but then immediately left, when he'd seen the sharp dropoff looming. The result was a car that had slewed right after hitting Ryakhin's vehicle, with the front wheels aimed more or less straight ahead.

"Looks good," Tracie muttered.

Smith watched with a quizzical look on his face. "Okay, I'll bite. What looks good?"

"Take the bolt cutters and slice through the guardrail cables directly in front of Speransky's car. Then get back here and help me push. This poor guy," she nodded at the dead man buckled behind the wheel, "is going to suffer a serious car accident, not the minor fender-bender we orchestrated a few minutes ago."

Smith smiled and shook his head. "You look innocent but you're a devious little thing, aren't you?"

"You have no idea."

That was when another car came around the curve and approached the scene of the accident.

24

Tracie and Ryan Smith instinctively moved toward one another, closing ranks to stand directly in front of the driver's side door. Their bulky winter parkas helped screen the dead man strapped in behind the wheel from view, and Tracie thought that unless the approaching vehicle contained police, they might be okay.

There was nothing she could do about the splash of blood staining the pavement.

A look down the road eased Tracie's concern about police. This was just another civilian. The car slowed as its driver gawked at them.

Tracie spoke under her breath to Smith. "We're just two drivers who had a minor traffic accident. We're exchanging telephone numbers and blaming each other. Look angry and unhappy."

Smith scowled and Tracie frowned and the driver of the approaching car continued past the scene of the crash. His head appeared to be on a swivel, as he kept his eyes glued to them until he had driven well clear.

Unlike the old lady a couple of minutes ago, he didn't stop to see if anyone was hurt. Didn't offer to find a phone and call for help. He simply motored past at a snail's pace, then returned his attention toward the road ahead and hit the gas.

They maintained the fiction of two angry motorists blaming each other for the damage to their cars until the passerby drove out of sight, then immediately dropped the act.

Tracie said, "Our luck is gong to run out any second now. Let's finish this."

Without another word, she opened the driver's side door and began heaving her weight against the car's frame as Smith sprinted to the guardrail and snipped through the pair of rusty cables.

This vehicle was bigger and heavier than Ryakhin's compact Lada. The added mass would be a benefit once they had achieved a little momentum, but it also increased the difficulty of overcoming inertia initially.

Smith finished with the guardrail in seconds and then double-timed to the passenger side and opened that door. Even with his slight build he was much heavier and bulkier than Tracie, and after one horrible second where the car simply would not budge— *Dammit, the damage must be worse than I thought*—it inched forward, stopped, and then began rolling reluctantly toward the side of the road and the dangerous dropoff.

Once again the road's slight downhill grade aided their efforts, and the car began picking up speed. It rolled through the guardrail and Tracie and Smith gave one final shove. They stepped clear and watched as the car teetered on the edge of the dropoff and then, with a loud *creak* of rebuke, went over the side.

The big car picked up speed, crashing through underbrush and hard-packed snow and careening down the hill until smashing into a grove of trees maybe one hundred yards from the road. The wind whistling around her ears muffled the sound of the impact somewhat, but Tracie could still hear crunching metal and shattering glass.

She turned toward Ryan Smith, one eyebrow raised. "So what do you think? Did he survive?"

"Seems doubtful, given his condition *before* the accident."

Then Smith turned serious. "Do you really think this is going to fool anyone?"

"Oh, hell no. Not even close. Your bullet blew half the operative's head off. There would be no possible way for this car accident to account for the kind of damage that agent suffered. It will take the authorities maybe five minutes of investigating to conclude that guy wasn't killed in a car accident.

"Not only that," she gestured toward the guardrail, "even the most casual of investigations will determine the cables had been cut, rather than frayed as would have happened if they'd snapped from the impact of the car."

"It's too bad I cut the cables," he said. "They were so corroded, they probably would have snapped from a high wind."

Tracie shook her head. "We couldn't risk it. If we'd pushed the car into the cables and they had held, we would have been screwed."

Smith ran a hand across his eyes. He looked as exhausted as Tracie felt. "If it's going to be obvious to the Russians that our friend down there wasn't killed when his car went off the road, then why take the time and go to the trouble of staging the accident?"

"Two reasons. First, the authorities who do the investigating aren't going to be the first responders. The rescue team is going to be concerned with pulling the victim out of the wreckage, not so much with determining how he died. The longer it takes to recover his body, the farther away we can be by the time they do. Even if it's only a couple of hours before it occurs to them that the damage to the guy's head is inconsistent with a car wreck, that's a couple of hours more than we would otherwise have had."

"Okay. I'm certainly in favor of a clean getaway. What's the second reason?"

"I have a mission to complete. Even after the Russian police determine the guy died from a gunshot wound, it's not going to be immediately apparent to them that the victim was KGB."

She pictured Yuri Ryakhin, tied up in his kitchen and waiting to tell his story. "The clock is ticking on my time in the Soviet Union, at least for this mission, and the longer it takes the KGB to learn one of their agents was killed by a bullet to the head, the better chance I have of completing my mission and getting the hell out of Russia alive."

Smith nodded. "Okay. So what happens now?"

"Now it's time for us to split up. You've done a hell of a job on very short notice, and I owe you for it, big-time. You ever need a favor, look me up. But for now, your part in my mission is over.

Pick up all your gear and hike back to the cars we stashed in the woods. Grab the one you came in and get as far away from here as quickly as you can. Sooner or later—and my guess is sooner—all hell is going to break loose and you don't want to be anywhere near here when it does."

"What about you?"

"I think Ryakhin's car is drivable. I'm going to leave Speransky— or whatever his real name is—trussed up in the trunk and hightail it back to my safe house. Once I get there, Comrade Speransky and I are going to have a little heart-to-heart and get to know each other.

"Now that I think about it," she said with a grim smile, "you probably don't want to be anywhere near there, either."

25

Evgeny Domashev would have sworn on his mother's life that he was at least passingly familiar with every section of Moscow. He'd grown up in the area, had spent most of his time haunting its streets and neighborhoods as a child, and had worked in and around the city for the majority of his adult life.

But when the redheaded bitch popped the trunk and motioned him out at gunpoint, he could not say with complete certainty he was even *in* Moscow. He guessed he was, because the timing seemed right, but he wasn't positive.

He'd lost consciousness when the *cyka* kicked him in the head, but had awakened in the cold and dark of the trunk before the vehicle's engine had even started. Checking his watch was out of the question given the way his wrists had been secured, so the glow-in-the-dark numerals it featured did him no good.

But Moscow was roughly a six-hour drive from Kremlyov, and his internal clock told him approximately six hours had passed since his humiliation at the hands of the tiny woman who had somehow gotten the drop on him.

He could only thank the fates that none of his KGB peers had witnessed it. Not even Nikolay Mineyev, whose head had been blown apart by a high-velocity sniper round, and who, Evgeny was certain, had been dead before his body hit the frozen Russian roadway.

The car squealed to a stop and the engine died, and a moment later the trunk lid opened and Evgeny squinted against the watery grey light. His head pounded and he assumed he'd suffered a concussion. The woman was small but her boot was heavy, and she hadn't held anything back with her kick.

Bitch.

She leaned over him, weapon aimed at his midsection, and spoke quietly. "I'm going to slice through the tape on your ankles. Then I'm going to help you out of the trunk. If you try to kick me, or try to escape, or even look at me like I have spinach in my teeth, I'm going to shoot you in the stomach. You won't die—yet—because we need to have an important conversation. But you *will* wish you were dead, and I promise to maximize your suffering for every last second of what's left of your life. Do we understand each other?"

He tried to keep the smoldering anger out of his expression, but doing so became more and more difficult as the little *cyka* droned on. No one spoke to Evegny Domashev in the tone that bitch was using.

No one.

Even his KGB superiors were deferential.

They requested, they did not demand.

They were solicitous, they were not arrogant.

They understood that Evgeny Domashev had ended more lives, and in more creative ways, than they could count, and understood also that staying on Evgeny's good side was not just good sense, it represented the key to a long and healthy life.

This woman understood none of that, and he could feel his pulse racing and his temper shortening. The building anger made his head pound even worse and made any kind of clear thinking that much more difficult to achieve.

Still, she was the one with the gun—for now—and thus she controlled the situation.

For now.

Evgeny forced a placid look onto his face and nodded. *Da, I understand.* He couldn't actually answer, because the little bitch had taped his mouth closed.

"Good," she said. She reached into the truck with her right hand while holding her weapon rock-steady with her left. Sliced through the duct tape on Evgeny's ankles with a combat knife.

She slipped her knife into its sheath and grabbed Evgeny under the armpits. Then she lifted him roughly to his knees and supported him as he clambered out of the trunk.

Despite her warning, Evgeny immediately assessed the situation, searching for a potential escape route and attempting to determine his whereabouts.

He was unsuccessful on both counts.

He had assumed immediately upon the trunk's opening that there would be no potential witnesses. The little bitch's level of comfort in displaying her weapon told him that before he had even glanced at the surrounding area.

And his assumption was a good one. They were alone in a very narrow, trash-filled alley. It felt claustrophobic, with dirty concrete block walls looming over them on either side.

As far as Evgeny could see, the walls were windowless, meaning the location must be industrial. The buildings were clearly not residences; therefore they were either factories or warehouses.

His captor stepped behind him and prodded him forward, shoving the barrel of her gun roughly into his back.

He considered his options. His feet were now free. Could he pivot and sidekick her in the knee, disabling her before she had time to squeeze the trigger? Could he—

"Do not go there, Comrade. Do not even think about it. I am faster than you even when you're uninjured. With your head pounding and your wrists secured, you would have no chance. Trust me."

Chert voz'mi. This little bitch was good. He must be careful not to underestimate her any more than he already had.

He reluctantly trudged forward, moving deeper into the alley. Night was falling quickly, and between the setting sun, the overcast grey skies, and the walls that seemed to stretch upward for hundreds of meters, light was minimal.

After perhaps twenty meters, a third wall loomed in front of them. It was constructed of concrete block as well. A door that looked as though it belonged in a residence stood in the middle of the wall. It seemed bizarrely out of place in this industrial setting.

"Turn to your left," the woman hissed.

Evgeny complied, and as soon as he had, the woman shoved him in the back. He crashed into the concrete wall face-first and the pain blossomed in his head.

"Do not move," she said. "If you move, you die. Do you understand?"

If it's the last thing I do, I am going to kill this little cyka. He gritted his teeth and nodded. He knew what she was doing. She was well trained. Unlocking the door would require her to divert her attention from Evgeny, which would make her vulnerable. She was minimizing his chances of taking advantage of her distraction.

She was smart.

Shrewd.

He would still kill her.

The jingle of keys told him he was right, and after a moment the woman grabbed him by his parka and yanked him backward. He stumbled and she caught him, and before he could regain his balance she spun him around and pushed him through the door.

A dim light flickered on. They were in a small, mostly bare room. A sturdy wooden chair sat precisely in the middle of the room.

This was a safe house. Evgeny should know. He had spent more hours, days and weeks inside safe houses than he could possibly count.

And this particular safe house had been prepped for an interrogation.

For *his* interrogation.

He had already long-since come to the conclusion the little bitch was CIA. It was the only explanation for how she could have managed to overcome the difference in their sizes and taken him down. This safe house only served to confirm what he had already deduced.

For the first time, a thread of real fear snaked through his bowels. Getting assaulted had not fazed him. Being threatened with a gun had not fazed him. Even being knocked out and tossed into the truck of a car like a bag of garbage had not fazed him.

Evgeny Domashev had lived through all those things and worse, many times in the past.

But this. This was different. The prospect of interrogation by this grimly determined young woman, who seemed to possess not a shred of empathy, or a drop of concern for his wellbeing, or even a morsel of humanity, was cause for real concern.

Maybe more than concern. Maybe fear.

Because ever since the trunk cover lifted and he found himself staring into the face of his captor, she had reminded Evgeny of someone. It had taken him a few minutes and a little bit of pain to figure out exactly *who* she reminded him of.

But now he knew.

She reminded him of himself.

And he knew better than anyone else in the world what he was capable of.

And that was terrifying.

26

January 24, 1988
4:35 p.m.
CIA safe house
Moscow, Russia

Tracie frog-marched Speransky across the room. She shoved him constantly, keeping him off-balance, not allowing him the luxury of an easy trip. His anger was still building, but he didn't resist.

Smart move on his part.

Before leaving for Kremlyov yesterday, Tracie had screwed the heavy wooden chair—to her it looked a lot like the electric chair that this cold-blooded murderer deserved—to the floor. She had taken a few minutes to modify the chair by attaching a heavy metal L-brace to each leg. Each brace she had then screwed into the floor. Her modifications would prevent the chair from skidding across the floor or tipping over.

No matter how…spirited…the interrogation became.

Speransky was doing his best to project an image of stoicism, but she could tell he was getting more and more nervous.

Concerned.

Afraid.

The last thing an animal like he could stand was loss of control, and once Tracie had finished strapping him into the lookalike electric chair, he would have even less control over his fate than he had now.

He would have absolutely none whatsoever.

And he knew it.

Tracie stopped Speransky next to the chair and moved in front of him. Stood silently, gun trained on him, staring into his face and waiting for him to meet her gaze. He seemed to want to look everywhere but at her. Eventually, though, he'd taken in every object in the room—it didn't take long, this portion of the safe house was nearly barren—and with obvious reluctance he lifted his eyes to her.

She held his gaze for three seconds.

Four.

Five.

Then she very slowly looked from his face to the chair. To punctuate her point, she flicked the barrel of the Beretta from his midsection to the chair and back again.

Playing out the little vignette was not strictly necessary. Speransky's hands were still secured behind his back at the wrist and his mouth was still gagged and taped. She had the gun. He would wind up sitting in that chair in a few seconds, one way or the other.

But it was all about control. About reinforcing the notion of who had it and who did not. About establishing the type of psychological dominance that would enable her to pry information from this experienced KGB operative.

Information that he was undoubtedly determined not to share.

Physical torture could be effective. Every human being, no matter how strong and how determined, had a breaking point. Everyone could be turned.

Eventually.

But Tracie could not afford to take the time it would require to break Speransky's resistance using only physical means. Sooner or later someone was going to find Yuri Ryakhin bound and gagged in his kitchen, and when that happened, Tracie's assignment would instantly morph from difficult to nearly impossible.

So her plan was to combine physical means with psychological. To create in Piotr Speransky a certain mindset: that his captor was smarter and stronger and better prepared than he.

To break him mentally.

She thought she knew just how she was going to do it, and her plan was to start right now.

Speransky followed her gaze. He looked from her face to the chair and then back again.

Didn't move.

Tracie stepped forward. Lifted her gun and placed it under his chin. Pushed steadily upward until he was gagging and struggling to breathe.

He would know or strongly suspect—and rightfully so—that Tracie would be reluctant to shoot him. If she'd wanted to do that she could have done so back at the ambush site and saved herself a lot of trouble and risk.

Her intention to interrogate him would be obvious, and since a man who was dead could not provide answers, the prospect of taking a bullet became much less likely in his eyes, which made the threat the Beretta represented that much less effective.

But it didn't mean she was out of options. She swiveled her wrist and clubbed him in the jaw with the butt of the gun. He stumbled back a step with a brief groan of pain. His eyes watered and he blinked rapidly to clear them.

Then they narrowed until they were nothing more than slits, the barest of openings, his fury and humiliation plain.

Still he held his ground.

Tracie drew back her arm to strike Speransky second time, in the exact same location, and abruptly he moved forward. Turned and slumped into the chair, making certain to hold his head up in clear defiance of her.

But the damage had been done and her point made.

She was fully in charge.

Now she had to get down to business.

*   *   *

January 24, 1988
8:15 p.m.
CIA safe house
Moscow, Russia

Speransky's hair hung in his face, sweaty and stringy, and he moaned through his gag. Five minutes had elapsed since she'd removed one of the fingernails on his left hand—the second one she'd taken—and now she approached him again, pliers prominently displayed in front of his wide bloodshot eyes.

Blood dripped from his left pointer finger and middle finger, and Tracie knew the pain must be immense. But even worse than the throbbing in those fingers with each rapid beat of his heart would be the knowledge that a third nail was about to be ripped from a third finger.

The pain would again explode in his hand and he would again scream into his gag and a third finger would join the first two in becoming swollen, bloody, disfigured pulps of useless flesh.

Tracie hated inflicting pain on another human being. She felt sick to her stomach resorting to physical torture but maintained a mask of steadfast determination. She knew she was making headway and showing any reluctance to Speransky at this point would only stiffen his weakening resolve.

"Let's see," she said. She leaned over his hand and pretended to examine it closely. "Which finger to choose?"

She raised her head and looked into his eyes. "Or maybe it's time to start on the *right* hand. You're going to have a hell of a time tying your shoes or buttoning your shirt or wiping your ass when you can't use the fingers on either hand, aren't you, Piotr?"

He whipped his head back and forth, eyes still angry but now pleading rather than arrogant.

She lowered the pliers to the pointer finger on his right hand and began digging the nose into the tender flesh between nail and forefinger.

Speransky whimpered. He was panting heavily behind his gag, sweat pouring down his face, his agony obvious. He had started out this portion of the interrogation with a determined look on his face and had managed to maintain dead silence until screaming into the gag as the nails were ripped from his fingers.

This single whimper represented major progress and Tracie paused.

Held his gaze.

"Had enough, Piotr?"

He could of course not answer. At least, not with spoken words.

But he whimpered again, a reaction she knew was unintended. He meant to resist, the inflamed nerve endings in his injured fingers simply would not allow it.

"Would you like me to remove your gag? Maybe have a friendly conversation, like two civilized human beings?"

This was a critical juncture. Tracie hoped she was not moving too quickly. Her intention again was to establish psychological dominance over the KGB man. She needed him to bend to her will.

If he toughened up and refused her offer of gag removal, it would be a victory for him. An extremely painful victory to be sure, as she would have no choice but to then rip another fingernail off his hand, but it would be a victory nevertheless, and would add potentially hours more onto the interrogation.

Hours Tracie could not afford.

He hesitated, pausing at the question, and she shrugged. Began digging the long nose of the pliers deeper under the nail, and that was when he screamed into his gag.

It wasn't a scream of pain, although she knew he had to be experiencing plenty of that. She had not been gentle with the pliers, and even now blood began to well up around them and dribble over Speransky's fingertip, pooling on the chair's wooden arm.

But previous screams had been mindless, nothing more than his body's natural expression of severe agony. He couldn't have stopped these screams from erupting even if he'd tried, which at the time he'd been beyond doing.

This scream had a point. It was meant to convey a message.

Tracie stopped what she was doing. Withdrew the pliers and said, "I'm sorry, you're going to have to speak more clearly. Did you say you *do* want me to remove your gag, Piotr?"

He closed his eyes, perhaps from pain, perhaps from sheer exhaustion, or perhaps from shame at his loss of self-control.

Then he nodded, just once and so abruptly as to be easily missed. But Tracie didn't miss it.

She said, "Listen to me closely, Piotr. This safe house is in an industrial area, as I'm sure you are well aware. It is a Friday night, which means no one is near. Additionally, this building has been soundproofed."

She had no idea as to the truth of the statement and seriously doubted the CIA would have spent the time and funding it would require to soundproof a simple Moscow safe house, but Speransky would have no way of knowing, either. And given the dynamics of the current power structure, he could not afford to question her assertion too rigorously.

She frowned and continued. "You could scream at the top of your lungs with a fellow operative standing right outside, ear pressed to the exterior wall, and do you know what he would hear?"

He stared, eyes unblinking. She took that to mean he did know what his hypothetical rescuer would hear, but she told him anyway.

"He would hear nothing, Piotr. No one will hear you if I remove your gag and you scream. Trust me on this."

She held his eyes with a dark gaze and continued. "But one thing *will* happen if you scream. You will make me very angry if you scream. And if I get very angry, do you know what will then happen?"

Another unblinking stare.

"If I get very angry, Piotr, your gag will go right back into place and I will immediately continue removing your fingernails until they are gone. There will be no five-minute breaks between removals, either. They will disappear one after the other. And then I will start on your toenails. And when your toenails are all gone I will shoot you in the knees, one after the other. All of that will happen before I take my next break.

"Do you understand all this, Piotr?"

The briefest of head nods told Tracie that, yes, he understood.

27

January 24, 1988
11:40 p.m.
CIA safe house
Moscow, Russia

The key to accomplishing successful physical torture lay in regulating pain. The interrogator's challenge was to make the subject uncomfortable to the point where he or she would become willing to provide whatever information the interrogator required, but not so uncomfortable he or she lost consciousness or, God forbid, died.

Tracie hated physical torture. The notion that it could very well be *her* strapped into a chair, on the receiving end of the pain being dished out, was always uppermost in her mind even when she wished it were not so.

Thus far, although Piotr Speransky would likely disagree, Tracie had managed to avoid inflicting any serious, lasting damage on her subject. He was in considerable pain, but that was the whole point. She needed to break him quickly, and to accomplish that she had to soften him up physically so he would be less able to resist the psychological manipulation coming next.

And it was all or nothing. As much as Tracie believed in backup plans, in this instance she had none. If her gambit failed, there would be nothing to fall back on.

After removing Speransky's duct-tape gag, she had started off slowly, doing her best to play both of the good cop/bad cop roles herself. The bad cop had just yanked fingernails out of Speransky's hand, leaving him bloodied and whimpering in the torture chair.

The good cop began by speaking quietly, almost soothingly, initially working on nothing more complicated than getting Speransky to provide honest responses to simple, non-confrontational questions. Questions to which she already knew the answers.

Questions like whether he worked for the KGB.

The file Tracie had removed from Yuri Ryakhin's office at the Arzamas-16 nuclear plant in Kremlyov yesterday had been thin, but still it contained enough information to permit her this line of questioning.

And it had taken little time to establish that, yes, Piotr Speranksy was, in fact, employed by the Soviet Union's intelligence agency.

"And you work as an assassin for the KGB, is that correct, Piotr?" The key to successful psychological manipulation of a subject was to keep that subject off-balance. That had been Tracie's goal with the physical torture—to give Speransky no choice but to concentrate on the pain radiating outward from his fingertips.

This would theoretically make him less likely to be able to follow meandering questioning and rapid subject changes in questioning, which would, again theoretically, make him more likely to provide his interrogator with truthful answers.

She walked behind Speransky as she asked the question. Disappearing from sight of the subject after physical torture had been administered could be extremely effective as a psychological manipulation technique. The subject immediately begins to fear a return of the physical pain he'd received earlier.

The human brain was an amazing organ, but it could also be the most effective weapon in a savvy interrogator's arsenal.

Speransky mumbled something Tracie could not make out, and she immediately bent and whispered into the man's ear, "Speak up, Piotr."

He of course had not been able to see her approach, and he jerked against his bindings in surprise at her closeness.

He raised his voice—slightly. "I said I do whatever my superiors ask me to do. Just like you."

"And your superiors ask you to murder people, isn't that right?"

"I have been forced to kill, yes. Again, just like you, unless I miss my guess."

Tracie laughed. She had ignored, and would continue to ignore, his comments directed at her. She was in control of the interrogation, not the prisoner, and she would direct the course of the questioning.

"Forced to kill," she said. "That's a good one, Comrade. The fact is you enjoy your work, don't you? You enjoy raining death and destruction down on the enemies of the Soviet State."

He shrugged and then winced as the motion reverberated through his injured fingertips and cranium. "I do what I must."

She stepped back in front of Speransky and smiled coldly at him. "As do I, Comrade. As do I."

Now Tracie began pacing away from Speransky, then spinning abruptly on her heel and returning to her position directly in front of him. "And this 'doing as you're told.' Does it include the radioactive poisoning of unsuspecting American—and occasionally, Russian—citizens?"

Now it was Speransky's turn to flash a cold smile. He did it through lips quivering from pain, but he did it nonetheless. "It would be silly to pretend otherwise, my little red-headed *cyka*, would it not? I already know you forced Comrade Ryakhin to lure me to Kremlyov. Thus, I know you are aware of my patriotic activities."

Tracie nodded. It was time to play good cop again. "True," she said. "But there's something I don't understand. Weren't you concerned about contracting radiation poisoning yourself? Handling Polonium-210 more than a half-dozen times? Weren't you at least a little worried about that?"

He stared impassively and she continued. "I can understand accepting orders from your superiors, misguided though those orders may be. But you don't strike me as the selfless type, as someone who would willingly sacrifice his own life in service to his country. How could you be sure you wouldn't end up just as sick—and just as dead—as the men you were sent to assassinate?"

Speransky's relief at the line of questioning was obvious. Here was a chance to placate his interrogator in a way that would permit him to feign cooperation without actually giving up any useable intel. Tracie smiled inside while keeping her face an unreadable mask.

"There was never any real danger to me," he said. "Polonium-210's radioactive isotopes are formed in such a way as to be unable to penetrate human skin."

Tracie began moving slowly toward a small table at the far end of the room onto which she had tossed her backpack. As he spoke, she unzipped a pocket and reached inside.

He continued to talk as she turned and paced back in his direction, hands clasped behind her back. He had clearly become suspicious but he had no alternative but to continue. "In order to be deadly, Polonium-210 must be ingested by the subject. Inhaled, or swallowed. That was how it was explained to me."

"And you believed what you were told? It didn't occur to you to question whether your KGB superiors might simply be using you as a pawn and sacrificing you in pursuit of their own goals?"

"Of course it occurred to me." He sounded insulted that his interrogator would think so little of his operational awareness. "I took nothing for granted. The first time I met Comrade Ryakhin, we had a little chat that was not so different from this conversation."

"Is that so?"

"*Da,* it is so. I was the one asking the questions, of course, and my method of achieving cooperation consisted of placing my Makarov to Comrade Ryakhin's skull instead of removing his fingernails. But by the time we had finished our little discussion, I felt comfortable that as long as I was extremely careful working with the Polonium, the risk to me was minimal."

Speransky had gotten suddenly talkative. His desire to extend what he believed to be the "safe" portion of the interrogation was obvious.

And misguided.

Tracie pretended to consider his words while watching his expression change from one of relative openness to suspicion.

"But you would already have known all this from speaking with Ryakhin," he said slowly. "It was what you were counting on. You had to lure me to Kremlyov, and you knew—or at least Ryakhin knew—that the fear of accidental exposure to radiation would be the one thing that might cause me to override my own concerns and drive there anyway."

Tracie's smile was cold and hard. "Very impressive reasoning, Comrade," she said. "Especially under the circumstances."

She shrugged and withdrew her hands from behind her back. His eyes widened as he glimpsed what she held: a small, lead-lined spray bottle.

The bottle she had liberated from storage at Arzamas-16.

The bottle designed to hold the deadly solution of Polonium-210.

"So," she said conversationally. "What you are telling me is that there is little danger to me personally, as long as I am very careful not to inhale when I spray this solution into your mouth?"

28

Speransky's eyes widened and he recoiled reflexively at the sight of the spray bottle. His head struck the chair-back with a thud and bounced forward. He didn't seem to notice.

"Where did you get that?" His voice showed little sign of stress, which was impressive. He'd recovered from his initial fright quickly and well, but he'd clearly been rattled. Tracie needed to take advantage of this crack in his composure.

She ignored his question. Undoubtedly he already regretted asking it, since the answer was so obvious.

Instead she said, "You know what surprised me about my visit to Arzamas-16, Piotr?"

He shook his head but remained silent. His eyes remained glued to the little bottle in her hand.

"No, surprise isn't the correct word." She stroked her chin as if concentrating. "Shocked might be the better description. I was really shocked at how easy it was for the plant to manufacture a dose of Polonium-210."

She spoke conversationally. Not friendly, not exactly. But close. Bus stop conversation. Cocktail party conversation. Like two strangers thrown together for a few minutes finding a way to pass the time.

Speransky ripped his gaze from the spray bottle for a second, focusing on her, his fear and confusion plain.

Good.

He returned his attention to the bottle and she continued. "Yeah, it was kind of a long shot, asking Ryakhin to manufacture a dose. I almost didn't even bother trying, because, you know, it seems like accomplishing nuclear fusion should be a long and complicated process."

She tilted her head and stroked her chin. "Or is it nuclear *fission*? Do you know?"

He was breathing heavily, eyes wide, and she shrugged. "I don't know either, and I suppose it doesn't really matter, does it?"

He stared at her in horror. She'd taken a calculated risk with this approach, because she had little more than the most basic knowledge regarding the operation of a nuclear plant or the process of creating radioactive isotopes. If Speransky *did* have that knowledge, it could blow her interrogation to hell.

She felt it was worth taking the shot, though. Despite working on the opposite side of the geopolitical fence, Piotr Speranksy was a lot like Tracie. Uncomfortably similar, in fact. But her experience as an intelligence field operative had taught her that most of the time, case officers were far too busy studying intel needed to complete assignments to waste time learning nuclear physics.

It was worth the risk.

And judging by Speransky's reaction, her assumption had been right on. He at least seemed to accept the possibility she was telling the truth.

"Anyway, the fact of the matter is," she continued, "the process is a pretty simple one. It only took a couple of hours and a little arm-twisting, and I had exactly what I needed.

"I gotta tell ya, Piotr, it was a real eye-opener. The fact that somebody like me was able to get something like that so easily, in a closed city deep inside a supposedly fortified Soviet stronghold like Russia..."

She shook her head ruefully. "It really makes you question everything you thought you knew about security, don't you agree?"

She had been pacing continually, keeping his eyes on the move, trying to prevent him from having any time to reason things through. *Keep the subject off balance* was Rule Number One of a successful interrogation.

He didn't answer. At least not out loud. But his face had grown steadily paler as she talked and she supposed that was enough of an answer in itself.

She stopped pacing and stood, feet planted, directly in front of her prisoner. The conversational manner was instantly gone and in its place, a hard brutality.

"So. Now that we've laid our cards on the table—those of us who have any cards to play, that is—it's time to get down to business. I'm sure, Piotr, as a fellow professional, you can appreciate my desire to move things along."

He was trying to maintain his composure but doing a poor job of it. He was simply too rattled.

Tracie's voice was quiet and cold when she spoke. "I visited one of your Polonium-210 victims recently, Piotr. He was at the end. Did you know he was in so much pain he'd practically chewed through his own lips?"

Speransky swallowed heavily but said nothing.

Tracie continued. "I want to know the name of the KGB officer who dreamed up the bright idea of using Polonium-210 on American CIA operatives in Russia, of condemning good men to such a painful and unnecessary death.

"That's what I want to know," she said. "You *will* tell me his name. And after you tell me his name, you're going to tell me where I can find him."

Speransky finally found his voice. "You must be joking. If you are, as you say, 'a fellow professional,' I am sure you must know I cannot give you that information. It will make me a traitor to my country and a condemned man. I cannot."

"Do I look like I'm joking, Piotr? Do you think I'm risking my life in this country, dealing with the likes of you and Yuri Ryakhin, because I enjoy a good joke? Is that what you think?"

She had begun lowering her face toward Speransky's as she spoke, and by the time she finished, her eyes were inches from his and she was screaming at the top of her lungs. He blinked as spittle rained into his upturned eyes.

"I promise you that you will not get that kind of information out of me," he said, his voice shaking. "But even if you could, you would never be able to get close to your target. It is impossible. It would be a suicide mission."

"I'm touched by your concern for my well-being, Piotr, really. And to think we just met. But why don't you let me worry about the mission's difficulty. Just tell me what I want to know and maybe, just maybe, you'll avoid chewing through *your* lips in pain as you await the end."

He shook his head. "I told you, I cannot—"

"Open up," she said.

"What?"

"I said open up. And while you're at it, say 'ah.' I'm done playing games. It's time for your medicine."

The little spray bottle was still clasped in her right hand, and she lifted it quickly, holding it in front of his rapidly blinking eyes. He clamped his jaws together with an audible *clack*, the muscles in his neck straining.

Tracie laughed. "Really, Piotr? You think you can avoid what you have coming to you? Haven't you forgotten something?"

He was breathing rapidly, his nose flaring as he tried to draw in air without opening his mouth. His arms shook under their bindings, his injured fingers flopping against the wooden armrest.

"All I need to do," she continued, "is place this little spray nozzle against your nostrils and squeeze. I'm certain one nostril would be sufficient for my purposes, but my daddy always told me anything worth doing is worth doing right, so I'd probably spray both nostrils. You know, just to be sure."

She'd been holding the spray bottle perfectly still, and Speransky's eyes had been focused on it like it held the key to life.

Which, as far as he was concerned, it did.

But now he began shaking his head side to side, as if vehemently punctuating a negative reply.

She thought the psychological intimidation might be just about complete. She hoped so, anyway, because the ruse had nearly been played out. Hopefully a few more seconds of reflection would be enough.

She straightened suddenly and chuckled. "Wow, Piotr. That

was a close one. In all the excitement, I damned near forgot one important detail. I swear, sometimes I can be so scattered."

Spinning on her heel, Tracie crossed the room to the little table holding her backpack. She pretended to rummage through the bag, although she'd left the item she wanted sitting right on top of her other gear.

"Ah! Here it is," she mumbled just loud enough for Speransky to hear. She lifted the medical facemask out of the backpack and slipped it over her head, patting it into place over her mouth and nose as she returned to the chair holding her terrified subject.

"Can't be too careful," she said, her words muffled as they floated through the mask.

By the time she had crossed half the distance, Speransky had resumed his violent head thrashing. His efforts this time made his previous attempt look half-hearted, and Tracie hoped he wouldn't break his own neck before surrendering the information she needed.

"Now, Piotr," she chided. "Don't be silly. You can't avoid your medicine forever. I can just stand here and wait for you to tire, then spray the Polonium into your nostrils."

He continued to shake his head as if he hadn't heard a word she said. Probably he hadn't, given his panic level.

"Or I could just do this." Her left hand flashed forward and clamped onto his forehead, smashing the back of his skull against the chair back. He was much bigger than Tracie but she had all the leverage, and the best he could manage was to grunt and groan as he tried to continue shaking his head.

"That's better," she said. "Now, let's get this over with. I really don't like how I look in this mask. It doesn't match my eyes at all."

She loomed over him and brought the tip of the spray bottle to Piotr Speransky's nose.

29

January 25, 1988
12:10 a.m.
CIA safe house
Moscow, Russia

"Marinov!" Speransky shouted. "Marinov! Slava Marinov!"

Tracie pulled back, her heart hammering in her chest. She stared at Speransky for two seconds. Three.

"Bullshit," she said. "You just made up a name to delay the inevitable." She leaned over the KGB operative again, returning the spray bottle to his nose.

"No, it is true." Speransky was panting, breathing so hard Tracie thought he might hyperventilate and pass out. "I swear it is true. That is the name of the man you want. But it doesn't matter, you will never—"

"Shut up."

Speransky slammed his mouth shut and tried to shake his head. All he could manage were tiny lateral movements.

Tracie removed her left hand from Speransky's forehead and stepped back. He blew out a deep, shaky breath and his head dropped forward onto his collarbone. "I swear it is true. God help me."

"You know what's going to happen to you if you lie to me, Piotr?"

No response. His chin remained on his chest.

Tracie stared at the top of his head for a moment before continuing. "If you lie to me, even God won't be able to help you. If you lie to me, I'm going to do what I threatened before. I'm going to pull out the rest of your fingernails, Piotr. One after the other. Then I'm going to pull out your toenails. Then I'm going to shoot you in the kneecaps. Then your elbows."

She bent down and whispered into his ear. "And only then, Piotr, only after I have put you through unimaginable pain, will I spray this solution down your throat. Then I will leave you here to die in this filthy Moscow tenement, alone and forgotten."

She pulled away again. "Do you understand me, Piotr?"

"I understand." His voice was muffled and weak, and she thought she might have heard a brief sob between the two words.

She walked to the table holding her backpack and pulled a second chair across the floor with a screech.

Speransky jumped at the sound and lifted his head. He watched as Tracie placed the chair directly in front of his own and sat in it.

"Tell me about Slava Marinov and the plan to poison American CIA officers with radiation."

Speransky sighed deeply. His eyes were bloodshot and wet and his face pale. He looked exhausted.

Tracie knew how he felt.

After a long moment, Speransky started talking. He spoke slowly and haltingly. But at least he was talking. "The mission was code-named 'Project Kremlyov Infection,' for obvious reasons. Marinov has been in charge since its inception in early 1984. To the best of my knowledge, it was conceived and developed by Slava."

"Where in God's name did this man come up with the notion of radiation poisoning as a method of assassination?"

He shook his head slowly. "I cannot say specifically, but study your history, *cyka,* and you will learn that the KGB has a long history of developing poisons and other methods of eliminating enemies that appear natural, or at least that do not immediately suggest the likelihood of assassination."

He raised his eyes and met Tracie's gaze, the first time he had done so since breaking under her interrogation. "I must add, my cold-hearted friend, that your CIA has a long history of doing exactly the same thing."

"Let's not get off-track. We're not discussing the CIA. Get back to the subject of Project Kremlyov Infection."

"My point, *cyka*, is that when an organization has long searched for methods of quietly assassinating its enemies, the prospect of doing so using nuclear radiation will probably not be rejected by the men in charge if it seems to be feasible from a practical stand-point. I do not doubt that was the case with Comrade Marinov and Project Kremlyov Infection."

"Thank you for clarifying," Tracie said drily. "Let's get specific, shall we?"

Speransky raised his eyebrows and waited for her to continue.

"How were your targets identified for elimination?"

"I do not know that. I was merely the hammer in this construc-tion project. The blunt instrument. The blueprints were drawn up by Marinov, and Slava Marinov is far above me in my organization's chain of command. Comrade Marinov was not in the habit of discussing strategy—or anything else, for that matter—with me."

"How did Marinov learn the identities of the American oper-atives who were targeted for assassination? Where did he get his information?"

"I told you already, I do not know."

Tracie shook her head sadly. "You know, Piotr, you're going to have to do better than this if you want to remain useful to me. I'm sure you can guess what will happen to you if you do *not* remain useful."

"You know already I do not wish to die. Ask me a question I can answer and I will."

"Okay. How do I get at Marinov?"

"I told you already, you do not 'get at' a man like Slava Marinov. His office is buried so deeply inside KGB headquarters that it would take forty minutes of walking to reach him in the unlikely even you were ever able to infiltrate the facility. And then once you reached his office, you would encounter layers of armed security. It cannot be done."

"So Marinov lives at KGB headquarters then?"

Speransky's forehead wrinkled in confusion. "What?"

"Well, I assume by the way you're speaking that the man must live inside the fortress that is KGB headquarters. Come on, Piotr, cut the crap. You're really trying my patience. I may radiate your ass just on general principles."

He closed his eyes and Tracie said, "You're going to have to try a little harder. Where does Marinov live?"

"I do not know where Slava Marinov lives. Why would I know that?"

"I think you know a lot more than you've been willing to admit to so far. Even if you don't know his specific address, can you verify he lives in Moscow?"

"*Da,* Comrade Marinov lives in Moscow."

"How does he get to work in the morning? And I swear to God, Piotr, if you say 'by armored car,' I'm done with you. If you say you don't know, I'm done with you. Give me some goddamned intel and do it now."

"Why should I tell you any more?" he whispered. "You are only going to kill me when you've gotten what you need."

"That's not true."

"Of course it is true. We are in the same line of work, remember? You have nothing to gain by allowing me to live and everything to lose. If our positions were reversed, I would kill you the moment I no longer needed you."

"Well, I guess that's the difference between you and me. I have no desire to commit cold-blooded murder. Don't get me wrong, if you cross me I'll cut you down before you even know what hit you, but if you give up Marinov, and I'm able to complete my mission, I will allow you to live. I give you my word."

Tracie could see Speransky didn't believe her. She didn't blame him. *She* didn't believe her. The fact of the matter was that eliminating the operative doing the actual poisoning was just as much a part of her assignment as eliminating the man who'd *ordered* the poisoning.

Which meant Speranski would not survive when all was said and done.

But if it would take a little white lie—or even a gigantic black mushroom cloud of a lie—to finish this damned mission when she was so close to doing so, then a lie it would be.

"Now," she said. "I've given you my word. It's time for you to give me what I need."

Speransky sighed. It was obvious he didn't believe her, but what choice did he have? Give her what she needed and probably die later, or keep his mouth closed and definitely die now.

"Slava Marinov takes the train to work. His schedule never varies. He is as punctual as is humanly possible, given the variables associated with Moscow public transportation."

"What station? Which train?"

"He arrives at Belorussky Station every morning on the 7:10 local. The 7:10 is, of course, almost always late, but if you are looking to intercept Comrade Marinov during his morning commute, that would be the way to do it. He exits the train and moves immediately to a limousine awaiting his arrival in a secure location outside the station. The car then drives him directly to headquarters."

Tracie gazed thoughtfully at Speransky. He had nothing to gain by lying and everything to lose. Her Polonium-210 radiation threat was a lie, but he didn't know that, and at this point it didn't even matter. He knew she could put two 9mm slugs in his head any time she wanted.

She thought her silence might unnerve the KGB man after all she had done to him, but that didn't seem to be the case. He appeared perfectly willing to sit quietly in the lengthening silence.

Maybe he thought silence was preferable to the sound of a gunshot or of nuclear radiation being sprayed into his system.

Maybe he actually believed her assurance that she would let him live if he provided actionable intelligence regarding his handler.

Or maybe he was just so goddamned exhausted and injured and beaten down that he didn't have it in him to worry.

Finally she nodded.

Glanced at her watch.

"Okay Piotr. I believe you. But we still have a long night ahead of us. You're going to tell me every last thing you know about Slava Marinov: his personal history, his schedule, his family situation, his favorite goddamned color. And when you've finished, we're going to start over and do it all again."

He closed his eyes and his head sank back down to his chest.

"Do you have a problem with that, Piotr?"

For a long time he didn't move. Then he slowly shook his head.

30

January 25, 1988
7:40 a.m.
Belorussky Station, Moscow

Tracie had been standing on the platform outside Moscow's Belo-russky Railway Station for close to an hour now. She was tired and wired. She hadn't slept in nearly thirty-six hours, but adrenaline pounded through her system as the interminable wait for Slava Marinov's train stretched on.

The station had seen better days. It looked as though renovations had been begun and then abandoned. The windows Tracie could see were filthy and a long, serpentine crack ran through one of them. The cobblestones that made up the passenger platform were warped and cracked and had needed to be replaced for probably at least a decade.

And the platform provided little shelter from the bitter Moscow cold. Wind whipped seemingly in all directions, stinging exposed skin and ruffling the great tufts of fur surrounding the hoods nearly everyone had drawn around their heads and faces.

Tracie had purchased a large cup of tea en route to the station, arriving well before Marinov's scheduled 7:10 arrival but determined not to miss the KGB murderer should Speransky's statement about the train's chronic lateness be inaccurate.

Her intention had been to observe the station from a distance before entering, and she had done so, but the surveillance had been perfunctory due to the cold. She was able to plan out a potential escape route and verify the absence of law enforcement or Red Army soldiers—at least for the time being—but that was all.

By the time she entered the station, her tea had been stone cold, and she dumped it into a trash bin with a disappointed frown after having consumed barely one-third of the contents.

It was probably just as well. She already felt jittery from nerves and lack of sleep. Adding caffeine to the mix would be a mistake.

She had found over the course of her career that the tension she inevitably experienced while waiting for the action to begin always melted away once things started happening. At that point she would feel calm and strong and in control. In the meantime, a family of butterflies circled inside her stomach, and her hands felt shaky and foreign.

And cold.

She had of course worn heavy, fur-lined gloves, but upon arrival at the station had removed them and stuffed them into the deep pockets of her parka. For what she was planning, gloves would be impractical, and even though she knew Marinov would likely not arrive for quite some time she didn't want to be stuck trying to yank off her gloves at the last possible moment, when quick action would be critical.

So she kept her hands mostly buried inside the same pockets holding her gloves and tried her best to appear unmemorable. Avoid drawing unwanted attention to herself.

The weather conditions were helpful in that regard. Inside the station, which might have seen better days but at least was warm and toasty, passengers removed their coats and hats while awaiting their trains. But outside, men and women were forced to bundle up. This would make identification by witnesses problematic, even in the unlikely event Tracie was observed.

That was the positive.

The negative was that Marinov would undoubtedly be bundled up every bit as much as she was when he stepped off the train.

As would every other disembarking passenger.

Identifying her target would not be easy.

Speransky had provided a unique identifying characteristic during the long hours of overnight interrogation, which Tracie hoped to use to her advantage. Assuming the KGB assassin had been telling the truth, which was of course a questionable assumption.

And even if he had, the number of passengers getting off the train at a Moscow station concerned Tracie. If the crowd was too big and too unwieldy, it might simply be impossible to check every male before the passengers swarmed across the platform and down onto the city streets. They would be moving quickly with these low temperatures and high winds.

There was nothing she could do about any of that now except worry. She gnawed on her lower lip while stomping her boot-clad feet on the platform in an attempt to keep the blood flowing. A few other hardy souls stood outside, but the majority of people—*the sane ones*, Tracie thought—had chosen to remain inside, in the warmth and out of the wind, until the train's arrival.

Tracie checked her watch as she had been doing obsessively for the last half hour. It was not an easy process, since she had to remove her hands from her pockets and then push up the heavy left sleeve of her parka with her bare right hand, but she guessed she must have done exactly that at least ten times in thirty minutes.

Seven forty-five.

Speransky wasn't kidding about the train always arriving late. Tracie shook her head impatiently. *I thought the supposed benefit of an authoritarian government was that at least they got the trains to run on time.*

Apparently that wasn't even true.

She had begun shivering and was considering returning inside the station to warm up, just for a couple of minutes, when the decision was abruptly taken out of her hands and rendered moot.

Because the train was coming.

It rounded a corner a quarter-mile from the station and then brakes squealed loudly as the heavy engine and the line of cars behind it began to slow. The ground under the platform rumbled, and moments later the engine crawled past the platform and screeched to a halt.

It had turned out Piotr Speransky was considerably more knowledgeable about his handler's routine than he had initially admitted. So much so that Tracie suspected Speransky had been gathering intel on Marinov in an effort to protect himself. To find something incriminating he could hold over the man's head in the event Marinov ever decided Speransky had become expendable.

One of the things Speransky had told her was that Marinov had a superiority complex a mile wide. He was an important cog in the KGB machine and he expected to be treated as such, and not just by people aware of his status. He wanted and expected ordinary citizens to bow and scrape.

"He will be on the first passenger car," Speransky had said confidently. "The one closest to the engine and thus closest to the station upon arrival. He would no sooner arrive at Belorussky Station on a rear car than he would steep his own tea at the office."

Tracie said a quick prayer and began to move. Already she could feel her nerves calming, the familiar clarifying focus of concentration narrowing her field of vision.

Everything melted away except the mission.

Tracie Tanner had come to realize she lived for these moments. Colors brightened when she was working an active mission. Sounds became more acute. Odors were stronger. Sensations magnified.

She positioned herself on the platform halfway between the station entrance and the steps leading to the city sidewalks. Speransky had said the limo waiting to drive Marinov the rest of the way to KGB headquarters would be parked behind a barricade on the street just north of the station, and she prayed he was telling the truth.

If the target exited the train and turned south, she might never catch him in the dense crowd of passengers.

The situation was less than ideal, but without backup, Tracie had no choice but to play the odds.

Passengers began streaming from the front and rear of the cars and Tracie narrowed her eyes, studying each as they climbed down onto the platform.

The women she ignored.

A few children exited and she ignored them as well.

The men she locked onto, examining each as closely as possible and then eliminating them one-by-one when it became clear they were not her target. Fur-lined hoods snugged up against wool-en-masked faces rendered most of the disembarking passengers virtually unidentifiable.

But none of that should matter. Tracie wasn't concerned about identifying her target facially. There would be another way. Speransky claimed Slava Marinov had started his KGB career as a field operative, performing for the Soviet Union the kinds of dirty and thankless missions Tracie had been performing for the United States over her nearly eight-year career.

Marinov's time in the field had come to an immediate and permanent end when he took a bullet in the spine fired by a West German FSB officer during a mission gone sideways. The KGB officer had been badly injured, and for a time doctors had said he would never walk again.

But the doctors had been wrong.

He *did* walk again.

However, he did so with the aid of a cane, suffering a noticeable limp. Over the years, Speransky said, the severity of Marinov's limp had lessened, but it had never disappeared.

If you look closely, Tracie's reluctant informant had told her, *you will see the limp. You cannot miss it. That is how you will identify your man.*

The first people to exit the train began streaming past, most heading straight for the outdoor stairway, preferring to get the chilly walk to their destination over with right away.

A few entered the train station instead.

None were Marinov.

Tracie shifted her gaze to the people exiting the lead car by the rear stairway.

No luck.

She scanned the crowd exiting the second and third passenger cars, determined to be thorough despite Speransky's insistence Marinov would disembark from the first car.

Nothing.

She scanned constantly, reverting her attention to the car directly behind the engine as passengers continued to exit. This was a popular stop.

The platform was now filled with people, the crowd churning toward her, and Tracie began to fear she would miss Slava Marinov.

He would slip past her in the mass of humanity.

Maybe he already had.

She choked back a rising tide of concern that was edging close to panic. This had to work. There was no backup plan. It was Monday morning, and if Yuri Ryakhin had not yet been discovered bound and gagged in his kitchen, he soon would be.

Dammit.

An odd motion from inside the crowd drew Tracie's attention. It was unlike the rest of the expected movements of people within the seething crowd.

She narrowed her eyes and focused on where she thought she had observed something...different.

There it was again.

People's heads bobbed up and down slightly as they walked, but one head in particular stood out because its bobbing motion was more pronounced than the rest.

Someone was limping.

And that someone was a man.

As the bustling group of people approached, Tracie stared, trying to catch a second glimpse of the man between the constantly shifting heavy winter coats.

There it was again: and the man walking with a limp was using a cane.

It had to be Marinov.

She'd identified her target.

31

January 25, 1988
7:55 a.m.
Belorussky Station, Moscow

Tracie had assumed the KGB officer would bypass the train station's interior, preferring to move directly to his waiting car via the outdoor stairway. Her assumption had been a good one. Marinov showed no inclination to turn toward the warmth of the building.

He was more or less boxed in by a small group of people all with the same plan in mind: to hit the stairs and get started toward their destinations. That was why she'd nearly missed seeing him. He wasn't tall, and he was surrounded by men. They dwarfed him in height and rendered him nearly invisible.

The crowd moved right to left past Tracie's position. Marinov didn't seem to take notice of her, and neither did anyone else. No one was talking. The commuters didn't know each other. They were just all strangers of a single mind.

Marinov's position, tucked away inside the small group, was far from ideal. It was almost as if the travelers had formed an unwitting protective phalanx around Tracie's target. To be successful she needed to get close to him, and doing so the way the pedestrians were currently positioned would present a major problem.

She tracked their progress as they approached the stairs and then fell in behind them. The crowd had finally stopped surging off the train cars, but there were still plenty of people following Tracie and her target across the platform.

Marinov moved more slowly than the average walking adult male, thanks to his limping gait, and given the bitter cold, none of his fellow travelers seemed inclined to dawdle. The KGB officer began to fall back in the pack. As they reached the top of the wide staircase and began to descend toward the street, the men behind Marinov parted, one to his right and one to his left, and passed him.

Tracie picked up her pace and moved closer. If at all possible, she wanted to finish this before Marinov reached the streets and came within sight of his car. She had no doubt the limousine was being driven by a KGB case officer, and also no doubt that officer would be armed and inclined to protect his boss.

Tracie had chosen a parka to wear that was too big for her small frame. The large size made for a cold walk, as the coat struggled to contain her body heat.

But she hadn't chosen the winter wear for comfort. She'd chosen it for operational advantage, and now her discomfort would pay off.

Hopefully.

She kept her coat zippered and held her right sleeve at the cuff with her left hand. Pulled her right arm in toward her body and slipped it out of the sleeve. Now the right sleeve of the parka hung limply to the side, her arm free inside the coat.

She snaked her hand up her ribcage, resting it on the butt of her Beretta. Her shoulder holster was big and bulky and more than a little uncomfortable, but it was specially designed and customized to hold not just the weapon, but the weapon with sound suppressor already threaded into place.

Tracie eased her gun out of its shoulder rig. It had been specially modified with a pair of nylon straps encircling Tracie's ribs and waist, securing it in place with the butt of the weapon forward of its positioning in a standard shoulder holster.

The placement provided the extra room necessary to allow Tracie to do what she did next: lift the butt of the Beretta toward her left shoulder with her right hand and pull the gun—now with a much longer barrel than usual, thanks to the suppressor—out of the holster.

She continued walking as she worked the weapon free. Marinov was now halfway down the stairs, supporting himself with his left hand on the rusted iron railing as he held his cane above the steps with his other hand.

The group of commuters with whom he'd exited the train had pulled ahead of Marinov, and now Tracie had the opportunity she'd been waiting for: the target positioned in front of her and slightly to her left.

No innocent bystanders between them.

Nobody on the far side of Marinov who might take a bullet if Tracie missed the shot.

No reason to hesitate.

But Tracie hesitated anyway. A niggling concern nagged at her in the back of her mind.

What if it was the wrong man?

The odds were against it. What was the likelihood of two men, with identical disabilities, riding the *same* train car and disembarking at the *same* Moscow station at the *same* time, with Tracie's target disappearing into the crowd and the innocent victim taking a bullet?

The odds against that scenario were astronomical. This had to be Slava Marinov.

But still…stranger things had happened, and she could never forgive herself if she gunned down an innocent man.

She wasn't entirely sure she could ever forgive herself for what she was about to do, anyway. She'd killed before, been in gunfights and taken bullets that, had they been placed differently, would have killed *her*.

But she had never assassinated an unsuspecting, unarmed person without warning. She knew she was about to cross a line, about to take an action from which she might never recover.

Still, her concerns and misgivings were fodder for another day. Or another thousand sleepless nights. She had her assignment and was determined to carry it out.

But she had to be sure.

The target had now nearly reached the bottom of the steps. She closed the distance between them and spoke softly. "Comrade Marinov?"

The man swiveled his head instantly, searching for the person who had called his name.

It was the right man.

Marinov met Tracie's eyes for a split-second and then he turned his attention back to navigating the stairway. It was wide and steep and he risked falling. He had apparently decided he'd imagined hearing the near-whisper of his name.

Tracie adjusted her aim. The first rule of shooting a pistol was to aim center-mass at the target. It was true in normal circumstances, where the weapon was held eye-height in a two-handed shooter's grip and it was even truer now, when she would be firing almost blindly through a thick winter parka, with no opportunity to sight down the barrel.

She hoped for the best.

Squeezed the trigger.

Once, twice, three times, then a fourth, firing her silenced semiautomatic pistol in a lethal burst of 9mm slugs.

Marinov stumbled forward. He was still clutching the railing but his body swung left from the force of the bullets ripping into his body. He struck the iron railing and bounced off and then he was tumbling down the remaining stairs.

He struck the sidewalk with a wet splat, his skull cracking the cobblestones hard. He lay face down and unmoving.

Tracie swept past him, walking at a normal pace but not slowing, acting as though she had not noticed the pedestrian tumbling down the stairs outside the train station like a rag doll.

She glanced sideways, not turning her head but looking at Marinov in her peripheral vision. No blood was visible, as the slugs had torn through his parka, but it soon would be.

She wanted to kneel and feel for a pulse, to be certain she'd succeeded in her assignment, but didn't dare. Already a buzz of excited confusion was audible from the crowd of people descending the stairway behind Marinov.

She would have to take on faith that four slugs fired at close range into the body of an older man would be enough to finish him off. He wasn't moving. He was likely already dead.

Tracie continued along the sidewalk, just another commuter heading into Moscow to start another long workweek. She slipped her Beretta back into its customized holster but didn't bother trying to maneuver her arm back into its sleeve. The awkward motions it would require to do so would draw more attention than simply allowing the sleeve to hang limply at her side.

Behind her, the screams for help started. They faded into the background as she turned a corner and left the Belorussky Station behind.

32

January 25, 1988
11:20 a.m.
CIA safe house
Moscow, Russia

Tracie took her time returning to the safe house, wandering the streets of Moscow despite the bitter temperatures on yet another slate-gray, overcast winter day.

She tried to convince herself part of the reason for the delay was operational. That she wanted to make absolutely certain she wasn't being followed. That she wanted to minimize the chances of leading the KGB back to Piotr Speransky if she'd been compromised.

And as far as it went, she supposed the rationalization was even true. Working alone in a hostile environment, caution was always a prime consideration. It was just as important to avoid revealing the location of agency assets such as informants and safe houses as it was to avoid capture herself.

But she had to admit that caution wasn't the reason for delaying her return to the safe house and to Speransky. She could make a beeline for the safe house and there would be virtually no chance the KGB would follow.

Because if the KGB had been tailing her she would already be in custody. Hell, if the KGB had been tailing her, they would likely already be well into her first torture session. They would waste little time dealing with the American who had assassinated a high-ranking Soviet intelligence official.

She sighed and wrapped her arms around her body in a vain attempt to ward off a chill that was only partially due to the temperature.

Be honest with yourself.

Her delay in returning to the safe house was due mostly— almost entirely—to a reason other than operational necessity. Her delay in returning was due to the knowledge that once she stepped through the door, she had to finish her assignment.

And finishing her assignment meant killing Piotr Speransky.

And she didn't know if she could do it.

Logically, there was no difference between putting bullets into Slava Marinov outside the Belorussky Train Station this morning and putting bullets into Piotr Speransky inside the CIA safe house this afternoon. Both had been directly responsible for the deaths of multiple CIA case officers, good men whose only offenses had been the willingness to work toward nullifying the threat the Soviet Union represented to freedom and democracy.

Marinov had been the brains of the operation and was now gone. Speransky had been the "blunt instrument," as he called it, and deserved to go as well.

It was her mission.

But as difficult as it had been to pull the trigger on Marinov, it would be doubly so to pump Speransky full of bullets as he sat, secured and defenseless, in the chair to which Tracie had left him tied.

She was wandering Moscow, risking detection and capture, because she wasn't sure that when push came to shove, she would have the ability to look a helpless man in the eyes and pump 9mm bullets into his body until he was dead.

Be honest with yourself.

That was the long and the short of it. Her actions were irrational and dangerous. Self-destructive. The more time she spent alone inside the heart of the Russian bear, the less likely it became, not just that she would complete her mission, but that she would ever escape Russia alive.

If Yuri Ryakhin had not yet been discovered in Kremlyov—a

possibility that became less likely by the hour—and the KGB hadn't already begun scouring the country for her, they certainly would now. She'd assassinated Slava Marinov in front of dozens of witnesses, and while it was highly unlikely any of them had gotten a good look at her, dressed in anonymous clothing and buried inside a massive winter coat and a hat and scarf, her gender and small size would immediately eliminate probably eighty percent of Russians from suspicion.

She had to return to the safe house and finish this.

* * *

Without conscious thought, Tracie's travels around Moscow had drawn her closer and closer to the safe house and Piotr Speransky. It was as if, while trying to drum up the fortitude to complete her assignment, her subconscious mind had been pointing her in the direction she would eventually have to travel to do so.

She sighed angrily and turned toward mission completion.

* * *

Twenty minutes later she unlocked the safe house door. Even at midday and in the middle of a gigantic Russian city, Tracie was forced to take only minimal precautions to avoid being observed. The safe house was tucked away in a rundown industrial neighborhood, with the vast majority of the crumbling structures standing empty and unused. Aside from the occasional homeless drifter attempting to stay warm in front of fires blazing in rusting trash barrels, potential witnesses were few and far between.

She stepped inside, relishing the warmth of the interior after hours spent outside in the cold. Her stomach pitched and rolled. It felt like a ship on stormy seas, and she knew the queasy feeling would stay with her until she finished what she'd been sent to Russia to do.

She removed her winter coat and dropped in on the floor. Left her suppressed Beretta in its holster for the time being and walked across the room, stopping directly in front of Piotr Speransky.

Tracie had replaced the gag on her informant before leaving for Belorussky Station this morning, but despite his arms and legs being securely restrained, Speransky had retained some range of motion with his head. He tracked her progress with obvious concern, eyes narrowing steadily until they were mere slits by the time she positioned herself in front of him.

She lifted her combat knife out of its sheath at the small of her back and sliced through the duct tape holding Speransky's gag in place. Ripped the tape roughly off his head. A small clump of hair came with it and a bright red welt was left on the exposed skin of his face.

It had to have been painful but he barely seemed to notice.

"I want you to know something," she said before he could speak. "Thanks to the intel you provided I was able to rid the world of the cockroach known as Slava Marinov."

"Wonderful," he muttered as he looked away. The sarcasm was impossible to miss.

Tracie smiled grimly. "Just keeping you in the loop."

"I told you the information would be accurate."

"Yes, you did. And that is exactly why you're still alive to discuss the issue with me right now."

"But…" Speransky's body had gone rigid in the chair. His face looked every bit as pale as it had last night while Tracie was using a pair of long-nose pliers to dig into the skin under his fingernails. "There is a 'but' coming, is there not?"

It was phrased as a question, but it might as well have been a declarative statement. He knew what was going to happen next.

"Yes, there is a 'but' coming," Tracie said. The butterflies were still swarming in her stomach, but her earlier moment of self-doubt had passed. A little time considering the fate of Charles Fowler and the other dead CIA case officers had been sufficient to harden her resolve.

"But you are a professional, as I am," she continued. "And while your dedication to duty is in some ways admirable—although mostly just twisted and horrifying—there can be no excusing your actions. Condemning a half-dozen good men to the kind of death you inflicted upon them is simply inexcusable.

"Plus," she smiled at him, "I have my mission to consider. Eliminating Marinov was only one-half of the equation. You represent the other half, and I'm sure you can understand the importance of completing my assignment. We're on opposite sides of the fence, but some things, even a hated enemy can relate to."

"So you are going to spray the Polonium-210 down my throat or into my nasal passages despite your promise to spare me if I gave up my KGB superior." He looked away and shook his head. "It figures. I don't know why I am even surprised. I would expect no less out of an…American." He grimaced as he spit out the last word, as if he'd just bitten into a sandwich filled with rancid meat.

"Please, Piotr, spare me the manufactured shock. You may have been *hoping* for a different outcome, but inside you've known all along how this was going to end."

He hung his head. Shook his head again in disgust but didn't argue.

"And your analysis is erroneous, anyway," she added.

"Is that so? Would you care to share how I erred before condemning me to weeks of suffering, followed by an agonizing death?"

"You are incorrect in your conviction that I'm going to subject you to radiation poisoning. Even though you, and Marinov, and everyone along the chain of command above him inside the KGB seemed to feel it an appropriate way to deal with your rivals, I wouldn't subject my worst enemy to the effects of radiation. I simply couldn't do that, not after having seen its effects up-close and in person."

"So that ugly scene with the spray bottle of Polonium last night was—"

"It was the most effective way to extract the information I needed. No more and no less. I decided that physical pain alone would not provide sufficient motivation for a longtime pro like yourself to cough up intel.

"But the prospect of suffering from radiation poisoning," she continued, "well, I thought that might be a different story. And I was right."

ALLAN LEVERONE

"So you were never going to spray me with the suspension."

"Oh, I would have sprayed you, absolutely. Perhaps you would have crumbled *after* receiving the dose. It would certainly have been worth a try, anyway."

"But you just said—"

"Come on, Piotr, use your head. I know you're tired and in pain and heartbroken to have been beaten at your own game by a woman—and an American woman at that—but still, you've been doing this a long time. Think about it for a second."

His forehead wrinkled in concentration, but only for a moment. Then his eyes hardened. He ground his teeth together so hard Tracie could see ropy muscles bunching along his jawline. "There *was* no Polonium-210."

"Congratulations, you're a winner. I figured when I took that little lead-lined bottle from the Arzamas-16 plant that if you saw it you would immediately associate it with the deadly radiation you've been carrying around inside identical bottles for the last three years-plus."

She grinned. "And you didn't disappoint me, Piotr. P.T. Barnum supposedly said 'there's a sucker born every minute.' Well, you lived your minute to the hilt."

"What was in the bottle?"

"What difference does it make?"

"Just tell me."

"If I'd sprayed you, you would have gotten a mixture of water and a little honey forced up your nose. Harmless. Hell, maybe it would have been good for your sinuses, I don't know."

He muttered something under his breath.

"I'm sorry, Piotr, I missed that. Could you speak up?"

"I said you are nothing but a dirty little *cyka*. When I get out of here…"

"You're not getting out of here, Piotr. Ever. At least not while you're breathing. I said I wouldn't inflict Polonium-210 on my worst enemy. That doesn't mean I'm not going to complete my mission."

She drew her Beretta.

Examined the still-attached suppressor with a critical eye.

Tilted her head and nodded theatrically. "I think this will still work just fine."

Speransky tried to shrink back into his chair but there was nowhere to go.

"It's time," Tracie said.

She lifted the weapon and trained it on the Soviet operative.

33

"Stop! Please! Do not shoot!" He was panting and cringing and trying to escape but there was nowhere to go.

Tracie ignored him and began to squeeze the trigger.

"I can tell you where we got the list!"

Tracie had long preferred a weapon that required substantial trigger pressure to fire, and that preference saved Speransky's life.

At least for now.

She eased off the trigger and lifted the Beretta's barrel toward the ceiling. Stared unblinkingly. "What did you just say?"

Sweat stains soiled Speransky's shirt, giant dirty arcs that testified to all he had suffered through since the staged traffic accident yesterday outside Kremlyov. He'd done a good job of maintaining his dignity and professionalism right up to the last moment, but then he had cracked.

He took a deep breath and blew it out shakily. "I said I know the source of the leaks that cost the lives of the American operatives."

"That cost the lives of American operatives? Don't you mean the operatives that you murdered?"

"Fine. Yes. The operatives I murdered. But changing the phrasing does not change the point. I can provide you with the name of

207

the man whose actions permitted the KGB to identify and execute American operatives."

Now it was Tracie's turn to narrow her eyes.

Speransky paused to catch his breath. He'd been panting like a tired dog as Tracie began squeezing the trigger and it seemed clear he was more than a little surprised to still be alive.

"With Marinov dead," he continued, "I am the only person left who knows the source of the leak."

"Bullshit," Tracie said.

Speransky shrugged slightly and nodded. "You are right. There are others who know. But those others are positioned so highly on the KGB chain of command you could never access them. You were lucky to get at Marinov. Extremely lucky. But it would have been nearly impossible to access high-ranking KGB officers before today. After your murder of Slava Marinov, it will *be* impossible. They will close ranks. Disappear. You will never even find them, much less kidnap and torture them like you have done to me."

The flood of words emphasized Speransky's desperation. Tracie understood his reasoning because she had employed it herself in his position. Get your captors talking and keep them talking.

Talking was much less dangerous than shooting.

She cleared her throat, stalling for time while she considered this new development.

Then she shook her head. "You're full of shit."

"Not true. Kill me now and you will never know what I know."

"You said you had no idea where the list had come from, that Marinov would never share such a secret with a lowly field operative."

"You are not the only one who sometimes finds it expedient to lie."

"Fine. But I still don't believe you. Your 'information' is nothing but a pathetic attempt to save your own worthless skin. No handler would allow his operative access to that kind of intel."

She wasn't lying. She believed everything she had just said—it would serve no purpose for a superior to share the source of intel with his operative.

But still…

A little voice in the back of her head told her Speransky was telling the truth.

He was desperate to save his life. That fact was obvious and indisputable. But desperation did not automatically translate into his words being untruthful.

This was a dilemma of the sort she had never before faced. Of the sort she had never imagined facing. Her orders had been explicit: eliminate the evil behind the radiation-poisoning deaths of a half-dozen American patriots over the last three-and-a-half years.

She had succeeded thus far against all odds. Had eliminated Slava Marinov and was one squeezed trigger away from completing her assignment.

There had been no equivocation to her orders. Stallings had been very clear, and there had been no misunderstanding on Tracie's part as to the nature of her mission.

She had accepted it and traveled to the Soviet Union with every intention of completing it.

But wouldn't the CIA director want to learn the source of the leak so it could be plugged permanently? Wouldn't this entire mission be rendered moot if the KGB retained the ability to acquire the identities of American assets?

Today's mission success would slow them down, certainly, but eventually they would dust themselves off and assign another operative the task of assassinating American assets one by one. And all she had accomplished here, at great personal risk, would be nullified.

She made her decision.

Lowered her gun and once again trained it on her captive.

"Talk."

Tracie knew there was no way Speransky would be able to guess whether she was about to put two slugs into his skull or not, because she had no idea herself. She had steeled herself to eliminate the KGB operative, had been prepared to complete her mission and get the hell out of Russia despite her aversion to the notion of executing an unarmed man.

"Why would I say another word when I know you will only kill me once I have given you what you seek?"

Tracie almost laughed out loud. Despite the stress, despite the tension crackling in the air like an electrical storm, invisible and deadly, Tracie almost laughed out loud.

Now that he had successfully gained her attention, Speransky needed to negotiate for his life, but the KGB man made a valid point. Tracie's credibility had evaporated with the promise to let him live if he gave up Slava Marinov. She had reneged on the deal, and that fact threw the current situation into chaos.

She could promise to spare him if he revealed the source of the CIA leak, but why would he believe her?

It seemed an unsolvable puzzle, but there was one last possibility. Speransky had kept his mouth firmly closed about the CIA leak until milliseconds away from a 9mm execution. Only then had he offered up what must be his final bargaining chip.

"Why would you say another word? Here's why, Piotr. Because if you don't reveal the leak, I'll pull the trigger in the next three seconds. It's your choice. Talk or die."

The blood drained out of his sweat-soaked face. Again.

Tracie gave him a moment to start talking, but all he could manage was "Please...no...please..."

She squeezed the trigger.

The suppressed weapon coughed and a slug ripped into the wall behind Piotr Speransky. It blasted a hole in the plaster and showered the defenseless man with fine white powder.

He screeched, and piss began to flow onto the wooden chair and the smell of urine filled the room as Speransky's bladder released.

But still he didn't speak beyond the nearly incoherent, desperate pleas for his life.

Goddammit.

The threat of violent death had been Tracie's last gambit. She had nothing left to hold over the man's head. He seemed willing to take the secret of the CIA leak to his grave.

Goddammit.

But...

What about the truth? What if she could convince him that he actually *could* escape with his life and that all it would take to do so would be to rat out one more person?

He likely wouldn't believe her. He had absolutely no reason to believe her. But if the choice was to believe in the *possibility* of life or face her Beretta again and the certainty of violent death, with the knowledge that this time she would not aim for the wall...

She had nothing to lose, and even if the odds of failure were high she decided she had to try.

"It seems we're at an impasse, Piotr, wouldn't you agree?"

His head hung as he took in the sight of his soaked trousers. He didn't seem to have heard her, or if he did he had chosen to ignore her.

"Comrade Speransky, look at me." She spoke softly, her voice almost a whisper.

After a moment he lifted his head and met her gaze. He looked as exhausted and terrified as he had before, but now he looked defeated as well.

"Just finish me and be done with it," he mumbled. His eyes skittered away from Tracie's and he started to drop his head again.

"Piotr!" This time her voice was strident and he jumped. His nerves were shot to hell. But he locked eyes with her again and this time held her gaze.

Tracie figured it was the best she was going to get. She said, "You've heard of the concept of going after the big fish, I assume?"

He shook his head, confused. "Big fish? What are you talking about?"

"I already told you my mission. To eliminate the men causing the horrific deaths of American CIA assets in the Soviet Union."

"*Da*, you did. Which is why I wish you would just get on with it."

"Listen to me, Piotr. You might find my words valuable."

"I'm listening."

"I fully admit I lied to you. I did what I had to do to get you to give up Marinov. I had no intention of allowing you to live. I admit that, and as a fellow espionage professional, I have every confidence that you can understand my reasoning."

He said nothing, but his eyes glittered with the beginning of what Tracie hoped was understanding.

"But now," she said, "things have changed. *I want to go after the big fish.* If you truly know the name of the CIA employee whose treason had resulted in the deaths of those American operatives, I want it. The ability to apprehend that person means far more to me than does killing you. Give up that CIA name and I give you my word I will walk out of here without pulling the trigger on you."

Suspicion clouded Speransky's eyes and Tracie continued.

"No bullets in the head. No execution. I swear to you as a fellow professional. I want the American whose treason has cost my people their lives much more than I could ever possibly want you, Piotr."

"Fellow professional, eh?"

"That's right. A fellow professional."

"There is one big problem with your reasoning, above and beyond the fact that you have demonstrated already you are completely untrustworthy. As a 'fellow professional,' I understand in a way no one else could that you are not in any position to *make* the offer you just made. If your mission is to execute Marinov and me, then that is exactly what you must do or face severe consequences upon your return to Langley."

Tracie blinked in surprise. Even as rattled as he clearly was, Speransky had instantly seized upon the weakness in her argument. Once more she realized that despite the oceans worth of differences between their governments' worldviews, their two intelligence organizations were not as dissimilar as either would like to believe, and Speransky had grasped that fact immediately.

But she wasn't about to go down without a fight. "As a longtime field operative, surely you have been in situations where you were required to make judgment calls that may or may not have gone against your specific orders."

"Of course. But why would you risk potentially severe consequences when you could avoid any chance of suffering those consequences by shooting me in the head after I tell you the name?"

"Because that's not how I operate." She knew how lame the words must sound to the man she'd already lied to once, and hurried on. "I could also avoid those consequences by lying to my superiors when I get home. I could advise them that I succeeded in eliminating the two men responsible for the Polonium-210 and they would never know the difference."

Speransky's eyes wandered, focusing on something—or perhaps nothing—over Tracie's right shoulder as he considered her words.

"Think of it that way if it makes your decision easier, Comrade. And remember this: you have nothing to lose by trusting me, and potentially everything to gain. If you do not surrender the name of the American traitor, you *will* die, alone inside this depressing little room, within the next few minutes."

She turned and walked away, giving the KGB operative a little time and space to think. She wandered into the tiny kitchen and poured a glass of water. She had given it her best shot and now the ball was in Piotr Spernasky's court.

She waited three minutes.

Four.

Five. Then she wandered back into the living room. "It's decision time, Piotr. What's it going to be? Do you want to live or die?"

34

January 26, 1988
8:40 a.m.
Alley near the CIA safe house
Moscow, Russia

Tracie had no desire to return to the cramped, dark and uncomfortable crawl space beneath the Russian-made ZiL-157 delivery truck. The hour or so she'd spent inside the hiding spot while being smuggled into Kremlyov had been more than long enough for this lifetime or any other.

But leaving the nerve center of the Soviet Union would have been challenging under the best of circumstances, and after the chaos she had wrought in and around Moscow over the last few days Tracie knew her chances of escaping the USSR without use of extraordinary measures would be virtually nil.

She could cut and dye her hair. She could add lifts to her shoes and artificial bulk beneath her clothing to transform from slim and petite to tall and heavy. She could wear glasses and change her complexion using makeup, but none of it would matter. Red Army personnel would be blanketing every airport within a five-hundred mile radius of Moscow, checkpoints and roadblocks would be established and manned with heavily armed security.

She would be sniffed out.

Captured.

And then she would be executed. That would have been the

likely outcome if apprehended before her elimination of Slava Marinov. It was a certainty now.

So when Ryan Smith backed the truck into the alley half a dozen streets away from the safe house Tracie had been using as a base of operations, she clamped her jaws together and tried to prepare for the better part of a day's journey locked away inside a space that felt roughly the size and dimensions of a desk drawer. The engine rumbled and coughed, diesel fumes filling the dirty Moscow air, and then air brakes squealed and the truck shuddered to a stop.

The rear bumper clunked off the frame and then Smith was climbing down from the cab. He approached Tracie with a smile that never made it to his eyes and she was reminded how much was at stake, not just for her but for him as well. If her hiding place were to be discovered at a roadblock, Tracie Tanner would not be the only one to suffer a brutal and lonely fate.

Ryan Smith would disappear without a trace as well, fated to spend the rest of eternity in an unmarked Russian grave.

"Nice to see you again, Quinn," he said and this time his smile seemed genuine.

"Likewise, Smith." After a nearly eight-year career spent mostly working on her own, Tracie was familiar with solitude and most comfortable when working alone. If you relied only on yourself, you were subject to far fewer variables you could not control. But she had to admit Ryan Smith exuded a quiet confidence in his abilities that went a long way toward easing her concern about being trapped inside the crawl space, utterly at the mercy of an operative who was barely more than a stranger.

Many of the operatives she'd met were brash and bold, arrogant even, self-confident beyond all reason. But Smith seemed different. She decided if she had to place her fate in the hands of anyone not named Tanner, Ryan Smith was a pretty good alternative.

"Glad to see you're okay," he said as she tossed a small bag into the hiding place.

"Right back atya. Have you seen or heard any fallout from our KGB friend's tragic 'car accident' outside Kremlyov?"

Smith stared in shock. "Are you kidding me?" he said. "It's been all over the news. The guy was identified on state TV as a 'law enforcement officer,' rather than an intelligence specialist, but we stirred up a massive hornets nest. This little excursion is not going to be easy."

"What about Yuri Ryakhin?"

He shook his head. "Nothing, about him or about Arzamas-16 being compromised. I'm sure the Soviets are squashing that story because they don't want anyone knowing we successfully infiltrated a closed city."

She nodded. *Wait until they find Speransky*, she thought to herself. *Things will really explode then.*

She locked eyes with her fellow operative. "We need to get out of this city now. Not this afternoon. Not in a couple of hours. Now. Let's move."

Tracie crawled into the darkness as Smith refitted the removable bumper onto the truck frame. A moment later the engine roared and the truck rolled out of the alleyway and into the early-morning Moscow traffic.

* * *

January 26, 1988
Time unknown
Somewhere northwest of Moscow

The first roadblock came a short while after they'd left Moscow and its stop-and-go city traffic behind. Tracie could have checked her watch but didn't bother hauling her flashlight out of her pack to do so.

The time didn't really matter. This trip would take the better part of a day, and focusing on the slow-moving hour hand of her watch would make the time drag even more than it already was.

The truck stopped and then eased forward.

Stopped and then eased forward.

Continued to do so for perhaps ten minutes, and then it was their turn to be searched. Tracie didn't even know what had been loaded into the ZiL's cargo box, but she knew that whatever it was, it would be legitimate enough to pass the scrutiny of suspicious Red Army soldiers, and would be accompanied by an equally legitimate bill of lading. Smith would have made sure of it; his life depended on it every bit as much as Tracie's.

Problems would arise only if one of the soldiers were particularly sharp-eyed, enough so that they noticed the slightly lowered customized truck frame. That such an occurrence had never happened over the years of CIA use of the modified ZiL-157 provided a little peace of mind, but there was no way to avoid the racing pulse and sky-high adrenaline level Tracie experienced while lying helplessly beneath the idling truck as men with automatic weapons stood literally just inches away.

She had drawn her weapon during the several minutes Smith spent sitting in the line of vehicles waiting for the vehicle to be searched. She was determined to defend herself if discovered, all the while knowing such a defense would prove futile.

The cargo bed was searched, Smith's paperwork was examined, and after a few minutes that seemed much longer, the truck pulled away and left the roadblock—the first of undoubtedly several—behind.

* * *

January 26, 1988
Time unknown
Somewhere northwest of Moscow

They stopped a couple of times for fuel and to allow Tracie to stretch her legs and both of them to relieve themselves, but that was all.

No food breaks.

No other breaks of any kind.

The Soviet government would never reveal to their citizens or anyone else that the purpose of the intense manhunt underway was to apprehend an undercover CIA operative who had executed a high-ranking KGB official in the middle of Moscow, just steps away from his KGB-driven limousine.

They would never admit to being victimized in such an audacious manner. To anyone. Ever.

But the lack of admission would do nothing to quell their desire to catch the perpetrator. They would quickly put two-and-two together, tying the kidnapping of Yuri Ryakhin and the assault on the Arzamas-16 nuclear plant in with the murder of the unidentified KGB operative outside Kremlyov, the disappearance of Piotr Speransky, and their own "Project Kremlyov Infection."

They would tie all of those events together and reach the only logical conclusion possible: CIA.

Probably angry Russian calls were already being made to U.S. representatives, both inside and outside the intelligence community, demanding explanations and official apologies.

Those calls would be met with protestations of innocence and completely legitimate denials. After all, nobody knew of Tracie's mission inside the Soviet Union but Aaron Stallings and now Ryan Smith.

And neither of them was about to say anything.

The ZiL-157 jounced and stuttered over frost heaves and potholes, leaving Tracie to wonder whether any part of her body would escape the ride bruise-free.

Of course, bruises were better than bullet holes, and an uncomfortable ride beat the hell out of a blindfold and a firing squad.

Before she knew it, the truck was slowing to a stop again.

Another roadblock.

* * *

January 26, 1988
Time unknown
Northwest of Moscow, approaching the Baltic Sea

Two more roadblocks came and went without incident. They seemed to be getting farther apart the more distance Smith put between the truck and Moscow.

Tracie tried to doze but even as exhausted as she was, sleeping seemed too much of a challenge. Between the relentless bouncing of the truck and the recurring rushes of adrenaline every time she heard Smith apply the brakes, Tracie realized she would simply have to suck it up and arrive at the escape boat not just hungry and sore, but tired as well.

So be it. Regardless of how famished she was, or how bruised and battered, she was a damned sight better off than the poor bastards who'd been dosed with radiation by Slava Marinov and Piotr Speransky.

She chewed on the information Speransky had finally given up during those last tension-filled hours in the safe house and found her mind wandering inexorably to her old CIA handler, Winston Andrews.

He was not a subject about whom Tracie enjoyed reminiscing. In fact, she had thrown herself into her work with a nearly manic zeal over the last eight months for a number of compelling reasons, one of which was to avoid, as much as humanly possible, having to think about Winston Andrews III.

About his treachery.

An intelligence specialist who had served the CIA and its fore-runners for more than four decades, beginning during the Second World War, Andrews had guided the first seven years of Tracie's career. He'd officially been her handler, but the reality was that he'd been much more than that: the professional equivalent of a father figure, a confessor, the rock upon whom a young single woman feeling her way through the world of espionage, with its snakes and tricks and backstabbers, could lean.

And he'd been a traitor.

Andrews had been working with radicals inside the USSR to facilitate the Soviet assassination of Ronald Reagan.

When Tracie had learned of the plot, Andrews had tried to have her silenced.

Permanently.

Andrews' last words had come seconds before his suicide, as a heartbroken Tracie desperately interrogated her handler to learn the location of the planned presidential assassination. The doomed man had said something that day that had haunted Tracie's dreams ever since.

His words were burned indelibly into her brain and she knew she would never forget them: *"You want to know who else is involved with the Soviets, is that correct? There aren't many KGB collaborators in positions of authority above mine, but there are a few..."*

It was a terrifying prospect at the time and it was a terrifying prospect now, not because Andrews' words represented the possibility of treasonous activity inside the CIA—that possibility always existed, human nature being what it was—but because the kind of treasonous activity Andrews hinted at had the potential to be so far-reaching, so damaging.

Winston Andrews had been an important player inside the Central Intelligence Agency. An all-star. An A-Team member. A man with the ear of senators and congressmen and even presidents.

There weren't many KGB collaborators above Andrews in the CIA chain of command because there simply weren't many *people* above him. If his dying statement was even close to being accurate, that kind of treachery could be devastating, not just to the agency but to the nation as a whole.

Tracie had brought his words to the attention of CIA Director Aaron Stallings, repeating them exactly and emphasizing that they had been spoken calmly and rationally and did not strike her as the paranoid ramblings of a suicidal man.

On the contrary, Andrews had seemed almost pensive, had given serious consideration to his words before speaking them.

Tracie had no way of knowing what Stallings had done with the information. Presumably he'd launched an investigation, but he was not in the habit of discussing the inner workings of upper-management CIA with someone like Tracie, so she doubted she would ever learn exactly what actions the director had taken regarding Andrews' words.

If any.

But she *did* know that nothing had ever resulted. No upper-level agency prosecutions, no unexplained removals from service.

With the passage of time, Andrews' explosive charges had faded into the background, and while they had continued to concern Tracie, she'd been far too busy with active assignments to do much beyond worry.

She had hoped and prayed—and even begun to convince herself in the intervening months—that there was no substance to Andrews' words, that he'd been doing nothing but obfuscating and delaying one last time before taking his own life.

But this was what had bothered Tracie so much about his charges: Winston Andrews had had no reason to lie. No reason to divert attention from his own betrayal of Tracie and of U.S. national security. He had known he was going to swallow a cyanide pill, and had known perfectly well what the result of swallowing that pill would be.

He had known he would be dead within minutes, which brought Tracie full-circle back to her original cause for concern: he'd had nothing to gain by lying.

Now she had proof that his words had been as truthful as any he'd ever spoken.

And the sense of betrayal came rushing back. It was personal as well as professional. Tracie didn't think she would ever recover from the knowledge that the man she had been as close to as any family member for more than half a decade had tried to have her assassinated the moment she became a threat to him.

She didn't think she would ever again trust anyone the way she had trusted Winston Andrews.

But with the knowledge that Andrews had spoken the truth came the hope that by eradicating the traitor her handler had spoken about in such a mysterious way, she could at last exorcise the memory of Winston Andrews from her nightmares once and for all.

That was why she had made the decision she chose regarding Piotr Speransky back in the Moscow safe house as she agonized over whether to allow the assassin to live or die.

It hadn't been an easy decision.

Tracie prayed it had been the right one.

* * *

After successfully slipping through the fourth roadblock, the remainder of the long drive to the shores of the Baltic Sea was completed without incident.

Tracie had used the waterborne escape route several times in the past to escort CIA assets out of the country. While still containing an element of danger—there was no such thing as safety for an American espionage agent operating inside the USSR—the reassuring familiarity of the process helped her regain her bearings after the agonizing hours spent torturing Speransky and then trying to decide whether to spare him.

One final time she said her goodbyes to Ryan Smith. The young man had surprised her with his reliability, strength and wit, and while it was never a good idea for operatives to become close—and she wasn't about to allow that to happen here—each succeeding goodbye had become a little more difficult.

Now she hugged him tightly.

Released him and drew back to arm's length, holding his gaze with an intense stare.

"You're a good agent," she said quietly. "It was an honor to work with you, and I would do so again without hesitation."

"Thank you." He seemed surprised but touched. "And the feeling is mutual."

"Be careful out there, Smith."

"You too, Quinn."

Then he climbed into the cab of the ZiL-157 and was gone. The truck pulled away with a diesel rumble and a blast of noxious black smoke, and Tracie was left—as always—to continue on alone.

35

January 26, 1988
10:45 p.m.
Washington, D.C.

The buzzing of Lisa Porter's secure satellite phone caught her off-guard. To say she was surprised at receiving a call would be an understatement. In all the time she had been immersed in American culture, all the years she had spent preparing for this mission and then the months spent executing it, there had not been one single unscheduled communication from her Moscow handlers.

Early in her training there had been much coordination, sometimes with sat phone exchanges coming as often as every day. But as time had gone by and she became more comfortable in her 'Lisa Porter' identity, the communications from Moscow had lessened.

The calls ramped up again when the time came to snare David Goodell, but they were always on a set schedule. Once Lisa had established firm control over the KGB's newest informant, they had lessened once again.

More calls meant greater risk. Despite the fact the sat phone signals were scrambled, every communication represented an opportunity for the CIA to uncover the KGB's Washington operations.

Capture would mean charges of espionage leveled by the United States government.

Charges of espionage by the United States government would

result in immediate denials from Moscow, of course. But of more serious concern to Lisa was that those charges would also result in her being cut loose by her Soviet handlers.

She would face the likelihood of execution by her captors. There would be the possibility of diplomatic intervention of course, perhaps an exchange of some sort: an American operative for a Soviet operative. But since the point of Project Kremlyov Infection was the elimination of as many American assets in Russia as possible, there likely would be few American operatives left to offer in trade.

And Lisa guessed the United States government would be in no mood to offer mercy, given the circumstances.

Thus, there was every reason for her handlers to avoid unscheduled contact and no good reason to initiate it.

The sat phone buzzed and she stared at it, eyebrows raised. During the time she'd been forced to live with that worm Goodell, keeping the sat phone hidden had been of paramount importance. It had obviously been critical she not raise the man's suspicions regarding her interest in him.

He'd been so desperate for someone to believe in him, so easy for her to hook, that she doubted much of anything *would* have raised his suspicions. But a satellite phone sitting in a charging base might have one of the few things to accomplish it.

Since establishing a more appropriate handler/operative relationship with Goodell and finally moving out of his apartment, Lisa had felt no need to hide the sat phone. Goodell had no idea where she lived, and neither did anyone else who mattered. Lisa brought no one here. She'd never had a single guest in this apartment, and barring a visit from the FBI, she never would.

So she'd set up the phone's charging base on her nightstand.

The fact that the unit buzzed in the first place was a very bad sign. The fact that it *continued* to buzz as Lisa considered the potential ramifications was an even worse sign.

She sighed and lifted the heavy handset off the base.

Activated the receiver.

Said "*Da.*"

Identification protocols were conducted, each side had confirming to their satisfaction that the entity on the other end of the satellite signal was, in fact, the appropriate contact.

Then Lisa said, "What is happening? Why the unscheduled contact?"

"We have been compromised."

"How do you know?"

"Comrade Marinov is dead. Assassinated in Moscow."

"Assassinated? How?"

"Shot at close range at Belorussky Station as he exited the train en route to headquarters."

"And Speransky?"

"Missing. We believe he is dead as well, although we have no direct proof of that."

"What happened? How did we get burned?"

"We do not yet know, but it has always been inevitable that the United States would eventually realize their people are being eliminated. Once they realized that fact, it was only a matter of time before the method of execution was uncovered."

"And that has happened now."

"As I said, it was expected. What we did *not* anticipate was the speed and ferocity of the American response."

"What happens now? I assume I execute my escape protocols?"

"Correct. However, our promptness in tying Comrade Marinov's assassination to Project Kremlyov Infection leads us to believe there is sufficient time for you to complete one last assignment before putting your escape protocols into effect."

Lisa Porter blinked in surprise. One last assignment? If the Americans had exposed the KGB plot to eliminate CIA operatives working in the Soviet Union—and had been able to assassinate the brains behind the project *while he commuted to work at KGB headquarters*—it meant two things, neither of which was good for her:

First, the United States was sending a message to the Soviets, telling them in no uncertain terms that none of their people were safe from retribution, even those working in Moscow.

Second, and of greater importance to Lisa, if the CIA had been able to target Slava Marinov, a man much higher on the Soviets' intelligence chain of command than she, they would be coming for David Goodell—and then almost immediately afterward, for *her*—sooner rather than later.

It seemed clear to Lisa that she needed to move *now*, while she still could, to avoid capture. Project Kremlyov Infection had already been successful beyond all measure, resulting in the deaths of American operatives working to undermine the Soviet state. The exact number of deaths Lisa did not know, but it had to be substantial.

The American intelligence community would be in no mood to show mercy to the KGB operative working inside the United States who had secured the names of the dead CIA operatives. They would come for her hard, and relentlessly, and once captured, Lisa could expect torture and pain and eventual death.

It was easy for her handler to assume there was enough time for one last mission. He was sitting safely—relatively speaking—inside KGB headquarters. Lisa's perspective was much different.

Hadn't she done enough to advance the Soviet cause?

Couldn't she just grab her go-bag and head out of the hostile land in which she'd spent so many years risking her life already?

Anger and resentment and especially fear began building inside her, more fear than she would have expected. But she was a professional, committed to her cause.

More importantly, she had no choice but to listen to her handler and implement his instructions. Were she to ignore him and attempt to escape the United States before completing his "one last assignment," then she could expect treatment upon arrival in Moscow—assuming she was even able to make it home—that would not be much friendlier than she would get from the CIA if captured.

It might be worse.

All those thoughts flashed through her mind in a matter of seconds. Her handler waited patiently. She guessed he could ascertain most, if not all, of what she was thinking.

She sighed deeply.

Said, "Go on."

Listened as the KGB officer outlined her final assignment.

When he finished speaking, she agreed to attempt its execution. Again, what choice did she have?

Maybe it was even doable.

Time would tell.

36

January 27, 1988
7:20 a.m.
Aaron Stallings' residence
McLean, Virginia

"Excuse me? Did you just say what I thought you said?"

CIA Director Aaron Stallings seemed testier than usual, even for him, even for early morning. Tracie wasn't sure whether his short temper was due to the words she had just spoken or the fact he hadn't yet finished his first cup of coffee.

Probably a little bit of both, she decided.

She met his stare unflinchingly. "Yes sir, I think you probably heard me correctly."

His eyes were flat and hard. "So let me get this straight. The United States government sent you halfway across the world, into the nest of vipers known as Moscow, Russia—at great expense, I might add, and great risk not just to you personally but to the U.S. intelligence community as a whole—and you took it upon yourself to leave the country with your mission half-finished?"

"I don't see it that way, sir."

"Oh, is that right? You don't see it that way?"

"No sir, I don't."

"Well, let's recap your assignment, shall we? Your mission was to uncover the source of the Polonium-210 assassinations of a half-dozen American intelligence officers operating in the Soviet

Union, not to mention at least one Russian informant. Is my recollection correct, Tanner?"

"Yes sir. More or less."

"Please enlighten me as to where I'm mistaken."

"I don't represent the United States government anymore. I'm no longer an official employee of the Central Intelligence Agency. I would think you might recall that, since my termination was your doing, sir."

Stallings waved a hand like he was shooing away a pesky mosquito. "A distinction without a difference. If you had been captured while on assignment in Russia, even while working under the official direction of the CIA, you would have been disavowed anyway. You know that as well as anyone, so stop being such a wise-ass."

"Just trying to be accurate, sir. You did ask."

His anger at her impertinence was plain, and his face had turned a shade of crimson not typically associated with human skin, but Tracie didn't care. The verbal sparring with a man who represented her only form of support in an otherwise utterly secret career got tiring. Why did every interaction with this man have to be so damned adversarial?

"Anyway," Stalling said, "let's get back on track. Your little sidestep maneuver notwithstanding, there is nothing significantly off about my outline of your assignment, would you agree?"

"Yes sir, I would agree. However, I would also argue that I *did* complete my mission. I eliminated Slava Marinov, the high-ranking KGB officer who conceived Project Kremlyov Infection and ordered the executions of the American operatives."

"And yet the man who actually sprayed the radioactive solution into the drinks of the American operatives—the actual instrument of their destruction—remains alive and breathing and capable of continuing his murdering ways, EVEN AFTER YOU HAD HIM IN THE SIGHTS OF YOUR WEAPON!"

The CIA chief's voice had steadily risen as he spoke until by the end of the sentence he was screaming more loudly than Tracie had ever heard.

And that was saying something.

His eyes bulged and his face bypassed crimson on its way to an ominous purple, and spittle splattered his desk blotter in a mini-rainstorm that would have been comical were it not for the severity of his wrath.

Tracie sat quietly and took it. She had long ago stopped being intimidated by the bullying tactics of Aaron Stallings, but had learned also that interrupting him during an angry rant was like trying to stop a freight train with a fly swatter.

And picking the right moment to defend herself would be critical. The proper sense of timing might be the only thing to save her career.

Again.

Tracie had learned a lot about Aaron Stallings in the months since being rehired as the most secret asset in an agency cloaked in secrecy. He was a bully, he used his size and personality as a battering ram to intimidate, he ruled with an iron fist, and above all, he *hated* having his instructions ignored by those below him in the chain of command, which included nearly everyone inside D.C. in any official government capacity.

But he was also the ultimate results-oriented pragmatist and a man who had devoted his life to American intelligence services. Treason against the United States by an employee of the Central Intelligence Agency was like a slap in the face to Aaron Stallings. He regarded such an occurrence as a personal affront.

In that regard—and maybe *only* in that regard—Tracie and Aaron Stallings were remarkably similar.

The CIA director continued ranting but sooner or later Tracie knew he would have to stop yelling to draw in a breath. It took longer than she would have expected, which offered perhaps the most accurate glimpse into his level of anger and frustration.

Eventually he did stop yelling, though, just for a moment. Tracie jumped in and spoke before he could resume his tirade. "May I explain my reasoning, sir, or would you rather just scream and yell until your heart gives out or your head explodes?"

"Explain your reasoning? I don't think there can *be* an explanation for ignoring a direct order. Jesus Christ, Tanner, I already fired you once for insubordination—for this exact offense!—and I *know* you're not stupid. You're anything but stupid, so what the hell is wrong with you? Why in the world would you put your career at risk *again* because of—"

"I know who's leaking the names of our agents to the KGB."

Stallings's mouth snapped shut. The thick flap of skin beneath his jawline flapped like a flag in a strong wind. His skin color began returning to normal but thunderclouds filled his eyes.

"What did you just say?"

Tracie realized the CIA Director's reaction was virtually identical to the one she'd had when Speransky blurted out the existence of the list under duress. She wondered whether it was a good thing or a bad thing to be thinking like Aaron Stallings.

She sighed and continued. "I said I know who's leaking the names of our agents operating inside the Soviet Union. You must have realized after the second case of radiation poisoning that we had a leak somewhere."

Stallings scowled. "Of course I realized it. One operative getting assassinated might have been caused by any number of scenarios, the most likely being his own carelessness. But the moment our second man went down I knew it could only mean one thing: we had a leak somewhere."

"I'm sure you've been investigating the source of the leaks."

"No, Tanner, I've been sitting behind my desk with my thumb up my ass as our people in the USSR are being cut down one after the other. *Of course* I've been investigating the source of the leaks!"

"But so far no luck?"

"I don't answer to you, goddammit. You answer to me. And this isn't even a subject I'm willing to discuss with a case officer, especially not with a case officer who's not even on the agency's official roster of operatives and who is about to be terminated. Again."

Tracie's anger had been building, and now she erupted in fury. "I see. So I'm good enough to be sent into the heart of our sworn enemy's operations, with little support or backup, and to put my life on the line to extract justice for our murdered operatives, but I don't even deserve the courtesy of a straight answer?"

Stallings's face had begun to darken again and Tracie steeled herself for the explosion she knew was about to come. The truth of the matter was that she probably deserved an upbraiding this time.

It was extremely uncommon for handlers to discuss the reasoning behind assignments with their operatives. It simply didn't happen. There were secrecy concerns to consider, and the reality was that the justification for a mission was usually irrelevant to the man or woman tasked with carrying out that mission.

Tracie deserved to be screamed at this time. She'd allowed her anger to distort her judgment and had unquestionably crossed a line. She cringed inwardly and sat silently, awaiting the chief's outburst.

But it never came. Stallings had screamed at Tracie more times than she could recall inside this very office. He had belittled her, had attempted to intimidate her, had ranted and raved and screamed, and every single time—without exception—Tracie had believed the abuse to be undeserved.

Now she deserved to be reprimanded, but none was forthcoming. Stallings appraised Tracie thoughtfully, leaning back in his chair until she heard it creak in complaint.

He seemed to have choked back his anger, at least for the time being. Aaron Stallings was nothing if not pragmatic, and although there was no question he was still seething at what he perceived as Tracie's insubordination, he also realized the number one priority was and had to be finding the deadly leak within the CIA and then plugging it.

He took what felt like a very long time considering his response. Then he nodded.

"Okay," he said quietly. "I'll grant that your situation is different from everyone else's in the agency. You're not an official employee. Your continued existence as an operative is unknown to virtually everyone inside Langley besides myself. Even given the high level of risk endured by the average case officer, yours is much greater.

"And I know you don't believe this, Tanner, but I like you. You're among the most dedicated and talented operatives I've had the honor of working with over the course of four-decades-plus in this business."

Tracie sat slack-jawed as her boss, the man she'd clashed with countless times over differences large and small, spoke words she never expected to hear. Not from Aaron Stallings.

"In some ways I think of you as a daughter, Tanner. That's why I tend to give you leeway I wouldn't dream of giving anyone else. It's why I cut you slack when you probably don't deserve it. Like now."

Cut me slack? All the times I've sat here while you go up one side and down the other, that was you cutting me slack? The words ran through her head but she was so stunned, so caught off-guard, so shocked by what she was hearing, she simply couldn't get them out.

And that's probably a good thing, she thought dimly.

"Anyway," Stallings continued. "Maybe that's my overly long-winded way of saying you've again dodged a bullet. So to speak. I'd tell you never to speak to me in that impertinent tone again, but I suppose we both know I'd be wasting my breath.

"I'll answer your question, but let me state the obvious, just in case you've somehow missed it: you claim to have identified the leak responsible for the deaths of a half-dozen good men. You'd better be right about that, or things will get very unpleasant for you very quickly. Do we understand each other?"

"You said you would answer my question," Tracie said levelly. "Care to do so?"

Stallings shook his head testily. "No, alright? The answer is no. We have not been able to identify down the source of the leaks. Yet. We've had our suspicions, but we believe the *number* of leaks has been limited. The treasonous activity has been extremely damaging, obviously, but the source has been careful not to go to the well too often, meaning our opportunities to apprehend the traitor have been necessarily limited."

The CIA chief's face darkened again. "So if you have a name, I'd suggest you give it to me right now."

37

January 27, 1988
7:40 a.m.
Aaron Stallings' residence
McLean, Virginia

"David Goodell," Tracie said.

Aaron Stallings closed his eyes upon hearing the name.

Then he nodded tiredly. "Dave was one of the relatively small number of administrators we felt could potentially represent the leak. As Assistant Director for Eurasian Operations he obviously had access to our roster of operatives in the region. Hell, he *controlled* the roster. He had financial problems as well, which always represents cause for concern. Those sorts of issues open the door to co-opting by the Soviets."

"I'm sorry," Tracie said, but Stallings either didn't hear her or ignored the remark.

"I didn't want to believe Dave was capable of such a betrayal," he mumbled. He almost seemed to be talking to himself, despite occasionally glancing into Tracie's eyes. "I've worked with him for a long time, and I selected him for the position of Assistant Director for Eurasian Operations above a slate of other candidates many inside Langley believed to be better-qualified and more deserving.

"This feel personal," he said, "although after the Winston Andrews situation, I suppose I should be used to it."

Stallings had clearly been thrown off his stride, and he plunked his elbows onto his desktop and clasped his hands together, resting his head on his hands and closing his eyes.

He sat like that for a long time. Eventually he said, "How certain are you of the accuracy of your intel?"

"I'm convinced Piotr Speransky was telling the truth when he gave me Goodell's name. I think by that point in our conversation he was beyond lying."

Stallings nodded. He looked old and tired to Tracie, older than she had ever seen. "It goes without saying we came down hard on David during our investigation, as we did with the other half-dozen or so employees we felt could have represented the leak. He vigorously maintained his innocence, but that was to be expected, obviously."

He raised his eyes and met Tracie's. "David went through a rough time a few years ago. His marriage fell apart, he was drinking heavily, and he had those financial problems I already mentioned. But he straightened his ass out and has been a model employee since."

Tracie cleared her throat and spoke softly. "How long ago did he clean up his act?"

"Three or four years." Stallings ran a meaty hand over his eyes and then rubbed his temples. "About the time our operatives in the Soviet Union began dying."

"He had to clean up his act if only to avoid suspicion once the bodies started to pile up."

"Exactly." The old spymaster seemed to have regained his footing. At least a little. He sat straighter in his chair, spoke with greater volume, and met Tracie's eyes.

"You said his marriage fell apart about the time the assassinations started. There was another woman, wasn't there." It should have been a question, but Tracie phrased it as a statement. She already knew it had to be true. The Soviets had gotten to Goodell somehow, and the traditional points of access were money or sex. She guessed that in this case, the KGB had been able to utilize both.

"We checked her out," Stallings said emphatically. "We ran her background six ways from Sunday. Everything about the woman Goodell took up with after he split from his wife checked out. Her name was Lisa Porter and she was practically the All-American Girl: grew up in Massachusetts, educated at Vassar, no known associates with foreign ties."

"She sounds perfect," Tracie said, raising her eyebrows.

Stallings nodded. "Exactly. Almost too perfect."

"Somehow the Soviets got to her. Maybe through her family, maybe through radicalization in college, who knows?"

Stallings fell silent. He was deep in thought and he ran a finger across his desk blotter, making random patterns on the paper. Tracie doubted he even realized he was doing it.

Finally he spoke. "We could sit here all day tossing out theories regarding the motivations of traitors and murderers. The truth will come out now. It always does once you turn over the rocks and shine a light directly underneath."

"The question is where do we go from here?"

"And the answer to that question is clear: you're going to plug the leak. Permanently. Eliminate the security risk."

"Me?"

"Am I not speaking clearly, Tanner? Did I lose my voice? Am I speaking in tongues?" If Aaron Stallings had been thrown for a loop by the news that one of his handpicked employees was a traitor, it hadn't taken him long to recover. He was already much closer to the acerbic, tough-as-nails bully Tracie had come to know than to the vulnerable, elderly man he had seemed just moments ago.

"Eliminate the security risk." She spoke slowly, trying out the words. They sounded almost foreign and the knot that had sat in her stomach since pulling the trigger on Slava Marinov suddenly seemed to mushroom.

"You heard me."

"Sir…" She stared at her boss and he returned the look, his eyes flinty.

She coughed into her fist and tried again. "Sir, with all due respect, I will not assassinate a United States citizen. I don't care what he's done or what he stands accused of doing. That's a line I cannot and will not cross."

Stallings's eyes narrowed as she spoke until by the end of her statement his pupils were barely visible. His lips had nearly disappeared, his mouth a bloodless slash.

The silence stretched out.

The air was electric.

The CIA chief was capable of a lot. Tracie had known that since her first hour of her first day working for him. But this was beyond anything she could possibly have imagined. He was sanctioning the murder of an American, on U.S. soil?

An icy chill enveloped her, colder than even the bitterest temperatures she had just endured in the middle of a Moscow winter.

She wasn't sure how long they sat facing each other. It might have been thirty seconds or it might have been ten years. It felt like a lifetime.

But Tracie didn't care how long Aaron Stallings remained silent or how angry he got. Or what the repercussions of refusing the order might be. She had reached her limit.

The silence stretched to the breaking point and then Stallings leaned back in his chair. His eyes widened and his expression softened.

He said, "Apparently we're having a bit of a miscommunication. I wasn't ordering the assassination of an American citizen, Tanner. I would never condone such a thing."

"Is that so?"

"Yes, that's so. When I say I want you to plug the leak and eliminate the security risk, I mean only that I want you to go get Goodell. Take him into custody. Bring him to Langley for debriefing."

His lie was transparent, but at least he had backed off his shocking instruction. Tracie didn't feel much better, though. The knot in her stomach remained just as large and just as virulent.

"Why would *I* go get him? Isn't that a job for the FBI?"

"He'll be turned over to the FBI. Eventually. But before that happens, I want to interrogate him. Personally. It was agency intelligence specialists who died because of this man's treason. I want him to answer to agency personnel for it. We owe the dead men that much. Goodell can answer to the law when I'm done with him."

"Sir…I understand the desire to interrogate a traitor, to try to understand the thought process that would allow a man to look himself in the mirror every day after being directly responsible for the deaths of innocent me, men whose lives depended on Goodell's discretion. But don't you think you might jeopardize any legal case against Goodell if you take it upon yourself to question him before turning him over?"

"I'm not worried about any 'legal case' against him. I want to look him in the eyes and ensure he understands exactly what his actions wrought. I want to read him the names of the men who died because of his actions, to list the wives who are now widowed and the children who will grow up without fathers. I want him to explain to me exactly why he thought his life was more important than theirs."

Tracie had learned long ago that the only person who stood a chance of changing Aaron Stallings's mind when he felt strongly about something was the president of the United States, and even then it wouldn't be thanks to the strength of his argument.

It certainly wasn't going to be accomplished by a lowly field operative, and an unofficial one at that. If Stallings were determined to speak face-to-face with the traitor he would do so, with Tracie's help or without it.

She sighed. "When do I meet my team?"

"Team?"

"Yes. When do I meet with the other operatives we'll use to apprehend Goodell?"

He snorted. "You should know better than that, Tanner. There's not going to be any team. You are the team."

38

January 27, 1988
7:50 a.m.
Aaron Stallings' residence
McLean, Virginia

"I'm going to take him myself? Sir, we're talking about a traitor directly responsible for the deaths of more than a half-dozen men. Don't you think approaching him with a single agency operative might not be treating the situation with the gravity it deserves?"

"Jesus Christ, Tanner, would you listen to yourself? You just returned from the heart of the Soviet Union, where you single-handedly eliminated one of the highest-ranking KGB officers we've ever removed."

"Ryan Smith helped."

"You know what I mean. Smith was nothing more than logistical support. That was your op and you handled it beautifully." His tone coarsened. "Aside from ignoring your orders to eliminate Piotr Speransky, of course."

"We've already been over that, sir. Speransky provided the intel that's allowing us to 'plug this leak,' as you put it, once and for all."

"Yes," Stallings agreed with a glower. "And there was absolutely no reason you couldn't have eliminated him after you extracted the intel. No reason other than a misplaced sense of morality, or fairness, or some other quaint but meaningless notion.

"But that's not the point," he continued. "The point is that after all the assignments you've undertaken in your career, nearly all of them solo missions, now you're worried about apprehending one ink-stained bureaucrat and escorting him to Langley?"

Tracie shook her head. "Why do you even need me? Can't you just get security to bring him from his office to yours? He works in the same complex as you. Hell, you probably don't even need guys with guns to escort him. Just call him into a meeting and then take him when he arrives."

"Thank you for telling me how to do my job," Stallings said drily. "But for your information, Goodell is on vacation. He's taking some time off. He won't be back at Langley for nearly two weeks. Given all that just happened in Moscow, I think it's a safe bet that the KGB will try to alert their operative here in D.C. and pull the plug on the operation ASAP. If we wait until Goodell returns to work we'll probably never see him again."

"Maybe he's disappeared already. We already talked about how easy it will be for the KGB to put together the assassination of Marinov and the disappearance of Speransky. Wouldn't notifying their operative here in D.C. be their first move?"

"Exactly. That's why we need to move *now* to bring in Goodell."

"I don't understand. I'm supposed to bring in Goodell, *and* a KGB operative who may or may not already be aware we're coming for her? And I'm supposed to do this with no assistance and no backup?"

"No, Tanner, you're not supposed to do that."

She spread her hands. "What am I missing?"

"Goodell and Porter haven't been living together for more than two years. Given what we now know about Goodell, it seems obvious that their live-in relationship lasted only as long as it took for Porter to determine she had sufficient control over Goodell. Once she made that determination, she abandoned the sham romantic relationship and took over more of a traditional handler's role."

Tracie squinted in concentration, trying to parse the CIA chief's words. There was almost always more to what Aaron Stallings was saying than what he was saying.

Then it hit her.

"You don't know where Porter is, do you?"

"I told you already, Tanner, we checked her out thoroughly

after our people started dying. She passed with flying colors. Of course we kept an eye on her while she and Goodell were shacking up, but at that point it was mostly routine. Once she moved out of his apartment, yes, we lost track of her. Our resources are not unlimited."

"So the KGB could already have contacted her. We have no way of knowing."

"That's exactly why I had your driver bring you straight here from the airport. That's exactly why you're talking to me right now instead of sleeping in your own bed. This mission isn't over yet. We have a team scouring the area for Porter, but she's not your concern."

"My concern is Goodell."

"Exactly. Your *only* concern is getting David Goodell here where I can have a little conversation with my former protégé before we turn the son of a bitch over to face prosecution. And if there's an ounce of justice in the world, a firing squad."

The knot in Tracie's stomach continued to grow.

Something was wrong here.

She'd felt it almost from the moment she sat down in front of Aaron Stallings's desk, and she had no doubt whatsoever the feeling was more than just exhaustion.

Stallings jotted something down on a small piece of notepaper and handed it across his desk. "The top address is Goodell's D.C. apartment. The one below it is the home of his ex-wife and children. I'll expect to see the traitor standing in my Langley office by noon."

Tracie accepted the slip of paper. She folded it and dropped it into her blouse pocket without looking at it. She gazed at Stallings appraisingly.

Now it was Stallings's turn to spread his hands. "Well?"

"Well, what?"

"What the hell are you still doing here? I gave you your assignment. Unless you think Goodell is hiding behind my bookcase, there's no reason for you to still be here. Get the hell out of here and round up a traitor."

Tracie stood without a word. She held her boss's stare a moment longer, then turned and walked out the door.

39

January 27, 1988
9:40 a.m.
D.C. Arms Apartments
Washington, D.C.

The apartment complex was called the D.C. Arms, and its condition emphasized the extent of David Goodell's fall from grace.

There was nothing wrong with the place, not exactly. Nothing Tracie could put her finger on. But the buildings seemed down on their luck, gone slightly to seed. It was definitely not the sort of place one would expect a government heavy hitter like David Goodell to live.

Tracie pictured Goodell driving into the pothole-strewn parking lot every day, wondering how things had gone so wrong in his life. To head up a CIA intelligence division like Eurasian Operations, especially at such a young age, represented a major accomplishment, and would of course be accompanied by a salary commensurate with the job's responsibilities.

For a rising star like Goodell to end up here, living in a lower-middle-class apartment complex whose best days were far behind it—if they had ever existed at all—would be humiliating in the extreme.

The apartment complex provided a perfect illustration of the financial difficulties that must have played such a major role in his co-opting by the Soviets.

Tracie felt a tug of sympathy for the man but then swallowed it back.

David Goodell was a traitor whose actions had led to the deaths multiple agents who had been serving their country honorably. Financial problems were a poor excuse for a man to sell secrets to another country. Hell, they were no excuse at all, and if he'd allowed himself to be seduced by a KGB operative it was even worse.

There was no reason to feel sorry for David Goodell.

None.

Tracie kicked herself mentally and then double-checked the slip of paper Stallings had given her with the pair of addresses jotted on it.

Apartment 3-B.

She glanced from the paper to the building located directly in front of her agency car. A carved wooden 3 hanging above the entryway told her she was in the right place. Goodell's place should be inside, presumably on the first floor.

The complex was relatively large, but the buildings had been laid out in an easy-to-follow manner and it had taken Tracie roughly ten seconds to pull to a stop in the proper lot.

There was no way of knowing whether Goodell was here—if the man was taking a vacation in January, she assumed he must be a winter sports enthusiast, meaning he could well be in Vermont, or Colorado, or any of a hundred other skiing destinations.

Or he could be here, holed up in his apartment, hiding from the world.

She hoped that was the case. If not, the next stop would have to be Goodell's ex-wife's home—the second address on her list—and she had absolutely no desire to face the woman the traitor had thrown over to be with a Soviet spy. Tracie knew exactly what the woman's first thought would be: here comes another of my ex-husband's conquests. What the hell does she want with me?

And if Goodell happened to be there, things would go from bad to worse. She had no legal authority to compel him to accompany her, so if he hesitated she would be forced either to get physical or to threaten him with her weapon. She would have to do so in front of his children. Tempers would flare. The likelihood of an ugly—and dangerous—scene would be high.

Please be here, she thought to herself. *Don't make me barge in on your family.* Dealing an angry ex or frightened children were not in Tracie's comfort zone. They were nowhere near her comfort zone. She would rather face down a Soviet operative or defuse a ticking bomb.

Tracie realized she was stalling for no good reason. She'd wanted to observe the apartment for a while before entering, but "a while" had gone by and the area was quiet.

Something was bothering her, the same sense of ill-defined unease she'd been feeling since leaving Aaron Stallings's home office, and she remained unable to identify it.

Goodell would pose little threat to her, even if he were armed. He hadn't served the CIA in any operational capacity. He'd never even been in the military. He'd had no operational training at all as far as Tracie knew.

It was possible—likely, even—the Soviets had alerted Goodell's KGB handler to the collapse of Project Kremlyov Infection, which meant it was possible she was out there somewhere.

But Tracie doubted that was the case. It was much more likely the operative had departed the area as quickly as she could. She would know the Americans were coming for her and would abandon her old identity immediately, shedding it like a snake slipping its skin.

Then she would adopt a new one and attempt to make her way out of the country.

It was what Tracie would have done in her unknown adversary's place.

She sighed heavily and pushed open her car door, then trudged across the parking lot to the building's entrance and pressed the buzzer to Apartment 3-B.

She noted with little surprise that Goodell had never placed his name inside the slot next to the button for his apartment. He'd probably told himself this location was only temporary, that he would be on to bigger and better things soon.

Or he didn't want to be found.

Tracie waited thirty seconds and when nothing happened she pressed the buzzer again. This time she held the button down a good long time. A few more seconds went by and she was trying to decide whether to pursue this location any further or move on to the ex's house when the tinny speaker next to the buzzer squawked to life.

"Yeah?" It sounded like a man's voice, but distortion from the old, cheap speaker made even that determination a risky proposition. The voice sounded lethargic.

Uninterested.

Hopeless.

Tracie assumed the microphone would be located next to the speaker. She leaned down and said, "Mr. Goodell?"

"Who wants to know?" Immediate suspicion.

"UPS."

A short delay, and then, "I don't remember ordering any packages."

Tracie had expected that response, and immediately came back with, "Are you...Mr. David Goodell? If so, this has your name on it." She hoped she'd put just enough hesitation into her voice to make it seem like she'd been peering at the name on a package.

"Fine." The suspicion never left the man's voice but he sounded resigned, and a moment later the buzzer sounded and Tracie was inside the building.

She entered into a small foyer, grungy and dimly lit even in the daytime. Scanned the doorways, which ran down both sides of a long hallway. 3-B was on the right side, and Tracie double-timed to the entrance, wanting to be standing right in front of it when Goodell opened the door.

Assuming, of course, he hadn't already exited a rear window and was even now sprinting through the parking lot in a desperate attempt at escape.

A moment later the door opened a crack. The apartment complex hadn't provided peepholes for the residents to see who might be standing in the hallway, so Goodell had no choice but to peer through the narrow opening.

The moment he did, Tracie slipped her foot into the gap. She hoped he wouldn't panic and try to slam it shut. The prospect of bringing the traitor in while hobbling on a broken foot held no appeal.

"You're not UPS." The voice was the same as the one that had floated through the speaker, minus the scratchy distortion. It hadn't lost the suspicious tone, though, and Tracie stiffened as Goodell started to close the door.

She jammed her foot in a little farther and stopped it before he could achieve any leverage.

"No," she agreed. "I'm not here from UPS."

"I knew I hadn't ordered a package," the voice grumbled. "Goddammit." Surprisingly, the suspicion left his voice even as the resignation seemed to increase.

"My name is Fiona Quinn," Tracie said. "I represent the same organization you do. In fact, we work for the same man. I'm here at his request, Mr. Goodell."

"I don't know what you're talking about."

"I think you do. May I come in, please? I won't take up much of your time, I promise."

"You work for..."

"That's right. Aaron Stallings. Please, Mr. Goodell, I'm going to have to insist you allow me inside to speak with you. Unless you'd rather I do it here, in a public hallway."

"You need to let me close the door so I can remove the chain lock."

"Fine," Tracie said. "Don't run. Don't make me chase you. You won't like what happens if I have to chase you."

She pulled her foot out of the opening and as soon as she did the door eased closed. She listened intently for the sound of panicked footfalls inside the apartment.

A raspy metallic sound on the other side of the door eased Tracie's mind. Apparently Goodell had taken her advice.

The door swung open and a tired-looking middle-aged man indicated the shabby apartment with his left hand like Vanna White revealing the next puzzle.

"Come on in," David Goodell said.

Tracie stepped into a small living room. It featured threadbare carpeting that had been recently vacuumed, and furniture that appeared to have been picked up at the local Salvation Army.

Jesus, she thought. *Treason must not pay what I would have guessed.*

"As I said outside your door, Mr. Goodell, I assume you know why I'm here."

He sighed. "It took a lot longer than I imagined it would."

"You've been expecting me?"

"Or someone like you, yes. For the last four years. Every three a.m. in my nightmares."

"Speaking of nightmares, I'm sure you can imagine you've been responsible for a few. Wives who are never going to see their husbands again. Children who will grow up without fathers. Aging parents enduring the losses of their grown sons. Those people have all undoubtedly had *their* share of nightmares as well, and will continue to have them for a long time." Tracie's anger was building as she flashed on Charles Fowler enduring the agony of a drawn-out death, locked away inside the CIA's Langley medical facility.

Goodell's shoulders slumped and he hung his head.

The scene was pathetic.

He was pathetic.

"Why did you do it?" Tracie whispered.

"It wasn't like you think."

"Then what was it like?"

Goodell shook his head, steadfastly refusing to meet Tracie's gaze. "I never intended to sell out my country. I didn't get up one morning and decide, 'Today I'm going to condemn innocent men to death.'"

"Then how did it happen?"

His eyes wandered around the room as he pondered the question. They were red and watery. In that moment Goodell looked old. Older than old. Ancient.

And tortured.

"Things were falling apart for me on a personal level, even as my career advanced. I could feel my wife and I growing apart. She spends money like it's an Olympic sport, and when you added in my kids' college tuition bills, everything was crashing down financially."

"Lots of people have money problems, Mr. Goodell. They don't sell out to the Soviets."

"It wasn't just the money problems. In fact, it wasn't even *mostly* the money problems. I…"

His voice trailed away and he was quiet for a moment. Then he took a deep, shuddering breath and continued. "My life felt completely out of control, like I was drowning and a hand was holding me underwater, and the hand was so strong that no matter how hard I fought and tried to get to the surface, I just couldn't do it. And…and then I met Lisa."

"And she was young and pretty and sexy," Tracie scoffed. "I get it."

He shook his head. "That wasn't it. I mean, she *was* young and pretty and sexy, she was all of that and more. But it was the way she looked at me that did it. She looked at me like I *mattered*, like my opinion meant something, like I was interesting and worthwhile and…and competent. Everything I hadn't been getting at home for years."

He finally met Tracie's eyes. It was almost as if he'd run out of other places to look and had no choice.

"I know what you think," he said. "I can see it just from the way you look at me. But I'm not stupid. Foolish and reckless, obviously. But not stupid. I was well aware of the potential for Russian infiltration. I knew full well the KGB would love to get their hooks into someone in my position. I just…"

He shook his head again, lost in a memory. "It's just that Lisa seemed so…so *real*."

Another sigh. "And then, once she got ahold of that first roster list it was all over. I should have gone straight to Stallings, should have told him immediately what had happened. My life would have gone down in flames, but maybe we could have gotten those agents out of Russia before it was too late, could have saved all their lives.

"But I couldn't do it. I didn't have the balls to admit such a horrible screwup. I was a coward. And thanks to my cowardice, all those people died, and now my life has gone down in flames anyway."

They stood face to face, still just a couple of feet inside Goodell's front door. Tracie wanted to hate David Goodell, *had* hated him as recently as fifteen minutes ago. His actions had condemned people just like Tracie to horrific deaths. She had spent most of her career working in the Communist Bloc and the fact *she* hadn't been marked for execution was due to sheer dumb luck and not a damned thing else.

But the hatred she felt for Goodell had evaporated as she listened to him speak. She still hated what he had done—nothing would ever change that; nothing *could* change that—but all she felt now was nausea. That sick feeling in the pit of her belly that she feared would never disappear, and disgust for the pathetic excuse for a human being who had caused so much suffering.

She shook her head sadly. "You know it's time to go, Mr. Goodell, right?"

"I know. Do I have time to pack a bag?"

"That won't be necessary. Where you're going, everything will be provided for you."

40

"Do you have to cuff me? I'll go with you but I don't want to be taken out of here in handcuffs."

Tracie thought about the deserted parking lot and wondered what possible difference it would make. Was Goodell worried there would be TV cameras and reporters and crowds of jeering citizens?

She could drag him to her car wrapped in chains like Jacob Marley and unless things had changed dramatically in the last few minutes, not a single person would be around to even notice. It would just be one disgraced bureaucrat crossing an empty expanse of pavement, on his way to face the music.

It wasn't like D.C. hadn't seen similar scenes over the years.

"I'm not going to cuff you, Mr. Goodell. I'm not a law enforcement officer. I couldn't handcuff you even if I wanted to, because I don't have any. However, it probably goes without saying—but I'll say it anyway—that if you try to run when we leave here, or if you make any move I interpret as threatening, things will not go well for you. Do you understand?"

"I understand."

Tracie couldn't imagine this defeated shell of a human being even considering attempting to resist, but there was no reason to take unnecessary chances, either.

"Then let's go," she said. "It'll just be two people walking to a car and driving away. Totally innocent and completely anonymous."

Goodell nodded. He shoved his hands into the pockets of his jeans and waited for Tracie to open the door. Then she ushered him into the dim hallway and they walked toward the building's entrance, Goodell shuffling slowly, Tracie by his side and a half-step behind, guarding against sudden moves by a man she knew would not be making any.

The morning was cloudless and cold, and as they exited the building the sun was dazzlingly bright in comparison to the weak light of the hallway. Tracie squinted and wished she'd thought to bring her sunglasses.

She pointed to the anonymous white K-Car backed into a parking spot directly across the lot. "That's mine," she said.

They were halfway across the open expanse of pavement when the shot came.

A *crack* Tracie instantly recognized as unsuppressed rifle fire, and Goodell dropped straight down like he'd been shot.

Which, of course, he had.

Tracie dived to the pavement, aware of a second shot following the first by no more than a second. She waited to feel the slug biting into her body, or for the curtain to come down and everything to fade to black, but neither event happened.

That was when she realized she was not the target.

She might yet *become* a target, but for now this was David Goodell's party.

She leapt into a crouch and grabbed Goodell by the wrists. Blood ran from his skull, a lot of blood, flowing from under his hairline where the first bullet had struck. She didn't know where—or even if—the second had hit him, but based on the accuracy of the first shot, she doubted it had missed.

A third *crack* and the slug thudded into Goodell as Tracie dragged him desperately behind the shelter of her vehicle. She fumbled for her key and unlocked the passenger-side door, her hands shaking with adrenaline.

Then she lifted her gun from its shoulder holster and returned fire. She had no more than the vaguest general notion of the sniper's location, and given the presence of apartment buildings in nearly a three hundred-sixty degree circle, her options were limited. She feared hitting an innocent bystander despite the fact she hadn't seen a single person besides Goodell since her arrival at the complex.

So she fired into the ground in the general direction from which the shots had come. Give the assassin—*KGB*, she thought. *Lisa Porter*—something to think about. Maybe Tracie could maneuver Goodell's limp body into the car before she took a bullet herself.

She squeezed off a second shot into the same mound of earth on the far side of the parking lot and then grabbed Goodell under his armpits. He wasn't a particularly large man, but he'd lost consciousness and his body lolled like a life-sized doll in her grasp. She shoved and tugged and finally got him into the car as another shot sounded.

Tracie picked up her weapon and fired again. Then she dived into the K-Car, scrambling across Goodell's bleeding body and into the driver's seat. She bent as low as possible and jammed the key into the ignition.

Another bullet. This one whistled into the car, shattering the driver's side window and missing Tracie by inches, and she cursed.

The sniper had changed her focus from Goodell to his captor.

Tracie was out of time. If she didn't escape now, she never would. The sniper had the advantage of location and surprise, and the moment it occurred to her to take out a tire in the K-Car, Tracie would become a sitting duck.

The engine wheezed to life. Tracie jammed the accelerator to the floor and the car leapt forward just as another bullet struck, this time shattering the rear window. She remained low, using the vehicle's body to shield her as much as possible, and spun the wheel to the left. Then she lifted her head just high enough to see over the dashboard, just high enough to avoid driving into a building or another car.

Then she turned a corner and left the shooter behind.

41

Tracie realized she hadn't even washed the blood off her hands yet.

The symbolism of that fact seemed as depressing as it was wholly appropriate.

After shoving/pulling/forcing David Goodell's limp body inside the K-Car and escaping the assassin's bullets at the D.C. Arms Apartments, she'd briefly considered driving to the nearest hospital or even finding a phone booth and calling for an ambulance.

But she hadn't done either thing.

Hospitals and ambulances meant calls to law enforcement followed by probing questions when the patient was suffering from multiple gunshot wounds.

None of those questions would come with easy answers. Tracie had no official ties to the CIA, which itself had no mandate to operate inside the United States. She'd been on an unsanctioned mission assigned by the agency director himself to escort a suspect to CIA Headquarters—using force of arms if necessary—who was as yet facing no charges.

And who was under no legal obligation to accompany her.

Anywhere.

So once she'd gotten out of the line of fire, she pulled to the side of the road and checked on his condition.

No detectable pulse.

Massive cranial damage from a slug that had exploded into Goodell's skull upon impact.

He wasn't breathing.

He was dead, or soon would be.

Tracie put the car in gear and drove as fast as she could to Langley.

* * *

Stallings had instructed Tracie to bring Goodell into headquarters via the entrance reserved for high-level agency employees. It was the same gate David Goodell himself would utilized every day during his tenure as Assistant Director for Eurasian Operations.

Tracie doubted he'd ever come into work unconscious and leaking blood from a gaping head wound, though.

It was clear the security officers had been advised to expect Goodell's arrival as a passenger in a car driven by a non-agency employee, and it was equally clear the officers had been told to expedite approval into the facility. The men's expressions had changed in record time from bored as they approached the K-Car to shocked concern when they got a glimpse of the car's bullet-riddled exterior and the gravely injured—if not already dead—passenger inside.

Medical personnel appeared almost in an instant, arriving seemingly out of nowhere. They removed Goodell from the car and secured him to a wheeled stretcher, then raced away. The last Tracie saw of her charge was as the stretcher clattered through an automatic door that looked exactly like an entrance to any decent-sized hospital emergency room.

She allowed the security personnel to frisk her and remove her primary weapon as well as her backup gun from its ankle holster and her combat knife from its sheath at the small of her back. The men seemed unsurprised—and unfazed—at the extent of her weaponry.

Once she'd been disarmed, the security officers called for an escort and in seconds, two additional officers arrived to accompany her through the complex to Aaron Stallings's office suite.

The men were polite and professional but cold. Distant. Tracie wondered—not that it mattered—whether these officers were aware she'd previously worked as an agency field operative and been fired for insubordination.

Or maybe the carefully cultivated chill was their default mode.

The walk was a quiet one. Tracie guessed the silence was meant to intimidate, and while it wasn't going to come close to accomplishing that goal, she was grateful for it anyway. Because it gave her time to think.

Quiet reflection had always been her friend. It was during those moments, when she allowed her mind to wander and her thoughts to crystallize, that she was often able to connect dots and reach conclusions not always plainly evident, especially during the non-stop frenetic activity of a mission.

And the last few days *had* been frenetic.

Exhausting.

Stressful.

Her only downtime since leaving for Moscow had been the few hours during her trans-Atlantic flight on the agency jet from Helsinki to D.C. after being smuggled out of Moscow by Ryan Smith. She'd used that time to catch up on much-needed sleep and had then been shuttled directly to Aaron Stallings's home upon her arrival back in the states.

Things had happened quickly since then, and now David Goodell was either dying or dead.

The walk through Langley with her two silent companions represented an opportunity for Tracie to reflect on the assignment the CIA director had given her this morning. Bringing in a man suspected of one of the most damaging acts of treason in American history, exhausted and alone and with no mission planning, had been highly unusual.

It was almost predictable that it would have ended badly.

That likelihood of a negative mission outcome was what Tracie considered during the walk through the Langley campus. She gnawed on it like a dog chewing a bone. She considered it from all the angles she could as she crossed the lawns and turned the corners of the massive CIA complex.

She didn't like the conclusions she was reaching.

And then they arrived at the office suite of CIA Director Aaron Stallings.

* * *

The security officers waited with Tracie outside the suite until receiving permission to enter. They had positioned themselves one on either side and slightly behind her during the walk, and they remained in that configuration now.

It was as if they feared she might suddenly make a break for freedom, like perhaps her fear of the legendary CIA chief might drive her to a panicked sprint for the exit.

But Tracie wasn't about to attempt an escape. She was exactly where she wanted to be.

Stallings's personal secretary called Tracie inside and dismissed the security officers, and a moment later Tracie stepped into the chief's office.

42

January 27, 1988
12:10 p.m.
CIA Headquarters
Langley, VA

Being inside the CIA complex felt odd, but this wasn't the first time Tracie had visited Langley since her official removal from agency duty last spring. In fact, she'd probably spent nearly as much time here following dismissal as she had prior to it, when the majority of her time had been spent overseas on assignments.

What did feel different, and somewhat disorienting, was being ushered into Stallings's inner sanctum. The man had spent more than four decades in service to the CIA, the last twenty-five-plus years as director, and most field operatives had never come within shouting distance of this office.

The air felt heavy with the weight of history, intimidating in a way the security officers could never be.

Don't let it get to you, Tracie told herself. *You've dealt with Aaron Stallings plenty, and he's the same shameless liar and manipulator inside Langley as he is behind the desk of his home office.*

Tracie breathed deeply and strode across the room without waiting to be invited. Stallings's head was down as he pored over a stack of papers on his desk. It was the game he liked to play to demonstrate the pecking order when summoning Tracie to his home for an assignment: pretend to be busy—or maybe he actually *was* busy—and make the visitor wait.

"How's Goodell?" she said.

"He's dead." Stallings said the words and then raised his head, meeting Tracie's eyes, his gaze revealing nothing.

"You knew," she said.

"Excuse me?"

"I said you knew."

"Contrary to what you apparently believe, Tanner, I'm not capable of reading minds. I know any number of things. Could you be more specific as to which one you're referencing?"

"It doesn't take a mind reader to know what I'm talking about. You knew exactly what was going to happen when you sent me to Goodell's apartment this morning, didn't you?"

"Ah. Now we're getting somewhere. You're talking about your failed assignment, then. You're talking about the fact I sent you to escort a man safely from his home to this building, a distance of maybe four miles, and you weren't able to manage it without your charge ending up on a slab in the morgue. Is that what you're referring to?"

"I don't think you look at it as a failed assignment at all. I think you got exactly the result you wanted."

He spread his hands and shook his head. "What the hell are you talking about?"

"I knew something was off this morning. If I hadn't been so goddamned tired, maybe I would have seen it sooner."

"I don't follow. But you'd better be very careful if you're going to start leveling charges you can't back up."

"There was *no good reason* to send just one person to apprehend the man responsible for the deaths of six field operatives. Bringing in Goodell wasn't even the CIA's purview to begin with."

"I told you this morning, I wanted the opportunity to speak with Dave Goodell myself, face-to-face, before turning him over to the FBI. It was an opportunity denied me, thanks to your incompetence."

She shook her head. "You're not going to use insults to goad me off the subject. Even accepting the notion that using CIA assets to apprehend Goodell was appropriate—something I made clear this morning I disagreed with you on—it never should have been done using only one operative. There should have been a coordinated operation, thoroughly preplanned, with a team of agents, not one exhausted operative fresh off the plane from Europe."

"Watch it, Tanner."

"You claim to have a team of agents pursuing Lisa Porter. That's not even true, is it? Or do you expect me to believe agency assets are so incompetent as to allow a KGB operative to set up a sniper's nest right outside Goodell's front door?"

Stallings stared, anger smoldering in his eyes, and Tracie continued. " I don't doubt you're going to go after Porter *now*, but I think you either dragged your feet starting the mission, or deliberately led our people in the wrong direction. I think you knew she'd try to take out Goodell and I think you're perfectly satisfied she succeeded."

"That's enough, Tanner!" Stallings thundered. "Goddammit! What in the hell would I stand to gain by David Goodell's assassination?"

"Oh, come on, how stupid do you think I am? You stand to gain *everything* from Goodell's death. If he had lived to answer questions and face a jury, the damage to the agency could have been incalculable. Secrets would have been revealed, national security potentially compromised. And even worse from your perspective, the agency would have been humiliated by public knowledge of the treason of such a high-ranking administrator."

Stallings continued to glower at her. He didn't interrupt, though, and Tracie pressed her luck. She had expected to be thrown out of the office by now and guessed she had nothing left to lose by finishing.

"But now, with Goodell dead, you can control the flow of information. This situation can be anything you want it to be."

"I've heard enough, Tanner."

She shook her head. "A gunfight in such a public place will be all over the news. I'll bet you a week's pay you already have the disinformation machine working overtime on damage control. What's the story going to be? That Goodell was the victim of a mugging gone wrong? A tragic drive-by shooting that he happened to stumble into? By the time you're done, David Goodell

ALLAN LEVERONE

will be a dead hero, and your precious agency's reputation will be secure. Tell me I'm wrong, I dare you."

She was shaking and could feel tears welling in her eyes. She was exhausted and angry, and the sick feeling in her stomach had continued to grow. By now it felt alien and evil, like a parasite eating away at her stomach lining.

"Are you finished?" Stallings's eyes looked black and dangerous.

Tracie knew she was foolish to go up against the man who had lasted longer by a factor of ten than anyone else in the history of the toughest job in Washington, but she just couldn't stop herself. It was as if a dam had broken and she had no better chance of stopping the water from gushing out of it than she'd had of stopping David Goodell's assassination.

She clamped her jaws shut and held his gaze defiantly.

"You said your piece," Stallings muttered, speaking so quietly his voice was barely comprehensible. "Now it's my turn. First of all, you won't be able to bet a week's pay on anything if you don't shut your mouth right now and stop with these outlandish and entirely unsupported charges. I'll fire your ass again and this time there'll be no coming back."

He leaned back in his chair. He looked angry but perfectly unruffled. "You'd be gone already if it weren't for the fact that you have a point. It was wrong of me to send you to pick up Goodell. It should have been a different operative, someone who hadn't just returned from an assignment in Moscow."

"That's it? That's what you took out of everything I just said? It should have been someone else? That just proves what I've been saying! A KGB sniper took out the most critical witness in one of the worst cases of treason this country has seen since the Revolutionary War and all you can say is you should have sent *one different operative?*"

"I'm telling you, Tanner, this is your last warning."

"Or what?"

Stallings stared silently, his eyes never leaving hers.

"Oh, that's right, you're going to fire me. Guess what, sir? I don't know if I want to work any more for a man who is so unconcerned for my safety that he'll send me out to face a sniper, alone, without even the courtesy of a warning."

"You deal with much worse than what happened this morning every single day in the field, Tanner, so spare me the 'poor me' rhetoric."

"But there's a difference, and it's chilling that you don't recognize it. In the field I have a specific assignment to accomplish, and more importantly, *I know I'm in the field*, which means I know to expect anything, at any moment and from any direction. This morning's situation was nothing but an ambush, pure and simple. You knew I was walking into it and allowed it to happen, simply because it served your 'bigger picture.'"

"Get out, Tanner. Get out right now, while you still have a job."

"I'll leave. But I don't know if I want this damned job. I don't know if I can work for someone like you anymore."

She spun and marched out of the CIA director's office, pulse pounding in her ears and struggling to keep herself from falling apart. She slammed the door behind her and ignored the angry glare of disapproval from Stallings's secretary.

She needed sleep.

She needed a drink.

She needed to cry.

43

Tracie had hoped some much-needed sleep would help make her feel better. Bring some clarification to her feelings. Put things into perspective.

She'd gone straight home after storming out of Stallings's office, her hands shaking and her head pounding. The tears continued to threaten to come and she continued to deny them their due.

The black ball that had begun growing in her belly continued to metastasize until she thought it would detonate, exploding like a nuclear bomb, destroying her from the inside in a white-hot blast that would at least bring relief from the pain and the guilt and the horror and the fear.

She made it inside her apartment before the tears came. They hit like a hurricane, despair sweeping through her and forcing them out in an unstoppable downpour of despair.

She crumbled to her living room carpet. Buried her head in her hands and cried. She thought she might cry forever.

She couldn't put her finger on exactly *why* she cried, but stopping the tears now would be impossible.

Maybe she cried for the loss of Shane Rowley last spring. He was the one man she'd truly loved and the one who had proven through his actions he would do anything for her. She'd never stopped to grieve his loss, had never even slowed down. The oppo-site was true, in fact. She had thrown herself into her work with a mindless frenzy that had to have been as destructive as it was necessary to her sanity.

Maybe she cried for the realization that she was truly alone in the world, in every conceivable way. She'd always known she would remain alone on a personal level after Shane's death. Professionally, Winston Andrews' shocking betrayal had demonstrated that no one inside the CIA was truly in her corner, either.

But in her heart she had desperately wanted to believe in Aaron Stallings, despite her clear understanding he was an amoral manipulator who would always advance his own agenda at any cost. Had wanted to believe that if push came to shove, he would do what he could to protect her, as her handler and the only person alive aware of her Black Ops status.

To her dismay, he'd proven otherwise with his decision to use her as bait to draw out a KGB sniper, to manipulate his desired outcome after Tracie had refused to eliminate an American citizen.

But there was one other possibility for why Tracie cried.

It was the most horrifying of all, and for that reason she refused to acknowledge it.

Maybe she cried for what her Kremlyov assignment had revealed about herself. That she possessed the stone cold heart of an assassin.

She had killed before in the line of duty. Had accepted that death and destruction were the cost of doing business in a dirty world, where freedom was constantly under assault by men and governments willing to go to any lengths to eliminate the United States and the liberties for which it stood. Had always gone into her assignments with her eyes wide open.

But she had never before walked up behind a man—unarmed, as far as she knew, and elderly to boot—and pumped multiple 9mm slugs into his body, strolling away like she hadn't a care in the world as that man crumpled to the ground and bled out on a frozen Moscow sidewalk.

Yes, Slava Marinov had been responsible for the horrific deaths of a half-dozen American operatives, men who did not deserve to die, certainly not in the manner they were dispatched.

Yes, Marinov had brought his death upon himself, and yes, Tracie believed the world was a better place with him gone.

But what did it say about her that she was capable of the act?

How could she look herself in the mirror from this day forward and see anything other than the cold, dead eyes of a killer staring back?

They were legitimate points, she believed, each —or maybe all of them combined—enough to account for her panic attack in Aaron Stallings's office and near-breakdown here on her living room floor.

She lay just inside her closed front door for a long time. How long, she did not know. Eventually the tears dried up, an occurrence for which she should have been grateful.

But they were replaced by a cold emptiness.

A black void.

She pushed herself to her feet, shaking and stumbling like a drunk at closing time, and shambled off to bed. Surely things would look better when she awoke.

* * *

Tracie was typically a light sleeper. Years in the field had trained her body to deal with potential danger by snapping awake at the slightest sound, fully alert and prepared to take action. Sometimes she found her eyes opening for no apparent reason, and yet she knew there always *was* a reason.

Today was different.

Today a helicopter could have hovered directly over her and she wouldn't have awakened. A bomb could have detonated outside her window and she would have slept on. An assassin could have crept into her apartment and placed a gun at her temple and she would have been as helpless as a newborn baby.

Today her condition was closer to unconsciousness than sleep. She dropped off within minutes of her head hitting the pillow and remained in a near-comatose state for several hours.

The room was dark when she awoke. She had drawn her

bedroom shade, but the sliver of light that always snuck between the window frame and the shade during the day was nowhere to be found. The blackness inside her apartment was as complete as the blackness of her spirit.

She sat up in bed and waited to feel like herself again. To feel normal.

It didn't happen, so she waited longer.

When several minutes had gone by and she still felt as empty inside as she had after drying her tears at the front door, she shoved the covers off and slipped out of bed.

Padded to the kitchen and looked at the clock.

The time was a few minutes after 8:30. She'd been sleeping for hours but it was still only early evening. The night stretched in front of her, endless and as terrifying as staring down the barrel of a Russian Makarov.

Maybe more so.

She was no longer tired and knew sleep would prove elusive the rest of the night.

Tracie wasn't much of a drinker. Never had been. Too much alcohol could prove deadly to a field operative, dulling the senses and promoting sloppiness. When she did drink she almost always stopped at one.

Tonight might just be the exception that proves that particular rule.

She rummaged around in a cabinet, eventually uncovering a dusty bottle of whiskey that was so old she couldn't remember putting it there. Walked to the fridge and grabbed a half full ginger ale. Twisted open the cover, unsurprised to discover the soda was mostly flat. She couldn't remember buying that, either.

She mixed a drink anyway, dropping ice cubes into a glass and then pouring too much whiskey into the bottle before filling the rest with the ancient ginger ale.

Took a sip and placed the glass on the counter, then held herself tightly. She wrapped her arms around each other and rubbed vigorously above the elbows, trying to dispel a chill that was coming from inside.

She grabbed her drink and walked into the living room. Cranked the thermostat and then padded to her couch and sat down.

She left the television off.

She left the lights off.

She closed her eyes and tried not to think. Sipped her drink too fast.

When it was gone she mixed another, grimacing when the last of the ginger ale dripped out of the bottle. Not only was it old, there wasn't enough of it.

She returned to the couch and repeated the process of drinking and trying not to think. She discovered she was much better at the first challenge than the second. Turned out shutting off her brain was damned near impossible.

Too quickly her second drink disappeared.

She went to drop her empty glass onto the end table and almost missed.

Didn't care.

Sat for a while in the dark. Suspected the room would be spinning if the lights were on. Didn't care about that, either.

After a while she rose unsteadily, grabbed her car keys and walked out the door.

44

Tracie knew she shouldn't be driving but she did it anyway.

Add this to the list of things contributing to the nuclear bomb waiting to detonate in my belly.

The irony of picturing a ball of radioactive material inside her stomach after eliminating the man responsible for assassination via nuclear radiation was obvious, even to a drunk young woman trying her hardest to shut down the cognitive portion of her brain.

If she hadn't felt so damned bleak she might have thought it was funny.

But it didn't seem funny. It just seemed appropriate.

The trip was a short one, but the closer she got to her destination the more tempting it was simply to turn around and go home.

She almost did exactly that, and more than once. But the prospect of sitting alone in the dark, drinking herself into oblivion was the only thing she could imagine at the moment that might be *more* pathetic than what she was actually doing.

So she kept going and in minutes had arrived.

Tracie parked her car and killed the engine, then stepped into the cold Washington night. She crossed the half-empty lot, approaching the apartment she thought—but wasn't certain—belonged to Marshall Fulton.

She stood just outside the door feeling embarrassed and stupid and ashamed.

Maybe he wouldn't be home and she could slink quietly away.

This is silly. What the hell do you think you're going to accomplish by coming here? They barely knew each other, despite having been acquaintances for years. An intelligence analyst at Langley, Marshall had been at the CIA since before Tracie was recruited.

He'd helped her immensely last summer after she was fired by Aaron Stallings, putting his own career on the line by sharing valuable intel that led to her rescue of kidnapped Secretary of State J. Robert Humphries. That rescue had resulted in her rehiring, albeit on an unofficial basis, by Stallings as his personal Black Ops specialist.

Tracie had been pleasantly surprised at how well she and Marshall had worked together on that operation. As a bonus, his attraction to her had been obvious.

She had felt the tug of attraction as well, despite their many differences.

Marshall was a massive black man from inner city New Orleans, an analyst who had never worked in the field but who possessed a sharp mind and a keen intellect. He was handsome and outgoing and warm, with a dazzling smile that took little to summon.

Tracie was a petite redheaded white woman from suburban D.C., the daughter of a military father and a diplomat mother who'd had every advantage growing up. She had never worked anywhere *but* in the field. She was reserved and suspicious and cynical, a young woman who had found it harder and harder to smile under the weight of all she had seen as a CIA operative.

And all she had done.

Now she stood outside Marshall Fulton's front door, nervous and drunk. She realized she needed to pee and ignored it.

She forced herself to ring the bell, torn between hoping desperately he was home and praying fervently he was not. The hand she had injured deep inside a tunnel under an old Nazi munitions factory in Wuppertal, West Germany last fall throbbed, and she distractedly stroked it with her good hand.

And then the door swung open.

This was the right apartment.

Marshall was dressed casually, in ragged jeans and a bulky Tulane University sweatshirt, and his brows knitted together in confusion at the unannounced appearance on his doorstep of a woman he hadn't seen in weeks.

For a second.

Then Marshall's familiar warm smile broke through, prompting a return smile from Tracie and the thought that maybe she hadn't just made the biggest mistake of her life. She couldn't seem to stop shaking and realized she'd been more at ease facing down trained Soviet assassins than she was right now.

Marshall spoke first, which was fortunate because Tracie had no earthly idea what to say. "Tracie Tanner, as I live and breathe," he said. "Did I fall asleep early and I'm having the best dream ever or are you actually standing on my doorstep?"

"If you're that excited to see *me*," she mumbled, "I have to question your judgment. But, yes, I'm actually here. And you don't look like you're asleep." She realized her face had colored at the enthusiasm of his greeting and she hoped it was dark enough in the doorway that he wouldn't notice.

Marshall stepped back. "You're shaking like a leaf," he said. "Come on in and get out of the cold." He stepped aside and waved her in.

Yeah, it's cold out. That's why I'm shaking. Get a grip on yourself, Tracie commanded. *For some unfathomable reason, this guy likes you. Don't ruin it by acting like a twelve-year-old girl talking to the cute guy in class.*

She stepped into a tastefully decorated living room that reinforced just how badly she'd dropped the ball when it came to furnishing her own apartment.

Marshall grinned as her gaze swept the room and he said, "You like it? I've added stuff here and there as I could afford it, and it's finally to the point where I'm not embarrassed to have anyone see it. And not a moment too soon, apparently."

"Are you kidding?" she said. He reached out to take her coat and she shrugged it off and handed it over. "This place makes me realize my decorating skills suck. My apartment redefines the term 'minimalist.'"

Marshall laughed. "Well, unlike some world travelers I could name," he said with a wink, "I actually spend most of my time *in* my apartment. It wouldn't look like this if I were in your situation."

He was obviously trying to put her at ease instead of demanding to know what the hell she was doing showing up at his door like a stray dog. Her tears had pulled back for a while, but they hadn't retreated very far, and Marshall's small kindness brought them a little closer to reappearing.

She blinked them back and smiled. "Thanks for the lie, but I doubt your place looked very much like mine even on the day you moved in."

She swayed on her feet and Marshall grabbed her by the elbow. "Have you been drinking, Tracie Tanner?"

He said it with a smile and a teasing tone in his voice, but his concern was clear.

And embarrassing.

Tracie tried to recall if she had told him, on the one dinner date they'd shared months ago, that she rarely drank alcohol—and why—but she guessed the subject must have come up based on his question.

Her face flushed again and she scuffed her toe on his carpet. "I may have had a drink or two."

His big hand felt good on her small elbow, warm and strong and reassuring, and she wished he would leave it there forever. He didn't leave it there forever, but he did use it to lead her across the room and ease her onto his couch.

"I'll be right back," he said with another of those heart-melting smiles. He walked into what she guessed was the kitchen, and a moment later her suspicions were confirmed as the smell of coffee began wafting through the apartment.

She had already begun to feel a little more relaxed. Talking to Marshall was unlike talking to anyone else she knew, probably thanks to his innate ability to put people at ease.

But with him puttering around in his kitchen, leaving her alone with her thoughts—and doubts—she began once again to question her decision to come here. The temptation to bolt out the front door began to build, but she couldn't do that to poor Marshall, especially given how kindly he was treating her.

But it was still tempting.

After a couple of minutes he reappeared, carrying two mugs of coffee. He placed one on the table in front of her and kept the other for himself.

He moved to a stuffed chair situated directly across the table from her and sat. "A splash of cream and one-and-a-half sugars, correct?"

"Excuse me?"

"Your coffee," he said. "When we ate at the Congressional Steak House, that was how you ordered it."

The tears made another run for her eyes and she swallowed hard, touched that he would remember something so trivial from a date that had taken place so long ago.

He noticed her hesitation and said, "Am I misremembering? I don't go on *that* many dates, but I suppose it could have been some other sexy redheaded spy I took out, and *that* girl drinks her coffee with a splash of cream and one-and-a-half sugars."

Tracie laughed. "I might have to dispute the sexy part," she said, "but that was definitely me."

She lifted the mug to her lips and took a sip. It was delicious.

"Thanks for remembering," she said quietly.

Another smile from Marshall, this one wistful. "I'm pretty sure I've committed every minute of that night to memory, especially the way you kicked ass on those two Neanderthals outside the restaurant and then were pissed off because you broke a nail."

They broke out laughing. "I'd forgotten about that," she said.

"I told you, I remember every bit of that night like it was yesterday."

They shared a warm glance and then Marshall said, "What's wrong, Tracie?"

Another sip of coffee, this time to avoid the question as much as to enjoy the flavor. Then she shrugged. "What do you mean?"

"Well, let's see. You show up at my front door—not that I'm complaining, mind you—half drunk, when I know for a fact you almost never drink at all. I don't know you particularly well, but I've seen you in and out of Langley for a long time, and right now it's obvious that you're about as down and upset as I've ever seen you."

A tear forced its way out of Tracie's right eye and she swiped at it with the back of her hand. She hoped Marshall didn't notice but doubted there was much chance of that.

"Talk to me," he said. "What's really bothering you?"

45

January 27, 1988
10:40 p.m.
Marshall Fulton's apartment
Washington, D.C.

She sighed and sipped her coffee. Tried to make sense of the thoughts and fears and emotions swirling inside her overstressed, exhausted brain.

"I can't give you a lot of specifics," she said finally. "Classified assignment and all that."

"Okay. Then be non-specific. Be as non-specific as necessary. But it's clear you need to get something off your chest."

"Aaron Stallings used me as bait today to flush out a Soviet assassin. He didn't warn me, didn't give me a chance to prepare for a sniper's ambush. He just sent me out to face possible execution the very same day I returned from completing a risky and dangerous assignment overseas."

She realized she was shaking again and she breathed deeply, choking back another round of tears.

She tried to settle herself and more or less succeeded.

Took another sip of coffee.

Realized Marshall hadn't responded. He sat motionless across the table, staring at her over his coffee mug, not saying a word.

At last he cleared his throat and came back with the last thing she would have expected to hear. "So?"

"Excuse me?"

"I said, 'so?'"

Anger sizzled through her. "'So?' That's all you have to say? The man treats me like a disposable razor and that's your response? He's nothing but an amoral, manipulating bastard who treats human lives like they exist solely for his own purposes, to use and abuse as he wishes, and all you can say is, 'so?'"

"Don't misunderstand me," Marshall said. His gaze was direct and penetrating and oddly arousing. "I don't blame you in the least for being angry at how you were treated. It was plainly unprofessional, not to mention dangerous. You *should* be angry. You should be royally pissed."

"Thank you," she said. His response to her flare-up was—again—the last thing she would have expected, and she was left feeling vulnerable and unsure of herself. "But if that's how you feel, then why did you answer the way you did?"

"Because I don't believe that's what's really bothering you. Yes, you should be angry with Stallings. Yes, the way he treated you was inexcusable. But unless I'm missing something, you haven't told me a damned thing you didn't already know about our fearless leader. That being the case, I seriously doubt what you've said to this point is responsible for what I saw shivering outside my front door."

Tracie blinked, stunned.

He was right.

She'd thought Stallings's treatment of her had thrown her off-balance, had been responsible for the giant ball of radiation waiting to explode in her belly, but it couldn't be that. She'd been treated just as cavalierly by the CIA chief a dozen times in the past, in ways large and small, and while every instance had served to remind her that he was only trustworthy as long as their interests aligned, never had he affected her the way she felt right now.

Not even close.

It had to be something else.

And then she knew. Just like that. Out of nowhere she realized what had affected her so deeply, and what she'd gone to great psychological lengths to ignore.

The realization struck her with the force of a speeding ZiL-157, and once again the tears tried to come. It was getting harder and harder to stop them, and now she knew why.

She was a monster. She was a goddamned monster.

Marshall waited while she worked through it. He sipped his coffee and gazed levelly at her.

Then he said, "What's really bothering you, Tracie?"

He spoke softly, almost as if to himself, and the words came at the exact moment her devastating self-revelation blasted into her mind. It was like he could see straight through her skull and into her brain.

She raised her head to meet his eyes and the tears began to flow silently down her face. Stopping them now would be impossible. There were no wrenching sobs, no gasping histrionics. Just a pair of salty tracks running down her cheeks and dripping into her lap.

And Marshall waited.

"I executed an unarmed man yesterday," she whispered, shame burning in her face until she thought the heat in her cheeks would evaporate her tears the moment they left her eyes.

"I'm sure you did only what was necessary for national security."

"And he wasn't just unarmed," she continued, lost in her self-loathing and self-recrimination. "He was elderly and unarmed. He was seventy if he was a day, and do you want to know what I did?"

Marshall held her teary gaze without answering.

"I walked up behind him and I pumped four slugs into him. He never knew what hit him. He died without ever knowing."

"You've killed people before in the line of duty."

"Of course. But every time the other operative was armed and taking action to directly harm the United States."

"Are you telling me the target *wasn't* a danger to this country?"

Tracie looked down through the tears at her shoes. "He was directly responsible for the deaths of six CIA covert operatives, plus at least one Soviet dissident that we know of."

"Well then, there you go. Sounds justified to me. It's an unfortunate part of the intelligence business, you know that."

"But this time was different. He couldn't have harmed me if he'd tried. I walked up behind him and filled him full of 9mm lead and walked away. I'm a—"

"You're an operative. A damned good one. And you were doing your job. No more and no less."

"But—"

"There *are* no 'buts,' Tracie. Do you feel those six agency men who died somehow had it coming? Maybe they weren't quite vigilant enough? Maybe their deaths didn't deserve a response?"

"Of course not!" Tracie's anger surged and she glared at Marshall.

"Then your point about executing an unarmed and thus harmless man is invalid. Maybe he couldn't have turned around and harmed you in that precise moment, but if he was able to eliminate a half-dozen highly trained, professional intelligence field officers, the assertion that he was harmless, or that he somehow didn't experience the fate he so richly deserved, is simply not supported by the facts."

She wanted desperately to believe him. In her head she knew he was right. Slava Marinov was an enemy of the United States and had more than proven it by developing and implementing the monstrous plan to use nuclear radiation to burn through the bodies of good men before finally, mercifully, allowing them to die.

Slava Marinov had deserved his fate.

But all she could think of was Piotr Speransky, the KGB assassin who had made a career out of spraying a lethal radioactive concoction into the drinks of every one of the CIA victims.

Speransky was cold and hard and unrepentant, a killer, an animal without a conscience who would eliminate Americans again without hesitation if given the chance. Tracie had allowed him to live, a spur-of-the-moment decision she knew she might well end up regretting.

In some ways, she already did.

But more importantly, when she pictured Speransky she also pictured herself. Their ideologies were opposed, obviously, as were the ideologies of their governments.

But their job descriptions were essentially the same. They performed similar duties, both being sent into the world by behind-the-scenes manipulators for the purposes of advancing their government's objectives by implementing their handlers' instructions.

When people looked into *her* eyes, did they see the same cold hard emptiness that had so shocked her in Speransky's? Was Marshall Fulton even now shrinking back in his chair at the emptiness within Tracie's leaking eyes? Trying to hide his disgust at the bare shell of a human being sitting in his living room?

"You're a good person, Tracie." He continued to speak softly, his voice a rich baritone, the soft southern drawl blunted but not eliminated by years of living in D.C. "The fact that you're so devastated by ending someone whose disappearance from this earth results in a net gain for humanity proves as much."

She shook her head. "But I don't know if—"

"I told you already, there are no 'buts.' You're a good, moral, decent human being working in a brutal profession. Don't let your job description make you question your essential goodness or your humanity. Nothing is worth that kind of loss."

Marshall rose from his chair and walked around the table, coming to a stop in front of Tracie. His eyes were kind and empathetic, and there was no indication he wanted to shrink away from her.

And she definitely didn't want to shrink away from him.

He reached out and took one of her hands in his, and then she was standing and he was pulling her into a tight embrace, and his body was warm, and it was soft and hard at the same time, and she lifted her head and his lips were there, and they were soft and warm too, and she was melting away, and suddenly Piotr Speransky no longer existed, and neither did Slava Marinov or Aaron Stallings or anyone else in the world.

It was just Marshall Fulton and Tracie Tanner.

46

January 28, 1988
3:40 a.m.
Marshall Fulton's apartment
Washington, D.C.

Tracie's eyes flew open and she came instantly awake.

She knew right away where she was, a relatively unusual occurrence for a young woman who traveled the world on dangerous assignments and who was just as likely to awaken in East Germany as D.C., or on an airplane rocketing over the Atlantic Ocean as her apartment bedroom.

But she knew.

Her first memory upon waking was of Marshall Fulton's kindness and calm logic in the face of her humiliating meltdown in his living room. She'd shown up drunk and uninvited and suffering a crisis of confidence the likes of which she had never before experienced.

Had never even imagined possible.

Marshall had taken it all in stride, and had gently but firmly forced her to look inside herself, to recognize the true nature of her inner turmoil. He had done so without shaming her or making her feel foolish or silly, and that was a good thing because she was perfectly willing to do all that herself.

Her second memory upon waking was of Marshall Fulton's kindness and gentleness after…accompanying her…to his bedroom last night. "Accompanying" was probably the most accurate word she could come up with, because Tracie had been overcome by a sexual energy and desire she'd never before experienced.

She had been like a hurricane, slamming into Marshall in his living room, molding into his body in a manner that left no doubt as to her needs. They kissed long and hard and then she took him by the hand and practically ran to his bedroom, leading him down the hallway and to his bed with unerring accuracy despite having never stepped foot in his apartment before last night.

She had no idea what had gotten into her. It had been eight months since her last sexual encounter—a single night with Shane Rowley in a cheap motel outside New Haven, Connecticut—so she supposed that long drought might have something to do with the fury of her passion.

But there was more to it than that. Tracie had been overcome with desire at a level that was almost frightening. Her self-loathing from having executed an old man in Russia, the adrenaline from narrowly avoiding execution at the hands of a KGB assassin in D.C., Marshall's ability to seemingly see inside her very soul, and his obvious and long-running attraction to her had all combined to explode into a nuclear blast of sexual energy.

And here I thought that ball of radiation in my belly would destroy me, she thought, smiling in the darkness.

Marshall had left the bedroom door cracked and the hallway light on, "In case you need to get up in the night to pee. Or, considering you've been drinking, to puke," he'd added, grinning as Tracie punched him in the arm.

A narrow sliver of yellow angled across the bed, just enough light to reveal Marshall's sleeping form. He lay on his side, one arm draped over Tracie's bare hip, snoring softly and breathing deeply.

He looked handsome and sexy and sweet and innocent, and she felt an overwhelming surge of affection. She had loved Shane Rowley with a fiery intensity, despite—or perhaps because of—the limited time they'd had together. And most of that time had been spent running for their lives and trying to stop the assassination of the president of the United States.

Shane had been the only man she ever loved and she'd been convinced he was the only man she *would* ever love.

Maybe that was still true.

She didn't know what she felt for Marshall, but it was different than the feelings she'd had for Shane. Was it possible to love two men equally but in different ways?

Affairs of the heart were foreign territory for Tracie Tanner. She was more comfortable by a country mile fighting for her life than she was deciphering her own feelings on any subject, and that was especially true when the subject was love.

She supposed that would have to change.

Maybe it was time for that change. Maybe dealing with feelings and emotions was the key to keeping a grip on the humanity Marshall claimed to have seen in her eyes last night, to not letting her soul slip away, as Piotr Speransky's had done and as so many others in her line of work had done as well.

The prospect of that kind of loss was terrifying.

She had a lot of thinking to do. A lot of self-reflection.

It wouldn't be easy because self-reflection was so foreign to her.

But she realized with more than a little surprise that she was looking forward to the prospect. The "Project Kremlyov Infection" assignment had brought her right to the edge of a line, had maybe even taken her over the edge. On the other side of that line was a cliff, and she knew two things with perfect certainty: she didn't want to learn what was at the bottom of the cliff, and if she tumbled over it she would never climb out.

She glanced at the clock on Marshall's bedside table. It was nearly four a.m. There was no way she was going to get any more sleep tonight.

Next to her, Marshall continued to breathe deeply and snore softly. She wondered whether he was a light sleeper and decided she was about to find out.

She lifted her head and placed her lips to his ear.

"Thank you," she whispered.

He stirred but did not awaken.

She kissed his forehead and then slipped out of bed.

Picked her clothes up off the bedroom floor and dressed quietly.

Then she eased out of the bedroom and down the hallway.

She double-checked the lock on Marshall's front door before driving away.

Tracie Tanner will return soon in her sixth action-packed thriller. To be the first to learn about new releases, and for the opportunity to win free ebooks, signed copies of print books, and other swag, take a moment to sign up for Allan Leverone's email newsletter at AllanLeverone.com.

Reader reviews are hugely important to authors looking to set their work apart from the competition. If you have a moment to spare, please consider taking a moment to leave a brief, honest review of *The Kremlyov Infection* at Amazon, Goodreads or your favorite review site, and thank you!

Also from Allan Leverone

Thrillers:
Parallax View: A Tracie Tanner Thriller
All Enemies: A Tracie Tanner Thriller
The Omega Connection: A Tracie Tanner Thriller
Final Vector
The Lonely Mile
The Organization: A Jack Sheridan Pulp Thriller

Horror/Dark Thrillers
Mr. Midnight
After Midnight
Paskagankee
Revenant: A Paskagankee Novel Book Two
Wellspring: A Paskagankee Novel Book Three
Linger: Mark of the Beast (written with Edward Fallon)

Novellas
The Becoming
Flight 12: A Kristin Cunningham Thriller

Story Collections
Postcards from the Apocalypse
Uncle Brick and the Four Novelettes
Letters from the Asylum: Three Complete Novellas